DEAR DOCTOR EVERETT

Janet's youthful friendship with Martin Everett was just a far-off memory; certainly it seemed no reason why it should prevent her from marrying Ellis, the brilliant surgeon, to whom she owed so much – until Martin suddenly came back into her life.

*Books you will enjoy
in our Doctor-Nurse series*

THE DOCTOR'S PROBLEM by Clare Breton Smith
ARCTIC NURSE by Elizabeth Gilzean
RUNAWAY NURSE by Judith Worthy
THE NEW REGISTRAR by Hilda Pressley
SURGEON, R.N. by Helen Upshall
SISTER AT RYEMINSTER by Ivy Ferrari
NURSE IN NEW YORK by Constance Lea
THE DOCTOR'S DELUSION by Marion Collin
THE LOVES OF SISTER NICHOLE by Elizabeth Petty
NURSE AT NOONGWALLA by Roumelia Lane
THE BETRAYAL OF DOCTOR VANE by Sonia Deane
FATE IS REMARKABLE by Betty Neels
SISTER ON MUSGRAVE WARD by Janet Ferguson
SHIP'S SURGEON by Celine Conway
THE SURGEON'S MARRIAGE by Kathryn Blair
NURSE WITH WINGS by Judith Worthy
SISTER IN OPPOSITION by Linda Shand

DEAR DOCTOR EVERETT

BY

JEAN S. MACLEOD

MILLS & BOON LIMITED
London . Sydney . Toronto

First published in Great Britain 1954
by Mills & Boon Limited, 17–19 Foley Street,
London W1A 1DR

This revised edition © Jean S. MacLeod 1979

Australian copyright 1979
Philippine copyright 1979

ISBN 0 263 73151 0

Set in Intertype Times

Made and printed in Great Britain by C. Nicholls &
Company Ltd.,
The Philips Park Press, Manchester

CHAPTER I

"When something is over and nothing can be done about it, it's best to sever it with a clean cut, like the healing knife in an operation – drastic but sure. It's no use leaving an old sore to fester and cause a lifetime's trouble and regret."

Janet Ferrier spoke with her back to the room, her trim, uniformed figure silhouetted against the oblong of the hospital window, her eyes fixed steadily upon the grey block of the opposite wing across the paved quadrangle outside. It was raining, and she watched the drops gathering on the window-pane and sliding down in a thin trickle to the outside sill like slow, difficult tears. They were the echo of something in her heart that she had never been able to explain, a deep welling loneliness which had threatened to engulf her at times and which not even Freya Allanson, her closest friend and companion, had been permitted to glimpse until now. It was several minutes before she turned from the window to look into Freya's surprised eyes.

"But, Jan," Freya protested, "the very last thing I should have suspected in you was cynicism!"

Janet was instantly sorry.

"I shouldn't have said that," she apologized. "I know how you feel about Ben and it's no use telling you that he isn't worthy of your love or that you'll forget him soon. You can't just force yourself to forget. No one can do that. It has to come gradually."

In the brief, memory-ridden silence which followed the vague sounds of the outside world came in to them: the chiming of a distant clock; the muted roar of heavy traffic on the main road running past the hospital gates; the crunch of a car's tyres, nearer, on the gravelled drive, and the sound of voices as the first visitors of the afternoon surged along the white-tiled corridors to the wards where their loved ones eagerly awaited them.

It was all so familiar to them both, all part of their busy lives here at the City General, where they had qualified and worked together, yet in some way it was also remote.

To Freya, stricken by unfaithfulness in a first love affair, it seemed that life could never be the same again, that the work she loved would always continue to remind her of the man who had told her so casually, less than a week ago, that he was about to marry someone else. The memory of the summer behind them when Ben Scarriff had constituted her entire world was never likely to be driven out of her heart, and she could not believe that Janet, of all people, should think otherwise.

"When something is over and nothing can be done about it . . ."

The words themselves held finality and she found herself looking at her friend with a new interest.

Janet was a born nurse. It was obvious as soon as she came into a room or walked along a ward. There was competence in her erect bearing and a world of serenity in her calm eyes, and the curve of her mouth was generous and kind. She would never lose her humanity in a sea of technical routine nor would she become bogged in sickly sentiment to the danger of her professional skill. She was calm, cool and deliberate, and all through her training she had taken things in her stride. Nothing had flustered her. She had gone doggedly on to her goal, picking up a gold medal and the Spencer-Wroe prize for surgical nursing on the way with the same quiet smile which had nothing to do with pride. There was nothing hard or superficial about Janet, yet for a moment she seemed to be admitting to a hardness which sat uneasily upon her.

"I had no idea you had ever been in love," Freya said, voicing the thought almost automatically. "It must have been a long time ago."

They had been too close together during the past six years for anything to have touched either of their lives without the other knowing about it, and certainly Janet had never given any sign of suffering from an unhappy love.

Janet's face cleared, although her eyes were still curiously remote.

"So long ago that I may be confusing the wish with the substance," she tried to say practically. "There wasn't any love story – not really. We were children together, but he wasn't even the boy next door. His people lived on the hill, in a house that seemed fabulous to me in those days, and he came to the

6

village occasionally to play tennis. He didn't dance, so we only really saw each other in the summer when we bought ice-cream at the kiosk beside the tennis courts. Even in those days he was destined for the medical profession," she added, as if to herself. "I've often wondered if that was my real reason for taking up nursing. The first stimulus towards the ideal."

"It could have been," Freya admitted, aware that she need not have answered because the question had not really been directed towards her at all. "There always is a first seed, I suppose, however casually it may be planted, and admiration —or love—would be as good a reason for its growth as anything."

"The groping after the ultimate desire?" It almost seemed as if Janet had not heard her. "There has to be something, I suppose, some sort of peg on which to hang the future."

"He may come back into your life one day," Freya suggested, but Janet shook her head.

"Men don't come back, Freya. Not men like Martin. He was too ambitious, too independent. Besides, there was nothing between us. I could be nothing more than a name to him now. Eight years is a long time, and even for me it has become a blurred sort of memory."

"But you've never met anyone else, no one you've really cared about?"

A slow, almost painful flush spread over Janet's fine skin.

"I've admired a good many people," she admitted.

"Including Ellis Spencer-Wroe?" Freya smiled. "I was going to say that isn't quite the same—admiration as opposed to love, I mean—but perhaps it is, for you. The City's most eminent consultant and a bachelor, to boot! Nice going, Jan, if you can make it!"

"Now you're being plain stupid," Janet reminded her, the flush on her cheeks deepening until she could feel it running like a swift tide up to her brow. "Everyone thinks that way about Mr. Spencer-Wroe."

"Sure!" Freya agreed in her best American accent. "Sure we're all plumb crazy about him, but none of us have got quite so near as you have! There was a look in his eyes when he handed over that surgical prize of his the other day that suggested he had noticed you as a human being as well as a nurse, and a very attractive one at that!"

7

"You've been fed far too much on fairy-tales in your youth," Janet suggested, turning away. "This is what comes of swapping histories, but I've finished for the day. It's my afternoon off, and I'm going home."

Freya laughed.

"You remind me of a story in one of our primary books at school," she said as they went towards the door of the common-room together. "Jan and the little Dragon!"

"Slaying the past, do you mean?" Janet smiled. "Perhaps we all have to do that, sooner or later."

Her tone and mood appeared to be light, but the suggestion of regret lingered and at the back of Freya Allanson's mind a restless question remained unanswered. Was the past ever really, truly forgotten, she wondered, or did it persist to haunt one for the remainder of one's days?

Janet's first experience of love had evidently been a brief encounter, scarcely recognized, even at the time, as the tenderest of all passions, and the chances were that she had built out of that girlhood attraction something which had never really existed outside her own heart, something warm and comforting to hold against life as it was. It must have been about that time that her mother had died, and although they had never spoken very much about it, Freya knew that the loss had left her friend completely desolate for many years. Maybe Janet had clung to a suggestion of love for that very reason, conjuring up a name out of the past with happy connections against the brightness of other days. Freya didn't know. She had no way of finding out, but it did help to know that Janet understood about her own heartbreak.

They went down the stairs together, feeling a firmer bond between them than ever before.

At the door Janet said:

"I wish we had this time off together, Freya. I'd like to have taken you home with me. It's Robin's birthday."

"Jan! Why did you let me forget?" Freya was instantly all contrition. "He'll never forgive me for not sending him a card. I've been a selfish pig, thinking of nothing but my own precious affairs all the time! There is a parcel, though. Will you take it to him for me, and then it might not seem so bad – to have forgotten my one remaining faithful love!"

Janet waited in the foyer while she ran back to her locker

8

for the treasured parcel, wondering how long it would be before Freya could really forget her lost love. Robin would be expecting his parcel, she mused. Freya never let him down at Christmas or birthdays, although this birthday had almost escaped her memory. Freya never let anyone down, yet Ben Scarriff had not hesitated to tell her that he was going to marry the daughter of one of the senior consultants to the hospital.

Janet's eyes went to the notice-board above her head, reading the list of consultants, all specialists in their own line. Hartley Stroner, the gynaecologist; "Piper" MacFadyn, who knew all there was to know about that most intricate of mechanisms, the human heart; "Jock" Ewart, the brain specialist, and Ellis Spencer-Wroe.

Her eyes lingered on the last name, half apologetically, as she wondered why the majority of nurses made such fools of themselves over an unattached doctor, and some that were not entirely unattached. Ellis Spencer-Wroe's progress down a ward was like a royal procession, with a dozen hearts aflutter under their starched aprons, yet he was a modest man, unassuming and unfailingly kind, who had given the best years of his life to the one subject which had engrossed his mind to the exclusion of all else. At thirty-five he was an acknowledged authority in his line, his technique for operating through the thorax a new and dramatic improvement on what had gone before. To all intents and purposes he was a Norminster man, but he had operated and lectured in all parts of the world. That he always came back to Norminster and the City General was put down to the fact that he had received his initial training there and that he had dreams of building it up into one of the greatest teaching hospitals in the country.

A man with a dream; a man who could make dreams come true.

Janet had often wondered about Ellis Spencer-Wroe, about the sort of life he led away from the hospital, and once or twice, when he had questioned her about a case, she had been conscious of something like loneliness in him, the surgeon groping for something that the man had missed.

All this, of course, was the greatest figment of imagination, she told herself as she turned away from the board. She knew nothing about Ellis Spencer-Wroe, no more than any other nurse who passed him a chart on a post-operative inspection of her ward or held a suture needle for him in the operating theatre itself.

Freya returned with the parcel, trying to make an inadequate piece of string meet across its bulky width.

"I hadn't got it tied up properly," she apologized, "but perhaps it will do. Boys don't mind much about the wrapping. It's what's inside that counts." She thrust the parcel, still untied, into Janet's hands. "Tell him that's with all my love, and save me a piece of the birthday cake!"

Her manner had completely changed. She was no longer the heartbroken girl, facing the future with little hope, but the cheerful nurse, bringing assurance and confidence with her, yet Janet knew that the hurt Ben Scarriff had inflicted had gone deeper than most people would expect. Freya might never refer to her broken romance again, but that revealing half-hour in the deserted common-room upstairs had told Janet much.

She sighed as she turned away, thinking that Freya was the sort of person to whom love might have been kind. Generous, impulsive and gay, she was one of the best-liked nurses on the wards, and although there had been a light-hearted escapade or two in her past which had caused Matron to frown and read her a lecture on the ethics of nursing, she was generally accepted as reliable.

Reliable! That's what we're all supposed to be, Janet thought. Reliable above all else. A nurse must never lose her head. She could, of course, lose her heart and have it hurt and bruised, but she would be expected to go on being thoughtful and cheering and doing her work without a flaw. How difficult it was all going to be for Freya, especially as Ben Scarriff had no intention of leaving the hospital.

Angrily, resenting Ben more than she had ever done in the two years he had been at the City, she made her way round the end of the hospital block to where her bicycle was stored with the others in a shed adjoining the boiler-house. It was here that the resident doctors parked their cars, leaving the quadrangle free for visitors and the consultants, and as she wheeled her bicycle out of the shed a sleek Alfa Romeo drove up and Ben Scarriff got out from behind the wheel.

None of the residents could afford such a car, and she was

not surprised when she saw Ben's passenger slip across into the driver's seat he had just vacated. She was a tall, fair girl, beautifully dressed in an expensive-looking grey coat, and she kissed Ben lightly on the cheek as he bent to the open window.

"Come to dinner tonight, darling," Janet heard her say as she wheeled her bicycle away. "I shall be frightfully bored if you don't!"

Ben murmured something and turned away, tall and slim and immaculate, and very pleased with himself. He was making a brilliant marriage in the material sense of the word, which he hoped would go a long way to furthering his career, for no one knew better than Doctor Scarriff, in his more introspective moments, that he would never be other than mediocre without the necessary influence in high places. One was either so good in medicine that one could not fail to be noticed or one made it a point to work with the right people. Such was Ben's philosophy and it had served him for a time.

Janet pedalled hard. Why was it that her thoughts went winging back eight years, today of all days, and the name of Martin Everett kept recurring to her? Was he a successful doctor by now? Had he gone abroad, as once she had heard it rumoured? Had he married?

Her thoughts caught on the last question. He would be twenty-eight by now, almost twenty-nine. Strange how she should remember all these details about him when there had been so little between them, a passing attraction never really sealed by words which had haunted her with a strange poignancy across the years.

Martin Everett. It was simply a name bound up with nostalgic memories of her former home. She could not even remember his features clearly, although she had preserved some sort of image in her heart. She could, in fact, have passed him in the street without recognition, and sometimes it was quite clear to her that she had built up something she had need of from an uncertain dream.

When Janet's thoughts were busy she rode quickly and soon she was jumping off her bicycle at the gate of a semi-detached villa in one of Norminster's suburbs where her father had set up house a year after her mother's death. They had come in from a country village ten miles away because it would be

11

more convenient for Robin's schooling and also to be nearer the hospital where Janet was to become a student nurse.

Nordene was a northerly suburb flanking the main link road which ran through Norminster and eventually found its way to London, and it, too, had once been a village. It possessed a village green flanked by Georgian houses and an ancient inn with a curious sign above the door where an enterprising landlord ran dinner-dances in the winter and catered for passing traffic in the holiday season, and beyond this green core the villas and semi-villas of twentieth-century suburbia fanned out in all directions.

Lavender Road was not by any means the most pretentious of the tree-lined avenues which led from the Green, but it was home to Janet and she wheeled her bicycle round the side of the house to the back door with a feeling of security. He father would be home to tea and Mrs. Cass would have set the table early to surprise Robin when he came in from school.

She was greeted by an unexpected whoop of delight as she opened the back door, parcel in hand, and her brother hugged her around the waist.

"Hullo! I thought you were at school?" she greeted him, ruffling his already tousled hair. "Surely they haven't given the whole class a holiday because it's your birthday?"

"No," Robin agreed, trying not to eye the parcel too eagerly, "but we *have* got a holiday. The whole school has got it because there's an election or something."

"Lucky old you!" She made an abortive attempt to smooth his hair into place. "Don't tell me you've eaten all the birthday cake!"

"No. That's for tea." The blue eyes went back to the parcel. "Thanks a lot for the trucks, Jan. They're GREAT!"

Janet had been waiting for the word. It was the current expression of enthusiasm and covered most things from sheer ecstasy to mild delight, but she had a shrewd suspicion that her modest addition to his accumulating electric train set was not the primary excitement of this special day. Robin was too kind, however, not to mention her present first, and he even opened Freya's parcel to admire yet another piece of rolling stock before he burst out:

"Jan, I've got a new bike!" He drew her towards the garden-shed, quivering with excitement. "It's in here. It's blue, and it's got ten speeds!"

When she had fully expressed her astonishment and the new bicycle had been duly admired, Janet said:

"It's Daddy's present, of course?"

Robin nodded vigorously, caressing the bright chromium handlebars.

"Daddy's an' Mrs. Cass's," he acknowledged without looking up. "They've kind of shared. Gosh, Jan, isn't it *super*? Isn't it really *great*?"

"Yes," Janet said, "really great," but she was wondering why Mrs. Cass, who was her father's housekeeper, had come to share so personal a gift to his son.

Gladys Cass had been with them for four years. She was a firm, capable woman in her late fifties whose husband had been killed at sea during the Second World War, and Janet had always felt glad that her father had someone reliable to look after him when she was forced to spend so much of her own time at the hospital. Like all the other nurses, she slept in. It was a rule at the City General, but she was fortunate in being able to go home during her off-duty periods and rarely missed an opportunity to do so.

"I'd better go in and tell Mrs. Cass I'm here," she said as Robin closed the shed door on his precious new possession. "There might be something I can do to help with the party."

Mrs. Cass met her at the door. She was a big woman of the buxom, fresh-complexioned type and she seemed rather more assured today than Janet had ever seen her.

"Oh, so you did get off!" she remarked, rinsing her hands at the sink. "I wondered if you would or if that old tartar of a Principal Nursing Officer would find you something to do at the last minute."

"Miss Lawson's usually fair enough about our time off," Janet defended the hospital. "It's only in cases of emergency that we're asked to stay."

Gladys Cass regarded her critically.

"I suppose you're suited to that sort of life," she said. "Do you never think of getting married?"

The question held something like resentment and Janet looked her surprise.

"I don't think anyone should consider marriage without first

13

falling in love," she said briefly. "At the moment, I find my nursing satisfying enough."

"It won't always be enough," Mrs. Cass assured her with conviction. "You're bound to want a home of your own one day like everybody else."

Again the personal note seemed pronounced and a sick little stab of apprehension found Janet's heart. She could not put a name to it, but it seemed to involve all that she cared about, her home, and Robin, and her father, and even her work at the hospital. She could not question Mrs. Cass, of course. She had no real proof that her father's housekeeper saw Lavender Road as a future permanent home and resented her presence there accordingly. She was relieved, however, when Robin followed her into the kitchen and the conversation became general, and when her father came in and they sat down at the tea-table she tried to dismiss the thought of that first impression of change. She tried not to think that he looked different, tried not to recognize the look in his short-sighted grey eyes as one of hesitant apology. He had always been kind and considerate to Mrs. Cass and to-day he was happy at the thought of his son's happiness.

Janet had always loved her brother with a possessive love born of the fact that he had been only a year old when their mother had died, and the long gap in years between their respective ages had fostered a motherly feeling in her, helping in some ways to soften the blow of her own irretrievable loss. Robin was still very precious to her and she was not yet too old to romp with him on occasion.

When she had helped to clear away the tea things and parcelled up the generous slice of birthday cake which she was to take back to the hospital for Freya they sat on the floor together and set up Robin's train.

Not until the clock struck six did she realize the time, and she jumped up hastily, smoothing her hair before the mirror above the fireplace.

"I've got to go," she said regretfully. "It will take me all my time to get back to the hospital and be punctual on duty. I'm on suppers."

"Let me come with you!" Robin demanded. "I can use my new bike."

"You'd be too slow."

14

"No – no, I wouldn't! It can go as fast as – as anything!"

"There isn't a lot of traffic on the road after six," Janet said, looking at her father. "What do you think?"

Bill Ferrier put down his evening paper.

"He should be safe enough," he said. "It isn't as if he couldn't ride."

"I'll put on my anorak – and my scarf." Robin was willing to go to any lengths if he was permitted to go.

"Mind you come straight back," Mrs. Cass cautioned as he bolted for the door.

Janet and Robin cycled away together, with Gladys Cass and her father standing at the gate to watch them go. They looked as if they belonged there, Janet thought.

"We'll go along the side of the Green and down Mulberry Road," Janet said. "It's quieter that way, and don't forget to come back by the same road."

There was only a short stretch of main road leading up to the hospital gates to negotiate, but Robin insisted on coming with her all the way.

"Take your time going back," she warned as he turned in the wide drive. "See you on Tuesday!"

He waved to her and rode away and a car turned in at the hospital gates, passing her at the bend in the drive. Then, almost immediately, she heard the squeal of brakes on the main road and a grinding sound, as if some heavy vehicle had been pulled to an abrupt and unpremeditated stop. It was followed by a lengthening and terrible silence.

Automatically she jerked on her own brakes and when she put her feet to the ground she was trembling. For a split second there was no power in her limbs. They would not move nor could her numbed brain send any message to them until, by sheer force of will, she was urging them to the effort of covering the two hundred yards or so back to the gates.

Before she reached the scene of the accident she saw the wreckage clearly. She saw a brightly painted blue bicycle tossed on the roadside as if it had been a discarded toy and the dark shape of a car beside a huddled heap at the kerb.

"Robin——"

She was through the gates and tearing at the wreckage of the car as if she would lift it bodily from the huddled figure of the trapped child.

The car's driver was lying against the steering wheel and she noticed subconsciously that he was an elderly man with a crop of thick white hair, but for the moment nothing mattered except Robin. It was only when she realized that her own hands were torn and covered in blood that the futility of what she was trying to do occurred to her and she knew that she needed help.

Struggling to her feet, she gave one desperate glance along the now deserted road before she began to run. She ran in the direction from which she had come, and the drive had never seemed so long or winding. The gaunt grey buildings ahead of her appeared to be miles away and her breath was forcing itself out between her teeth in painful gasps long before she reached their shadow. Training had come uppermost, however, and she was thinking more clearly now, but when a car drew up on the quadrangle almost abreast of her she felt that there was no need to make the remaining few yards to Casualty.

Here was help in a concrete form. She caught the arm of the tall man who alighted from behind the steering-wheel, scarcely recognizing him as she gasped out her request.

"There's been an accident. Down at the gates. Can you come?"

Ellis Spencer-Wroe did not hesitate, but for a split second he looked into her face as he steadied her with a firm hand on her arm.

"Go back to Casualty," he commanded, "and bring what help you can."

He was in the car and had re-started it before she moved. It will be all right, something kept repeating inside her. It's Mr. Spencer-Wroe.

There was no fuss in the casualty department. Everything was done in the minimum of time, but even the few seconds' delay irked her and she found herself running down the drive again in the direction of the gates without waiting for the ambulance. The stretcher unit passed her on the last bend.

After that she was hardly conscious of what happened. The inevitable group of spectators had gathered and were thrust back to a reasonable distance, but her uniform let her through. She heard somebody say that the child was pinned under the car but that Mr. Wroe had got to him, and then she

16

stood frozen, watching Anne Norman and another nurse working with the stretcher party. An obscuring mist seemed to rise before her eyes before she saw the car again, and this time it was being raised rather drunkenly on a very old jack. The unconscious driver had been removed from behind the wheel and deposited on a stretcher, ready to be carried to the hospital, when the whole car seemed to sag in the middle and finally collapse.

It was then that she knew that Ellis Spencer-Wroe was underneath and Robin was free.

"He's taken the full weight of the car on his back!" someone said as she passed them to kneel on the pavement by her brother's side, but the words meant nothing for a moment.

"It's all right, Robbie!" she whispered. "You're safe. You're out now!"

She could not gather him into her arms as she wanted to do, in case he was badly injured, nor could she bring herself to look towards the road where his deliverer still lay trapped, with the heavy chassis pinning him down. An overwhelming sense of guilt and selfishness flooded over her as she clasped Robin's seeking hand in both her own, trying to comfort his fear with the most reassuring words she could find.

"We'll soon have you in the hospital, safe and sound."

Safe and sound! Dear God, if that could only be the truth, she prayed.

Someone whose face seemed vaguely familiar stooped to fold another blanket over Robin for extra warmth, a tall man who stood aside as the orderlies lifted the stretcher and carried her brother away. She saw him fleetingly, and then she was hurrying beside the stretcher, holding the child's clinging fingers and seeing, too, that they were lifting Ellis Spencer-Wroe clear of the damaged car.

How could she ever thank him? How could she ever repay him for what he had done for her brother?

The thought did not seem at all incongruous at that moment because she was fully convinced that Ellis Spencer-Wroe had saved Robin's life, and the surgeon was to add to that debt within the hour.

Ellis Spencer-Wroe walked unaided up the hospital drive and before he would permit his colleagues to submit him to a thorough examination he operated on the child he had rescued. Robin's thigh had been crushed and Ellis Wroe set and pinned the bone before he collapsed ignominiously in the ante-room, still gowned and masked as he had come from the theatre.

The P.N.O., Eileen Lawson, who had been watching him critically during the final stages of the operation, said afterwards that he just seemed to fold up, but it was no time before she had him settled in one of the private rooms adjoining Ward B and had sent for the sister in charge.

"We must have a nurse here in constant attendance, Sister," she announced. "Whom have you available?"

"There's Nurse Ferrier, Miss Lawson, but——"

The remainder of the sentence was left unuttered. The P.N.O. had given Sister Oliphant one look which said quite clearly that there could be no qualifications about a nurse's duties. If she was on the ward and the only nurse available to deal with an emergency, she must do as she was told, in spite of the fact that her brother had just undergone an operation. As a matter of fact, she had added, the boy was doing quite well. Children had an amazing fund of resilience, as Sister well knew.

When Janet was sent for she accepted her new assignment without a word. She had been told that Robin would be up and about again within a month, but she knew that he had escaped lightly only because a brilliant surgeon had taken the weight of a falling car on his own shoulders.

It had seemed a miracle, even at the time, that Ellis Spencer-Wroe had been able to walk away from the scene of the accident and even go into the operating theatre afterwards, but here, indeed, was the reckoning.

She walked towards the end room of the corridor wondering what she was about to find behind its closed door.

The shaded lamp beside the bed cast deep shadows in the four corners of the room, but the bed itself stood in a pool of greenish light and the face of the man lying there was plainly discernible even from the doorway. Ellis Spencer-Wroe looked younger and strangely vulnerable in that moment, his clean-cut features etched sharply against the white pillows, his thick hair jet black in contrast. He lay very still, but not relaxed, so that she knew he was not asleep.

Softly, she crossed to the bed, her shadow falling across his

18

face as he opened his eyes. They were startlingly blue eyes and they seemed to pierce straight through her nurse's efficiency to the tumult of emotion lying in her heart. She wanted to thank him for what he had done, but no words would come and it was left to him to speak first.

"I thought it was you," he said, "as soon as you opened the door."

His voice sounded tired and he passed a hand rather wearily over his eyes. Janet saw that it was his left hand and that his right arm and shoulder were already encased in plaster. She saw, too, that the bedclothes were raised over a cage across his knees, and it was almost more than she could do to repress a sudden desire to kneel by his bedside and pour out her humble thanks in whatever words would come.

Her training steeled her to her duties as a nurse, however, and she knew that her gratitude must be expressed at a more appropriate time and in a more practical way than disturbing a patient who should be induced to sleep.

"Miss Lawson would like you to get some sleep," she said gently. "Do you feel comfortable enough? Perhaps if I moved your pillow a little your head would be in a more natural position."

His eyes followed her round the foot of the bed and he smiled when she eased his head.

"You're a restful sort of person, Nurse. I've always felt that," he said. "It seems that we're going to see quite a lot of each other in the near future. Miss Lawson knows that I hate changes."

His eyes had closed and he seemed to be assuring himself of something in that half-nebulous world of semi-consciousness which comes before sleep. Janet had forgotten that he was Ellis Spencer-Wroe, the eminent surgeon and senior consultant at the City General, for it seemed that he was nothing more than a man a little bewildered by his own sudden helplessness and in need of her care and attention.

Yet the very fact that he *was* Ellis Spencer-Wroe might make her position difficult in the future. There was no way that she could see of ever compensating such a man for all that he had done, nothing adequate she could do to prove her unending gratitude to him for saving her brother's life.

She could nurse him carefully, but that, after all, was no more than her ordinary duty, and a brief expression of thanks

19

when the time came seemed a poor return for all he had done.

Perhaps there will be some way, she thought, but what that way would be she was far from guessing.

The hospital seemed very still. There were not even the little muted noises of the night to disturb the solitude of the isolated room, and Janet sat on until she was sure that her movements would not disturb her patient.

Then she rose and crossed to the window, moving the curtain aside to look out. The night held a gleam of stars and down in the quadrangle the first evening visitors were beginning to arrive, yet somehow she knew that her patient would not have any visitors. For the first time she remembered how much of an enigma Ellis Spencer-Wroe had always been, a man alone, apparently without a home background. Almost instinctively she turned back to the bed.

Looking down on the strong face on the pillows, she could not feel pity, because she knew that he had achieved what most men sought in life. He was a man at the pinnacle of his career who had won fame at an early age and was already acclaimed a genius in his profession, and if he also appeared to be a lonely man, perhaps that was how he preferred it. He had no ties, no commitments apart from those of his work, and he was probably content with that.

Suddenly her eyes rested on the thickened shoulder and right arm in their plaster casing and a sickening fear cut across her mind. Would this make a difference? Supposing he was badly injured and might never work again?

Responsibility rushed in on her like a flooding tide and she bent forward, almost as if she expected to be able to read something of the truth in the pale, relaxed face on the pillow, but Ellis Spencer-Wroe was completely unconscious and oblivious to her fear.

Adjusting the light so that it shone away from his face, she wondered how long it would be before she knew the real extent of his injuries, and then she went back to her former position at the window and stood there gazing down into the quadrangle, not wanting to leave the room in case he might have need of her.

And down in the paved courtyard beneath her a man whose name was Martin Everett glanced about him at the great hospital buildings as if time itself had spun backwards for him before he straightened his broad shoulders and approached the main door. He sought out the matron's office and made himself known to her.

"I had an appointment with Mr. Spencer-Wroe for seven o'clock," he explained, "but I understand that will be impossible now. I shall write to him when I get back to London."

CHAPTER II

IT was two days before Miss Lawson sent for Janet.

"You're in for it, Ferrier!" the pert little nurse who brought the message informed her. "The P.N.O. wants to see you right away. What have you been up to to merit such a reprimand in high places?"

It was true that Miss Lawson rarely interviewed one of her nurses in person except on a serious charge. The more trivial matters were left to her assistant, a woman of lesser insight who made the most of her authority and was greatly disliked in consequence, and Janet felt almost glad that she was being summoned to the fountain head for whatever had to be said.

She made her way direct to the office on the ground floor, knocking on the door and waiting outside with a fast-beating heart for the word to enter. When she received it she straightened her shoulders and turned the handle.

Eileen Lawson was seated at her desk beside the window, a small, neat figure in a severely cut poplin dress with a high, starched collar, her white-frilled cap resting on hair that had already turned a harsh iron-grey. She had fine, regular features and small, expressive hands which she kept folded on the desk in front of her as Janet came across the room, but it was undoubtedly her eyes which held the attention. They were deep-set and widely spaced, with a warmth of understanding and quiet patience in them born of a lifetime's service to the sick and dying.

"Sit down, Nurse," she said, indicating the chair on the near side of the desk. "I want to speak to you."

The chair Janet sat on had been placed facing the light so that Miss Lawson could assess its occupant's worth almost at a glance, but before she spoke she referred to a typewritten card lying on the desk before her which Janet supposed was her own progress report. Individual histories were kept filed away in the two capacious cabinets which occupied the wall space behind the desk, and she had only to refer to them in order to discover what sort of ability a particular nurse was likely to possess, but it was generally accepted that she made her own assessment of character from time to time.

"I have had a daily report sent in to me on your brother," she said, looking up from the card, "and I have seen him several times since his accident. I also hear that you have visited him. It must be a great relief to you to know that there is no serious damage to his leg," she added kindly, although Janet did not feel that this was the main reason for the interview. "You must be very conscious of all you owe to Mr. Spencer-Wroe in the circumstances," she added.

"Oh, yes, Miss Lawson, I am!" Janet hastened to assure her. "I only wish there was some way in which I could repay it. I have tried to thank him personally, but he brushes it aside."

"It was nothing more than my duty as a doctor," was what he had said.

Miss Lawson was apparently of the same opinion.

"You owe him a deep debt of gratitude," she said, "and there is at least one small way in which I think you might be able to discharge your debt."

"I will do anything—most gladly," Janet assured her eagerly.

"Mr. Spencer-Wroe dislikes upset more than anything else and he has made a request to me that his nurses should not be constantly changed. He expresses himself as being very content with your ministrations, Nurse, so the least you can do is to give him your utmost attention and care during the next few weeks. If it means that you may have to work an hour or two longer or are especially tied to one case, surely that is only a small return when you think of all that he has done for you? Mr. Spencer-Wroe is a very brilliant surgeon and this accident must be very irksome to him. We must hope that it proves to be nothing more serious."

Janet rose unsteadily to her feet.

"Nothing could happen, surely?" she asked, her face quite devoid of colour. "He will get well. He must!"

"I think he will get well," Eileen Lawson agreed, as she, too, rose to her feet. "At least, that is what we must hope for and work untiringly to achieve."

"It's so little to do," Janet said as she turned towards the door. "So very little to do."

She went slowly back along the corridor and up the wide stone staircase to the first floor. The lunch trolleys were being wheeled into the wards and the cheerful clink of china and the sound of brisk, hurrying feet on the parquet floors were the sounds she had always associated with her work, but suddenly she felt cut off, as if a weighty, personal burden had been pressed firmly on her shoulders to rest there for a very long time.

She collected her patient's tray from the hatch where it came up on the food lift from the kitchens, inspecting it carefully before she carried it towards his room. The other private rooms were empty for the moment. They were in sole possession of that end of the corridor, shut away in an isolation which seemed to underline her new responsibility, but the truth was that Ellis Spencer-Wroe was the least exacting of mortals. It was often true of eminent men, she acknowledged as she opened the door.

"Good morning!" she said cheerfully. "Have you managed to sleep again?"

"Not a lot." His eyes were on her face, searching it with a whimsical expression in their blue depths. "That's the second time we've wished each other 'good morning', Nurse. Do you never go off duty?"

"I only came on at eight," Janet told him, "when I brought your breakfast."

"And you were here at nine o'clock last night," he reminded her, although she would have thought that he had been too ill the evening before to notice who was attending him. He had been suddenly feverish and restless, with a high temperature and a rapid pulse which had only subsided after Doctor Curran had given him an injection to ease the pain. "Surely that was infringing all the laws of accepted hours?"

"I had time off during the afternoon," Janet told him as she poured hot soup into a feeding cup and slipped an arm expertly under his head. "That sort of thing doesn't really matter when there's an emergency."

"Am I an emergency?" he asked, his blue eyes suddenly lit by an amused smile. "It's strange to be on the receiving end of hospital routine, I'll admit."

"We hope it will not be for long, sir."

"Don't use that stupid title," he objected. "I'm reduced to

24

the status of a patient now, you know, and a very dependent one at that!"

He was trying to make it easy for her, letting her see that a great surgeon could be quite human, after all, and she felt grateful and content to accept his offer of a change in their circumstances. He was to be her patient and she his nurse, and for the moment Ellis Spencer-Wroe, the eminent consultant to the hospital, was non-existent.

"You will soon be able to have visitors," she consoled, laying aside the feeding cup and slipping her arm out from under his pillow. "Doctor Curran was quite pleased with you this morning."

She had turned to the tray and it was several seconds before she realized that he had not answered her immediately. When she moved back towards the head of the bed his eyes seemed to be fixed on a point just beyond her, and he said, almost as if he were speaking to himself:

"I can't think of any visitors who might wish to come, apart from the members of the hospital staff. When a man has no family," he added, "no immediate background, he tends to convince himself that close personal friendships are a luxury he can't afford to have. A successful career very often robs you of the friends you might have made, and when a man gives everything he has to that career he is apt to find himself on a pinnacle of splendid isolation."

She wondered if he regretted his own isolation and did not know what to say to him.

"Perhaps it's only at a time like this that we realize the value of friendship," she suggested at last, uncovering the steamed fish and creamed potatoes which had been ordered for him. "It can be a very precious thing."

"I had an idea that you might know about that," he said with the same conviction in his voice which she had heard there when he had first recognized her by his bedside. "It is something I have missed in the scramble for success. Once or twice I've made a tentative sort of offer," he mused, "but the other fellow always proved busy, too, and nothing ever came of it. Perhaps I didn't offer enough."

"It is a case of giving and taking," Janet agreed. "But sometimes one has to give more than the other. In many ways it's like——"

25

"Falling in love?" He was smiling directly into her eyes now. "Have you ever been in love, Nurse?"

Utterly confused by the unexpected question, Janet felt a rush of hot colour flooding into her cheeks.

"No—I don't think so."

"Yet surely you want a home of your own one day? I understood that all girls want that."

"It's like an anchorage," she said, remembering how often she had made her way back to Lavender Road, feeling just that. "My mother died eight years ago, but my father and I have always clung to our home because we knew how much we both needed it."

"He hasn't married again?"

"Oh, no! I don't think he ever will." Janet stooped to help him with the fish. "He and my mother were so deeply, so wholeheartedly, in love."

"Are you like your mother?" he asked unexpectedly.

Janet smiled.

"I suppose I am. She was auburn-haired, like me, and quite small, but she was also very capable."

He smiled in turn at the description, and when she carried his tray away he looked after her almost regretfully.

It was not so easy, Janet discovered, to treat him like an ordinary patient. He was a "special", and the relief nurse who took her place when she went off duty made it only too clear that they were privileged in being allowed to attend him. She was a fussy little creature in her late thirties, with a distressing impediment in her speech, but she was also a clever and reliable nurse in whom the P.N.O. frequently placed her confidence.

Kathy Bennet took over from Janet in the afternoon and she found herself with an hour to spare to visit Robin.

To her great relief, Freya Allanson was on duty in children's surgical, and she was occupying the ward sister's office. She hailed Janet as she passed the door.

"Your father's in, Jan—and Mrs. Cass."

Janet paused and went back to stand in the doorway.

"How is Robin?" she asked.

"Fighting fit! Mr. Spencer-Wroe did a wonderful job on that leg of his and it looks as if he will be using it in next to no time."

26

"We've got so much to thank Mr. Wroe for," Janet said, and Freya looked up from her reports, blotting the top one carefully before she said:

"Sometimes one wonders where a doctor's duty ends and sheer gallantry begins. He risked his own life, I suppose, but he wouldn't think of it in that way. What is it like nursing him? Do you feel—limited?"

"No—not really. He's very human and he simply refuses to be thanked." Janet stood staring down at the desk with its neat array of charts and duty reports. "He can't be out of the wood yet, Freya," she added unsteadily. "He still has terrible bouts of pain and Doctor Curran has increased the strength of his injections. It doesn't seem possible that anything could go wrong now, but——"

She left the sentence unfinished and Freya gave her a long, searching look before she declared with characteristic briskness:

"You've been working too hard. Off you go and see that brother of yours for ten minutes and then I'll come for a walk with you across the park. You've been breathing in too much hospital atmosphere these past few days!"

Perhaps Freya was right, Janet thought as she went forward into the ward where her father and his housekeeper sat on either side of Robin's bed. Robin had begun to enjoy life in Ward Three after he had discovered that he was not the only ten-year-old with a limb in plaster, and the host of presents he had received, quite apart from those bestowed on him on his birthday, appeared to be compensating somewhat for his loss of freedom.

"Nurse Allanson said you would come!" he declared, adding in a whispered aside, "It's best for me not to call her Freya in here. You see, she's in charge of all these children an' lots of the other nurses have to obey her."

"Quite right, Robbie!" Janet laughed, kissing him. "It would be terribly bad for discipline."

"How are your patients?" he asked her seriously.

"I only have one patient at the moment," Janet told him as she greeted her father and Mrs. Cass. "His name is Mr. Spencer-Wroe."

Her father looked at her from the far side of the bed.

"That's the surgeon who operated on Robin's leg, isn't it?"

he asked, his fine face gravely concerned. "They tell me he was injured at the time of the accident, too. Would there be any practical way I could thank him?"

"I don't suppose there is anything you could do for a man like that," Gladys Cass said. "He'll have everything he needs."

Janet hesitated, and then she said quietly:

"I think he might appreciate a visit in a day or two, once he is a little better."

"But he must have hosts of friends," Mrs. Cass objected. "A man like that is sure to know everyone in a place the size of Norminster!"

Her attitude was almost dictatorial, Janet noticed with some surprise, as if she had some sort of newly acquired right to criticize their family decisions, but her father said quite simply:

"If he'd like to have me I shall be pleased to go."

The bell rang for the visitors to take their leave and there was a general movement round the beds as last goodbyes were said and final requests made by little patients reluctant to let their loved ones go.

Janet walked with her father to the door.

"You'll let me know what Mr. Spencer-Wroe thinks about my visit," he said. "I wouldn't like him to consider it presumption on my part, but we do owe him a debt of gratitude which we are never likely to be able to pay in the ordinary way."

Always that sense of obligation, Janet thought as she watched the tall, familiar figure of her father walking away by his housekeeper's side.

It was several days, however, before she was able to open the subject with her patient. For the next twenty-four hours Ellis Spencer-Wroe's life hung precariously in the balance as they fought a blood infection which threatened to affect his spine. He lay on his back while a small procession of his colleagues filed backwards and forwards between his bedside and the surgeons' common-room, a spirit alone in that vast wilderness of unconsciousness which borders on the realms of death and which none can share.

The crisis lasted for three days and then Sir Adrian Pepper came down from London to see him.

After the consultation Sir Adrian sat closeted in the P.N.O.'s office with the other specialists for a very long time, and when they finally went out to their respective cars they stood in a grave-faced little group in the quadrangle for more than a quarter of an hour before they shook hands and drove away.

Janet watched them from the window of her patient's room.

He can't die, she protested inwardly. Not after all this!

It seemed that all she had felt for Robin on the day of the accident was now centred on the man lying so still on the bed behind her.

The P.N.O. came up to the room to relieve her. They were desperately short-staffed and Kathy Bennet had been working almost as long hours as Janet and had gone off duty with a raging toothache.

"I'll take over for a spell, Nurse," Eileen Lawson said. "You must really try to get some sleep, otherwise we'll have you cracking up on us, too." She gave Janet a long, penetrating look. "This case means a great deal to you, I know," she added after a momentary pause in which her dignity and remoteness as a matron went down before her humanity. "Mr. Spencer-Wroe will live, of course. There seems to be no doubt about that now, but the possibility is that he may never operate again." Her voice had dropped to a whisper and she glanced towards the bed. "The infection, you see, has gone down into his arm and he may remain paralysed on that side."

Janet felt that she could not move. Her body felt tense and rigid, and she stood staring down at the still figure on the bed, not wanting to believe what she had heard. It was a full minute, in fact, before the full tide of Eileen Lawson's words and their meaning came flooding in, backed by all the horror of what they would represent to a man whose work was his life.

Not to operate again. Never to be able to use the skill which he had perfected. And all because he had stepped in to save a life—Robin's life!

"No!" she cried, finding her voice with difficulty. "It can't be true! It can't be. It's too cruel!"

Eileen Lawson turned towards the door.

"Life is often cruel, Nurse," she said. "It is only when it touches us personally that we come to realize these things."

She was being kind because she knew that Janet was so

deeply concerned over the accident, but she did not hesitate to add, after due consideration:

"I should deem it a privilege, if I were in your place, Nurse, to be able to serve him, even in a small way."

If only I could, Janet thought. If only I could do more than just what is, after all, my duty as a nurse. If only there was something he needed beyond anything else.

For days that thought went with her all the time, days when she took no part in the ordinary life of the hospital but worked and thought for Ellis Spencer-Wroe alone.

When the fever had subsided he seemed to be his old self again, watching her with a quiet smile as she went about her tasks in the room, arranging the flowers that were sent to him by his colleagues' wives or sorting out the periodicals that lay on his bed.

Janet thought that he must feel his lack of visitors most when the procession of eager relatives filed past his door on its way to the wards, and one afternoon, when he had been allowed to sit up for an hour, she mentioned the fact that her father would like to come in to see him.

"He visits Robin every evening," she explained, "and—I think he would like to meet you to thank you for all you have done."

The smile she had come to know so well during the past eventful week lifted the corners of his mouth.

"I wish you weren't quite so sorry for me because I haven't the usual stream of visitors," he said. "A good many of the people I know are better outside a hospital ward. But that doesn't mean to say that I wouldn't like to meet your father," he added slowly. "Bring him any time you like, but don't let him thank me!"

Janet wondered why she always felt so tongue-tied about her own expressions of gratitude, but perhaps it was because she felt that words alone were a poor return for what he had done and all that he might suffer because of it.

"You worry too much, you know!"

She turned back towards the bed.

"What about?"

"About my lack of company. I have always been a self-sufficient sort of creature and I'm not regretting my present isolation. The fact remains, though, that you've been pretty

30

well twenty-four hours a day in attendance on me since I was brought in here, and that's not good for anyone."

"You've had Nurse Bennet on occasion," Janet pointed out.

"Only when you went off to the Nurses' Home to sleep. Isn't there a boy-friend kicking his heels in the offing and wondering when you are ever going to have any free time again?"

"No," Janet said decisively, "there isn't."

"All the same," he persisted with a sort of a sigh, "you ought to be able to get home now and then. Too much concentrated nursing isn't good for anyone. Besides, you could do some necessary shopping for me on your way, if you will?"

"I'll do anything," Janet assured him. "And Miss Lawson did suggest that I should go out this afternoon."

"Then perhaps you could also call at my flat," he suggested. "It's in Minster Close and the caretaker's wife will go in with you. She knows where things are. She has been looking after my creature comforts for the past three years. I shall need some fresh pyjamas and a clean handkerchief or two, and perhaps you could bring along a few of my books and any letters there may be waiting for me?"

Janet accepted the commission with an almost pathetic eagerness, writing down a list of the few necessities he wished her to buy for him and carrying it across to the Nurses' Home as if it were an amulet against the feeling of frustration which always engulfed her when she considered her debt to him. This was the first direct request he had made of her, the first thing he had asked her to do for him beyond her ordinary duty, and although it was so small a thing she nevertheless prized it.

"Hullo, Ferrier!" one of the junior staff nurses greeted her as they passed on the stairs. "Going out? I thought you were chained to the bedside of one of the great men?"

"He's just undone the padlock for the afternoon!" Janet retorted lightly. "Anything you want while I'm in town, Sylvia?"

The other girl smiled mischievously.

"The only thing I fancy at the moment is a mink coat."

Janet went on her way, thinking that it must be at least three days since she had last seen Freya Allanson, and as if the thought had conjured up the reality, Freya herself came towards her along the upper corridor of the Home.

"What luck!" Janet smiled. "Are you off duty?"

It seemed that Freya all but avoided meeting her eyes.

"Yes," she admitted, "but I've promised to meet someone." She hesitated for a fraction of a second before she said briefly: "It's Ben."

Janet bit her lip.

"Freya," she said, "are you sure you should do this? Are you sure you should go?"

"I've got to!" Freya burst out. "We haven't spoken—not really spoken to one another since he announced his engagement."

There was a dismal sort of hope in her voice, as if she could almost believe that things might be different, that some mistake might have been made, or that Ben Scarriff might conceivably have changed his mind.

"Did he say why he wanted to see you?" Janet asked.

"No. But he must have something to say."

Janet watched her go with a deep sense of protest in her heart. Why should love mean heartache and pain for some while it meant only joy for others?

Getting out her bicycle, she cycled home, stopping to make Ellis Spencer-Wroe's modest purchases on the way. A tube of shaving cream and some toothpaste and some fruit from the store on the corner of Lavender Road. His wants were really very few, and the fact sent a stab of something akin to pity through her as she contemplated his modest needs.

She had decided to call at his flat for the other things on her way back to the hospital, and it was only when she reached home that she remembered that the house would be empty. Mrs. Cass would be at the hospital for the afternoon visiting hour, but there had always been a family hiding-place for the back door key and she found it and let herself in.

She spent the next half-hour happily enough preparing tea and collecting the few things she wanted to take back with her, and at five o'clock Mrs. Cass came in to cast a critical eye over the tea table and say that she hadn't expected to see her.

"There's some fish for your father, but he'll be late getting in," she added. "He went to Bristol yesterday and he won't be back till the five-seventeen." She moved round to the fire, taking off her hat and patting her hair into place at the mirror over the mantelpiece. "A lot of his work is being done from

Bristol now, you know. He can manage it from there even better than he can from this end. When Robin gets well I think he will be wanting to move to Bristol altogether. The house and everything," she added, giving Janet a quizzical look.

It was the first Janet had heard of any such plan and she could not understand why Gladys Cass should be the one to tell her. Her father had always discussed such things with her in the past and she could not help feeling vaguely hurt that he had not done so now.

"What would you say if your father and I got married?"

The words came as a bombshell and Gladys Cass had uttered them defiantly. They were a challenge and Janet knew that it wouldn't matter what she thought about something which was already settled. She felt stunned and at a loss, baffled and a little jealous, perhaps, but deep down she knew that Gladys Cass was hardly the sort of person she would have expected her father to choose as a companion for the future. She was a rather bold, assertive woman, good-looking in a hard sort of way, with a taste for spectacular clothes and cheap perfume, and if, underneath it all, she had a heart of gold, it had been carefully hidden where Janet was concerned. From the very beginning, Mrs. Cass had resented her. She had been kind and generous to Robin, but the grown-up daughter of the house was quite another matter.

Janet's lips felt stiff, but finally she managed to say:

"If it will make my father any happier, Mrs. Cass, I can only wish you the same."

She hoped that she meant what she said, but she could not help wishing that her father had come to her and told her about this in his own way.

She felt lost, although she told herself that it was ridiculous to feel abandoned.

"Are you still nursing that Mr. Wroe?" Gladys asked, relieved now that she had broken the news and much more confident in her new position as the future Mrs. Ferrier. "He's one of the big men, isn't he? Your father tells me he's still a bachelor."

The inference was only too obvious, but Janet tried not to mind.

"No," she said, "he has never married. He has a flat in Minster Close."

33

"It must be a lonely life for a man." Gladys buttered herself a slice of bread with an air of great concentration. "I always say that people should get married whenever they get the chance. There's nothing like a home of your own, you mark my words." She paused to wash the bread down with a drink of tea. "D'you never think of getting married, Janet?" she asked pointedly when she realized that hinting was getting her nowhere. "After all, you're twenty-five, aren't you?"

"I am – every minute of it!" Janet tried to force a lightness into her voice which she was far from feeling. "I'm getting on, but people don't marry just for that reason, Mrs. Cass."

"Better call me Gladys," the future Mrs. Ferrier decided. "I don't suppose I could expect you to call me 'Mother' at your age."

Janet did not dispute the fact, but she rose to go as quickly as possible afterwards. Her own private little world seemed to be falling about her ears and her thoughts were in turmoil in consequence. There was little doubt that Gladys Cass would do her best to get her father away from Norminster because she would feel better about starting anew as Mrs. Ferrier in a strange locality and his business could be run as easily from Bristol.

Janet tried to tell herself that it might benefit Robin to get away from Norminster, away from the scene of the accident, but she knew that her family's departure would leave a tremendous gap in her life.

Almost listlessly she pedalled to Minster Close, that quiet, secluded square in the shadow of the great cathedral building where the houses were steeped in a gentle peace and shadowed by spreading elms.

Ellis Spencer-Wroe's apartments were on the second floor of the end house and they seemed curiously empty and deserted when the caretaker's wife finally ushered her in.

"Mr. Spencer-Wroe was never one for fancy things," the woman explained as Janet glanced round at the bare austerity of the sitting-room. "He dined out a lot and never kept much company. He was mostly at his books, sitting there for hours on end over a wood fire in the winter when he wasn't at the hospital. You'll find his books in there, Miss," she added, pointing to a communicating door. "I haven't had much time for dusting while he's been away, but I thought I'd give it all a proper going-through before he gets back."

Janet went through to the adjoining room, finding herself in a veritable paradise of books. In here the chairs were deep-seated and comfortable-looking and there were heavy claret-coloured velvet curtains to draw across the mullioned windows on a winter's night. The room looked down on the cloister courtyard with its brilliant emerald grass and cool fountain, and a silver birch raised its delicate tracery of leaves almost against the leaded window-panes. It was a room that had been well loved and often used, a man's room where contentment and peace could have been found.

She tried not to let the austerity of the outer room depress her as she passed through it again, but it was almost impossible to erase the impression of neglect which it had conjured up.

On the way back to the hospital she bought her patient some fresh flowers.

"Hullo!" he greeted her when she appeared with her purchases in her arms. "I thought you were never coming back!"

"It only seems a long time because you've had nothing to do!" she told him. "Didn't Nurse Bennet bring you something to read?"

"She did her best. Poor soul, she's still intimidated by the fact that I once walked the wards with a retinue of starched aprons behind me!"

Janet felt her heart contract at the thought that he might never do that again, but she endeavoured to say cheerfully:

"Sometimes I wonder why I don't feel that way, too."

"I'm glad you don't."

His answer had been swift and spontaneous and she found him looking at her with an expression which she had surprised in his eyes several times in the past few days. For an instant she felt trapped by it, and then she smiled.

"I've brought you all the things you asked for, I think. I hope the books are right."

She put them down on his bedside table, but he scarcely glanced at them.

"What did you think of Minster Close?" he asked.

"It's a lovely old place. So cool and restful tucked away there out of the rush and scramble of the High Street."

"It was the flat I meant," he said.

"I could have spent a much longer time in your library," she told him truthfully.

His answering smile was grim.

"Which means that the rest of the place didn't exactly impress you?" he suggested. "I should have expected that. It isn't quite a woman's cup of tea."

"It could be made comfortable," she qualified in an undertone, because something was suddenly choking in her throat and she wanted to cry.

"I suppose so," he agreed, but that was all.

"There were one or two letters at the flat," Janet said, taking them out of her handbag. "Mrs. Carling apologized about not having brought them over before this, but she thought you were too ill to be bothered with letters."

"I'll open them later." He ran through the bundle carelessly. "They're mostly bills and circulars. There's just this one from London." He slit the last envelope but did not take out its contents until Janet began to arrange his flowers. "It's from someone I should have met here on the day of Robin's accident," he explained after a pause. "A young surgeon I was interested in in London. He has applied for a residency here and I promised to see him that evening, but fate stepped in, I suppose. Millington-Brace told me this afternoon, however, that the management committee had accepted him, so he should be taking up his duties here next week. Perhaps," he added tentatively, "I could ask you to write to him for me? I ought at least to acknowledge the fact that he has written about my accident."

He held out the open letter and Janet took it from him, her eyes fastening on the bold signature at the foot of the page.

"Yours sincerely,
     Martin Everett," she read.

Martin Everett! Her heart seemed to turn over in her breast and then lie curiously still.

Martin Everett. It was only a name, a memory out of the past, magnified, perhaps, by a nostalgic longing for the happiness of her youth, but it had come at a time when youth had seemed to be slipping away from her and the uncertainties of the future had become very real.

She looked at it for a long moment before she folded the letter and put it away. It was strange, she thought, that she should be about to write to Martin Everett after all these years.

CHAPTER III

DEAR DOCTOR EVERETT,

Thank you for your letter. I am progressing favourably now, thanks to careful nursing and the ceaseless vigil of the hospital staff, and hope that I shall be on my feet quite soon.

I shall be most happy to welcome you to Norminster at the end of the month, my one regret being that we did not meet on the day of the accident.

Yours sincerely,

Janet's eyes remained riveted on the page when she had stopped writing. There was no movement from the bed, but she knew that Ellis Spencer-Wroe was looking at her fixedly, his head back against his pillows, his free left hand holding Martin Everett's letter.

I shall be most happy to welcome you to Norminster at the end of the month, my one regret being that we did not meet on the day of the accident.

She read and re-read the words she had written, as if they held some deep, personal meaning for her, shaken by an emotion which she could not understand. Long ago, in the remote country village where they had both been brought up, she had known Martin Everett. Long ago.

"Janet," Ellis Spencer-Wroe said, "is there anything wrong?"

She hardly noticed his use of her Christian name.

"No," she said. "I was wondering if you will be able to sign the letter with your left hand."

"I should hate to confess myself beaten," he laughed. "Everett will understand if it is not quite my usual style." He scrawled his signature laboriously at the foot of the page. "It's awkward to be handicapped," he remarked.

"It won't be for long."

Janet tried to meet his eyes with the utmost assurance in her own and must have succeeded, because he nodded his head vigorously.

38

"Once I'm on my feet again I shall feel better," he said. "I don't like this helplessness. It makes nonsense out of any plans for the immediate future. I thought, for instance, that I might have been able to install Everett as my right-hand man straight away, but now it looks as if old Hilary McGrath will have to stay put for a while. He ought to be retired, of course, at his age, but Everett should be able to find his feet with him just as well as he would with me."

"He's—in your line?" Janet asked almost stiltedly.

"Very much so. In fact, I might go so far as to call him the coming chest specialist of our day. He studied under Professor Wiengarten in Vienna for two years, so perhaps he has also something to teach me!"

"I don't think so," Janet said impulsively. "The debt will be all on his side."

"Why should it be a question of debt?" he asked. "A surgeon has no real moral right to keep the findings of experience to himself. There are always young men able and ready to profit by what he has to teach. It's rather like passing on a torch. The race is not to one man alone, and Everett is the type who will profit by his opportunities."

"You consider him—ambitious?"

"Very. And that's the way it should be. Ambition has come to mean something in a material sense, but a man can be ambitious to succeed for other things apart from money and position. I know that Everett is wrapped up in his work almost to the exclusion of everything else, because no man of his age could have achieved all that he has done in the past few years without giving every ounce of his energy and concentration to the task, and every minute of his time."

Janet wondered if she should say: "I knew Martin Everett. I knew him long ago", but there did not seem to be any point in the confession. Eight years was a long time and the boy she had known then was now a man with a man's ambitions and a man's restless desires.

"Do you want me to post the letter straight away?" she asked instead. "I can pop down to the post-box with it when I go off duty."

"That will be time enough," he agreed, forgetting about Martin Everett in the perusal of his own thoughts. "Your father came to see me yesterday, Janet."

"Oh!" She looked up, smiling. "I'm glad. Nurse Bennet said you had a visitor, but I wasn't quite sure who it was."

"We got on very well – after he had thanked me!" The whimsical smile made his eyes look bluer than ever. "He told me that he is thinking of moving away from Norminster."

There was a brief pause in which Janet's thoughts went to the conversation with her future stepmother and some of the desolation she had felt then at the loss of her home came sweeping back.

"My father travels over a large area for his firm," she explained, "and it would not really matter where he made his headquarters, but perhaps the move to Bristol would be a good thing for Robin's sake. The memory of his accident might fade more quickly if he found himself convalescing in a new environment."

"And you?" her patient queried. "What about you, Janet? You are very much attached to your home."

She found it necessary to swallow hard before she could answer.

"It is my father's home, too, and he is about to marry again. Perhaps Norminster and Lavender Road hold too many conflicting memories of the past. Perhaps he feels that he should make a clean break to ensure his future happiness."

Ellis Spencer-Wroe considered this possibility in a thoughtful silence before he said:

"So many of us have to make a clean break with the past, and one can't entirely blame your father, even though it is going to leave you comparatively stranded. You have friends in Norminster, though. I don't suppose for one minute that you propose to leave the hospital?"

There was urgency in the question, a tentative hope expressed without hesitation, and Janet wondered if he were perhaps nervous about a change of nurses on his own account.

"I've always been happy at Norminster," she told him, "and I can't see that there would be much point in going to Bristol. After all, my family will not be so very far away and I can visit them."

That was her hope, but suddenly she knew that Robin and her father might as well have been going to the ends of the earth. Gladys Cass was a possessive woman and the new home in Bristol would be very much her domain, planned and run

40

without the possibility of her stepdaughter ever staying there for any length of time.

"I hope you'll always be happy in Norminster," her patient said in a kindly, thoughtful way which brought the lump back into her throat and seemed to reduce her defences to nothing. "Happiness has a great deal to do with the smooth running of our lives—happiness and contentment."

She wondered if he had found complete contentment in his work and remembered thinking, not so very long ago, that she knew next to nothing about this man. Now it seemed that they were being drawn closer together with every day that passed, she lending him some of her youthful courage and he offering her a blueprint for the future.

Contentment in her work? Was that all she sought? Was her chosen profession enough, and would she be content to end up as P.N.O. of some worthy institution, as Eileen Lawson had done, respected for her humanity and generally loved in an abstract sort of way by most of the people she met?

Her heart contracted at the thought and she knew, without having to probe too deeply, that she wanted a home more than anything else that life might have to offer. The home-longing was uppermost. It always had been, and there was no use denying it.

She rose, holding the letter to Martin Everett against the stiff folds of her apron.

"When I am on my feet again, Janet," Ellis Spencer-Wroe said, "there's something I want to ask you. It's something rather special, but I don't want you to give me your answer while I'm still lying on my back."

"Whatever it is," she said without hesitation, "you know I shall be only too pleased to do it for you."

He smiled as she turned away.

On her way to the Nurses' Home she posted his letter, standing to gaze down at the name it bore before she dropped it into the pillar-box on the corner. Doctor Martin Everett, she read in her own handwriting, and within half an hour she found herself on the bus which would take her the twelve miles to Somerton.

She had not even waited to discover whether Freya Allanson was off duty and could come with her. She had obeyed an impulse which, as yet, she could not understand, and she found herself getting off the bus at the crossroads before she came to the village itself.

Somerton and the adjoining hamlet of Athersage lay to the north-west of Norminster, cradled in a gentle fold of the Cotswold Hills, with the steady stream of traffic on the main road passing them by. They had not really changed a great deal in the past decade; perhaps they had not even changed very much in the past century except for the advent of electric lighting and main drainage.

Between the two hamlets were the houses on the hill. There were four of them, and from the distance of the main road they appeared to be very much alike, all large and prosperous-looking, each secluded in its own small plantation of shady trees, and in one of them Martin Everett had spent his childhood.

Janet walked on towards Somerton. She did not know what had brought her. She only knew that she had felt impelled to come by a force stronger than her own will, and when she reached the village green she hardly knew what to do next.

Over there, between the Red Lion Inn and the post office, was the narrow lane leading to her former home, but somehow she knew that she would not go there to-day. Myrtle Bank held too many memories of her dead mother for that, especially when she was trying to adjust her life to the thought of her father's second marriage. Instead, she thrust open the door of the post office to the accompaniment of a jangling of bells above her head, and walked in.

She had no idea what she was going to buy or why she had yielded to sudden impulse and come in, but at least she could invest in a few stamps if nothing more interesting offered itself.

The bell echoed through the back premises and presently a small, stooped woman in a grey skirt and hand-knitted cardigan came through the glass-panelled doorway behind the counter. She was obviously short-sighted, peering through her thick spectacles at her visitor for a full minute before she came to the conclusion that this was not one of her regular customers from the village.

"You don't know me, Miss Spens?" Janet asked. "But per-

42

haps that's only natural. I must have changed a good deal since we lived in Somerton."

"You lived in Somerton?" Alicia Spens peered more closely. "Now, let me see. You wouldn't be the Ferrier girl, would you? I seem to recognize you from your mother."

Janet held out her hand.

"That was a wonderful guess, Miss Spens," she said. "It rather suggests that I can't have changed so very much, even in eight years."

"You were about seventeen when your father sold the cottage," Miss Spens reminded her. "Folk don't change so very much after that. The woman you will become is there in the face of the girl. If it wasn't that my eyesight was going I would have recognized you straight away."

Janet felt ridiculously pleased by the remark, asking eagerly:

"Somerton hasn't changed very much either, has it? Or Athersage? It all looks very much the same to me."

"Eight years have made a difference," the postmistress told her. "We've got main drainage now, you know, and there's been a new bridge built over the Cardle. Apart from that, though, and a few deaths and births, I wouldn't say that the village itself has altered much. The young folk go away, of course, but the old folk remain. You can't keep young people from trying their wings, I always say."

Janet remembered that Miss Spens had been noted for her "sayings", and most of them were not so much clichés as sound common sense garnered over a lifetime's experience.

"And what about the hill?" she found herself asking, conscious, suddenly, that this was part of her reason for coming to Somerton. "Are things—just the same up there, too?"

Miss Spens took time to consider.

"The Smiths are still up at Silverthorn, and Colonel Craven has still got Athersage Lodge, but Mrs. Westbury has left the Larches and the Everetts sold Normanscliff long ago."

"Oh!"

"They left very suddenly," Miss Spens continued. "The Everetts, I mean. Mr. Everett died, and the son was going to be a doctor, I understand."

Janet hesitated, wondering if she should add her quota to the local gossip, and then she asked:

"They've never come back? You would have thought that—Mrs. Everett would have visited her friends."

"There was some sort of talk at the time about financial trouble," the postmistress said, "but it may have been largely gossip. They went very quickly and that was all we ever knew about it, really, after they had sold the house."

"I see."

Janet told herself that it was senseless to feel disappointed, and whatever she had come to Somerton to find it was certainly not the solution to her own future. She chatted to the postmistress for a few minutes longer, bought half a dozen stamps, and found herself out in the autumn sunshine once more.

The bus back to Norminster was not due for another half-hour and she decided to walk along the road to the next bus stop.

It had rained during the morning and the ground underfoot was still wet, with the first drifted leaves of autumn making a border of saffron along the ditches, and the smell of damp earth and the resinous tang of a fir wood assailed her nostrils as she climbed to the brow of the hill, reviving all the nostalgic memories of childhood in a single breath.

She stood very still, with sudden tears in her eyes, looking down at the sun-kissed valley behind her. The houses on the hill were very near now. She could see their gables above the trees, and in the stillness the sharp, staccato barking of a sheepdog on a distant farm seemed to come back to her across the years.

Nothing had changed, yet everything was changed.

She left the road, following the horseshoe lane which led up to the houses on the hill, and suddenly it seemed that she no longer walked alone. The road she had taken had thrust the door of memory wide open, but before she had reached the gates of Silverthorn she turned. It was a quarter to four. She would have to go back or she would miss the bus.

A car pulled up on the main road coming to rest on the brow of the hill where the far end of Horseshoe Lane came out, and she watched it idly as she walked along. After a minute or two, its occupant got out and stood looking up towards the houses on the slope above them. He was a tall man in a tweed jacket, and with a suggestion of the open air about him, and he stood looking upwards for perhaps five minutes before he got into the car again and drove away.

It was the amount of time it would have taken Janet to walk to his end of Horseshoe Lane.

Just then the bus came grinding up the hill behind her.

Her fellow-passengers were mostly country people, travelling between the outlying villages, and they all seemed to know each other. She sat listening to their cheerful conversation till the bus reached Norminster, and then she had tea in the Minster Café and went back to the Home.

The lights went on in the hall as she reached the front door and she was just in time to see Freya Allanson disappearing round the bend in the staircase, but although she called her friend's name, Freya did not seem to hear.

Automatically she scanned the notice-board before she went up to her room, reading beneath a list of lecture times the announcement of the first staff dance of the season. Life at the City General was beginning to settle down to its winter session of work and gaiety, and Sister Tutor would be as much in the limelight as the various social sub-committees who ran the dances. You read the notices and, more or less, you took your choice.

Freya's bedroom door was closed when she passed it, firmly, conclusively shut against intrusion, but when she had deposited her coat and handbag in her own room Janet went back along the corridor to knock on that unresponsive door.

"Who's there?" demanded a stifled voice from within.

Janet paused.

"It's me, Freya." She had a feeling that the door was locked against all comers. "I've been to Somerton all afternoon. Can I come in?"

Footsteps sounded on the far side of the door and a key was turned in the lock. Freya let her into a room grey with twilight, and even when Janet sat down in the armchair by the window her friend did not offer to switch on the light. She stood looking beyond Janet into the gathering dusk, her face as grey as the greying day.

"I've—made up my mind to go to London, Jan," she said, at last, in a voice that she probably hoped was devoid of all emotion. It certainly sounded flat and listless as she added:

45

"It's the best way—the only way. Ben has no intention of ever leaving Norminster and he intends to get married before Christmas."

"But your midwifery!" Janet exploded. "What are you going to do about that? You were so keen!"

"I can take it in London. I've already applied, and there's a vacancy I can have if I'm prepared to go right away. Oh, Jan," she added, "I don't want to do this! I shall miss Norminster, and more than anything else, I shall miss you, but how can I bear to stay here seeing Ben day by day, seeing him happy with someone else when all the time I know that I could have made him equally happy if only I'd had the chance!"

Janet bit her lip. She could not tell Freya that Ben Scarriff was scarcely worth a thought, that he was the sort of man who could take and give love easily, according to his creed, because her friend had already invested him with all the finer qualities, although she must know in her heart by now that he had fallen lamentably short of her ideal.

"Who was it said that first love is always like this?" Freya tried to laugh but the sound was broken and hollow. "If it is, it's a wonder anyone ever loves again." She crossed the room in a rapid, nervous stride. "It's difficult not to be bitter or cynical, Jan. I feel as if love and life are laughing at me and I ought to strike back, only I don't know how. What is there to strike with? A man has a good many weapons, but a girl hasn't very many, has she? He's got his career and a niche he can still carve for himself in the world—"

She stood looking down at Janet for a moment, hopeless uncertainty in her eyes, and then she said defiantly:

"Well, maybe I've got that, too."

After that Janet knew that she could not argue against Freya's going to London. She would miss her even more than she realized at the moment, but for Freya's own sake the proposed change to London was the only way.

"When must you go?" she asked, trying not to betray her own despondency. "Have they given you a date?"

"They want me almost at once. I've asked Matron to make a special concession and she is willing to let me go." Freya pushed the heavy fair hair out of her eyes. "She said some-

46

thing about coming back, but I don't think I shall ever come back, Jan."

She crossed to the door and switched on the light, no longer trying to hide her ravaged face, and Janet glanced at the small travelling clock on the chest of drawers beside the bed.

"I'm on duty again at six," she said. "I hope you'll be happy in London, Freya. It isn't so far away, is it? We might sometimes meet."

"Of course we will meet!" In a good many ways Freya was more resilient than Janet and she could often dismiss a serious topic with a suggestion of lightness which she was far from feeling. "We'll meet for coffee and a good old gossip and we'll swap experiences till we're old and grey—or until you get married!"

"If you could tell me who I'm likely to marry, I should be grateful!" Janet laughed. "All the men at the City General are already someone else's property, with the exception of Hilary McGrath, and he's in his dotage!"

"Aren't you forgetting about your Interesting Patient?"

A flood of colour ran up under Janet's skin, staining her cheeks and brow.

"Mr. Spencer-Wroe!" she exclaimed. "Good gracious, Freya, one doesn't consider a consultant in the same breath as an eligible!"

"Why not? He's a bachelor, isn't he?"

"Very much so, I should think, and likely to remain one!"

"It's not the first time a bachelor has been known to change his mind!"

"You're finding food for romance where none exists!"

"Don't you be so sure! Bennet told me the other day that he's constantly asking about you."

"Which reminds me that it's five to six," Janet said.

"Nothing ever comes of evading an issue!" was Freya's parting shot.

Going across the park to the hospital, Janet tried not to think of that final sally of Freya's. It was trivial compared with the fact that her friend would be leaving for London so very soon and she would find herself alone in Norminster, and for the first time she was realizing to the full all that this friendship had meant to her. It had lasted six years and it had been bound up with Norminster and the City General all that time. The hospital could not possibly be the same with Freya gone and already she had begun to feel the gap, but there could be no arguing against the wisdom of her friend's decision.

The door of Ellis Spencer-Wroe's room was open when she reached it and she stood hesitating for a moment, wondering if there was someone in with him, but the silence remained unbroken and she went into the room to find him propped up among his pillows with a satisfied smile lighting his blue eyes.

"I thought you had a visitor," she said, "when I saw your door ajar."

"I have had one, as a matter of fact," he told her. "An unexpected visitor. Someone whom I should have liked you to meet."

Janet picked up his chart.

"Was it someone you've already told me about?" she asked as she noted Nurse Bennet's entries.

He waited until she had put the chart down before he answered.

"You've just written to him," he said. "It was Doctor Everett. He was in the district and he called to see me as he was passing the hospital."

"Doctor Everett?"

It seemed that she had repeated the name stupidly, her eyes still fixed on the chart, and suddenly the temperature curve took on fantastic lines, like a row of undulating hills, macabre, almost, in their deep plunges from height into abysmal depth.

"It seems that he's by way of being a local lad when all comes to all," her patient continued, "but I don't think I shall have to go back on my initial estimate of his worth because of that. We got on very well," he added. "He seems to be looking forward to coming here even more than I expected."

"He must be." Janet felt as if the words were being choked out of her. Had that been Martin Everett in the car at Somerton this afternoon, or was the supposition too fantastic even to be examined? If it had been, they had missed coming face to face a hairsbreadth. "It will be a great opportunity for him to be working under you."

The man on the bed moved uneasily among his pillows.

48

"Janet," he said, "I didn't mean to put this to you till I was properly on my feet again, but I don't think that time is really very far off. I feel amazingly fit, although I shall still have to suffer the plaster casing for a while. When that is off, however, I have decided that I shall have a great deal of adjusting to do."

The words stabbed deep into Janet's heart, although she knew that he was far from being aware just how much adjusting might be called for. The whole future might be changed for him when that plaster casing was taken off if the fear of paralysis became a reality, and all because he had been unlucky enough to be driving his car into the hospital quadrangle at a crucial moment and had saved a child's life.

Over and over again she had wondered what would have happened if she had ignored the car and run the extra distance to Casualty. Someone else would have been first on the scene of the accident, perhaps, but that did not matter now. She was well aware of the debt she owed.

Crossing to draw the curtains over the window, she paused by the head of the bed to adjust his reading light and he reached up with his free hand and caught hers.

"Janet," he said, "I'd like you to marry me."

She drew in a swift breath. Had she expected this? All the time, had she known that he was going to ask her to marry him? She thought of Minster Close and the loneliness of the rooms at the head of the wide oak staircase; she thought of their austerity and the way he had asked her about her own home, and more than anything else she remembered the growing friendship of these past two weeks which had seemed as long as a lifetime. They had come to know one another, slowly but surely, and they had found mutual warmth and comfort in each other's company.

"Has it been a surprise?" he asked. "I thought I had more or less prepared you for it."

"Perhaps you have." She half turned towards him. "What can I say but 'yes'?"

"Janet!" He gripped her hand more tightly, his strong fingers fastening possessively over hers. "This is more than I had hoped for."

But not more than I was prepared to give, she thought.

"The difference in our ages shouldn't matter," he assured
49

her, drawing her close. "After all, what's ten years measured against a lifetime's happiness? I'm not much use with words, but I do mean it when I say that I shall do everything in my power to make you happy, 'so long as we both shall live'."

Her voice caught in her throat as she tried to answer him, and then she thrust the contemplation of the future aside and knelt down by his bed, kissing him gently on the cheek.

"If I can make you happy, too," she said huskily, "that is all I shall ask."

He moved restlessly, as if his injured shoulder was beginning to irk him for the first time.

"I've been impetuous over this," he confessed. "I didn't mean to ask you till I was out of here and sound in wind and limb again, and I think that's still the way I would like it, Janet. You see, I don't want people to think that you are marrying me out of pity!" He laughed the deep-throated laugh she had come to love. "Would it matter to you very much if we didn't announce our engagement till I'm out of this?" He gave the plaster casing an impatient glance. "I'd like to feel that I was all in one piece before we start to celebrate."

"It won't make any difference," Janet agreed instantly. "The promise is still the same. After all," she added with that seriousness which was the greatest part of her charm for him, "a ring is only the outward showing and I'm quite prepared to wait for that."

He slid his arm up to encircle her shoulders.

"You won't have to wait long, Janet," he promised. "This will be enough to get me on to my feet in half the normal time!"

When she had kissed him again she stood up, her lips trembling a little as she said:

"Whatever happens, Ellis, nothing will ever spoil this."

"My dear," he replied gently, "I know!"

CHAPTER IV

JANET half expected to find her life changed from that moment onwards, but the routine of the hospital went on as usual. If Ellis had been going the rounds of the wards in the ordinary way it would perhaps have been more difficult to believe that they were promised in marriage. He would have been the eminent surgeon with the comet-tail of attentive lesser-lights following in his wake, and she, the least of these, would probably have been awed and unnatural in his presence. It was an emotion which might have been carried into their personal contact, but as they were nurse and patient she had time to adjust herself to the idea of being engaged to a consultant and not to be overwhelmed by it.

Ellis did not suggest any immediate plans for the future. He seemed content just to get well in the quiet atmosphere of his private room, listening to the pulse-beat of the great hospital which was life itself to him.

Janet began to realize that she would not know him completely until she saw him back in harness again. The surgeon and the man were indivisible and perhaps that was why he began to count the days till his new assistant reached Norminster.

"If I really thought he could get away any sooner I'd write and ask Everett to come at once," he said. "My waiting list is piling up and I can do nothing about it, but a man like Everett could operate under my guidance. He's young and keen and I know the answers. It sounds like a reasonable enough proposition to me."

Janet drew in a deep breath, trying to keep the tears out of her eyes. Supposing it always had to be that way? Supposing he was forced to spend the remainder of his life watching another man doing the work he loved, the work that his own keen brain might devise and guide although his crippled body failed him?

The thought would not bear examination, and on the morning when Martin Everett finally arrived at the City General

51

she found herself trying to avoid a meeting with him, although she knew that she was only postponing the inevitable.

The news swept round the staff rooms, of course, and there was much eager speculation about the new resident whom Mr. Spencer-Wroe would eventually take under his wing.

"He's quite young and unbearably handsome!" was the first verdict Janet heard, delivered by the languid Nurse Travers, who pretended a complete disregard for anything beneath the level of a consultant. "I ran straight into him coming away from the P.N.O's office half an hour ago. He appeared to know his way about and seems to be the arrogant type who'll be Somebody in no time."

"I expect the P.N.O. hurried out to introduce you!" Anne Norman reflected dryly, looking up from the *Norminster Daily Courier*. "There's a bit in here about Doctor Everett, as a matter of fact," she added to the room in general. "It would appear that he's a local lad who has made good."

"That's probably why he's come to Norminster," Jenny Rose observed. "No one but a native would come from choice!"

"Look, Rosebud," Olivia Manning objected, bristling immediately in defence of her native city, "Norminster's not so bad. I know it isn't London, but these things have to be borne with what fortitude we can muster. A few of us *belong* here, too, and we like it. Isn't that so, Ferrier?"

Caught off her guard by the unexpected question, Janet was aware of the eyes of the room turned towards her.

"I've lived round about Norminster all my life," she said, trying to forget that they had been discussing Martin Everett, "and I've grown to love it."

"Then you're bound to know our Doctor Everett," Diana Travers suggested, regarding her with more interest.

"I knew him in Somerton long ago," Janet confessed.

There was a murmur of surprise and Diana Travers mocked:

"What a dark horse you are, Ferrier! Could it be that there's something of a romance in our midst and we don't realize it?"

Janet put down her teacup and turned towards the door.

"I haven't seen Doctor Everett for over eight years," she managed to say steadily enough. "I don't think that sounds particularly romantic, do you?"

52

"Disappointing, to say the least of it! But then, you could have cherished a secret passion all these years, couldn't you?" Diana laughed unpleasantly. "Stranger things have happened, Nurse!"

"Oh, shut up, Travers!" Helen Gill expostulated bluntly. "You're always trying to winkle something unusual out of everything. If Janet is interested in the new resident, good luck to her, I say! She certainly won't make a fool of herself over him, anyway!"

Nurse Travers retired, disgruntled. She loved the limelight and Janet had stolen it from her for the moment, unwittingly, it was true, and with no apparent desire to be questioned about the past.

"What is Doctor Everett really like, Jan?" someone asked from the far end of the room. "Don't hold out on us!"

"How often has Jan got to tell you that she doesn't know?" Freya Allanson demanded, coming to Janet's rescue when she saw that her friend was disinclined to talk. "The trouble with nurses is that they are consumed by curiosity about each other's affairs when they find themselves with half an hour to spare!"

"You're taking a biased view of us this morning, aren't you?" Anne Norman remarked lazily, putting down the *Courier*. "Of course we're curious about the people we have to work with, Freya, but it isn't a spiteful curiosity. You sounded sour just now, and that isn't like you," she added in her generous way.

Freya got up and stood beside Janet.

"I'm sorry," she apologized, "but gossip always rubs me up the wrong way." She lowered her voice a little, so that it came swift and intense on the next words. "What if Jan *did* know Doctor Everett long ago? Eight years is long enough for her to have forgotten even how he looks."

"True enough," Anne mused without a great deal of conviction in her pleasant voice, because she had been watching Janet ever since she had put down the newspaper. "True," she repeated, "but strange, all the same."

They don't believe me, Janet thought. They all expect me to be half in love with Martin even before we meet.

"You're bound to be first to get to know Doctor Everett," Freya remarked as they walked away along the corridor together. "I hear he's going to work with Mr. Spencer-Wroe."

"He'll probably be on his own for a bit at first," Janet said, relieved that she could discuss the matter more sanely with Freya alone. "I suppose it wouldn't be quite what he expected, but if he's the arrogant type, as Travers seems to think, he'll probably take it all in his stride."

"What does Travers really know?" Freya returned scornfully. "She caught a single glimpse of him outside the P.N.O.'s office and now she's practically related to the man!"

They turned a bend in the corridor and Janet felt herself stiffen suddenly as a tall figure in a grey suit strode purposefully towards them from the far end.

For a moment her limbs seemed frozen and she stood rooted to the spot till he reached them.

"Could you direct me to the doctors' common-room?" he asked briefly. "I seem to have lost my way."

The remembered voice, the deep intonation of the commonplace words like an intimate whisper from the past, shattered the present with the impetus of an exploding shell and the cold whiteness of the corridor seemed to fade away, giving place to a country lane gay with flowers. The ceiling above them heightened and widened to a blue sky guiltless of cloud, and the sounds and scents and memories of Somerton were fresh and vivid in the air. Eight years had slipped away for Janet as she stood there.

She found herself unable to move. A strong spell seemed to hold her there, gazing at Ellis Spencer-Wroe's new assistant as if time itself had ceased to be, and then something seemed to snap within her and she found herself trembling from head to foot.

Freya was directing Doctor Everett to the common-room.

"If you go to the end of this corridor and turn sharp left . . ."

Ordinary, commonplace words, yet they seemed to ring and echo far above Janet's head. In a moment Martin Everett would thank Freya and walk on, passing so close to her in the narrow corridor that she might almost touch him.

Desperately she tried to pull herself together, making an effort that left her weak and shaken after it was over. She could not be sure whether Martin had recognised her or not.

He had looked at her with a puzzled frown in passing, but that was all.

Freya glanced at her as they walked on.

"Doctor Everett, I presume?" she said.

"Yes."

It was as much as Janet could manage.

"Look, Jan," Freya began after a pause, "I'm not being just idly curious, but *was* there anything between you and Doctor Everett in the past?"

Janet passed a hand over her eyes as if to obliterate a sudden vision.

"No," she said. "It's all so foolish, Freya. There's nothing for me to care about. Nothing, really."

"You may have to see a great deal of him in the future," Freya reminded her. "You may even have to work with him."

"I am only Mr. Spencer-Wroe's nurse for the present," Janet said.

She wished that she could have told Freya the truth, but somehow her engagement to Ellis Spencer-Wroe seemed remote and far away as they covered the last few yards of corridor to the door of his room. Nothing about her seemed quite real, in fact. It had all faded before that vision of Somerton and a country lane. It was the lane that led to the houses on the hill, the lane along which she had walked little more than a week ago, and she knew now that if she had not turned back half-way she would have come face to face with Martin Everett at the end of it.

His had been the tall figure standing beside the car on the brow of the hill that afternoon, and somehow she knew that he had returned there under as compelling a desire as her own.

Whatever had brought him back, whatever sentiment had taken him to Somerton that hazy autumn afternoon, it was part and parcel of the feeling in her own heart.

"Sometimes I wish I wasn't going to London, after all," Freya remarked abruptly as she turned away.

It was several seconds before Janet could bring herself to open the door in front of her.

"Hullo!" her patient greeted her, his blue eyes lighting up as soon as she came into the room. "I've just had a visitor."

"I think I passed him in the corridor just now."

Janet heard her own voice as if it came from a great distance.

"I've asked him to come back," Ellis said.

Her heart was beating much too fast, and she wondered if she should tell Ellis that she already knew his new assistant.

"You can tell me what you think of him," he smiled.

"Surely that wouldn't make any difference to your opinion?" she countered with an effort at lightness which she was far from feeling. "You've already made up your mind about him, haven't you?"

"As far as the job's concerned," he admitted.

She looked up sharply.

"But surely you would have to like the man himself before you could work amicably together?" she protested.

"I should have to be able to trust him implicitly," Ellis said slowly. "He doesn't give much away."

"Will he—live in the hospital?" Janet asked.

"I believe so." He gazed out of the window with a contemplative air. "I envy you both your freedom in this lovely weather, Jan," he said. "I ought to be at liberty to take you out on your days off and see that you get all the fresh air you need, instead of lying here waiting for you to come back to me and grudging you every minute of your free time."

"I know you don't really do that," she said, smiling down at him. "Ellis—I've always meant to ask you. Haven't you some relations of your own—someone who should have been told about your accident?"

He paused for a minute before he answered.

"I have a sister in Taiwan. That's all. She's a medical missionary out there."

"Is she a doctor, too?"

He nodded.

"It runs in the family! She went abroad several years ago with a friend—another woman doctor. It was touch and go whether or not I went with them at the time, but I decided against it in the end. I considered that I had more to learn here."

"It would have meant that you would never have been the great specialist you have become in these past ten years," Janet mused. "I don't suppose you have ever really regretted your decision."

56

"In some ways, no," he said, but she felt that his thoughts were very far away and that he had forgotten her for the moment. "I'm a great believer in destiny, Jan," he added after a moment. "I think that we all have our particular part to play in the game of life and that it works out in the end as it was meant to do. I believe in a Plan, you see. We may be only pawns in the game, but there's a place for each one of us and we find it in the end. But this is heavy stuff!" he added with a smile. "Tell me what you've been doing all morning."

"I've been checking stores under P.N.O.'s guidance," Janet told him as she took his temperature. "Which might possibly suggest that she considers you well enough to do without a permanent watchdog!"

He flicked the thermometer to the other side of his mouth with an expert movement of his tongue.

"My temperature ought to be going sky-high at that!" he declared as she took the tube away. "But I'm willing to be considered normal if only it will hasten the day when all this comes off for good!"

He looked down at the plaster casing as if it were a species of strait-jacket.

"Of course, it's irksome," Janet sympathized, "but you know how necessary it is for the time being."

"It makes me feel shackled and inadequate," he objected. "I even have to wait till you offer to kiss me, Janet!"

She came to stand beside the bed.

"What do you think Miss Lawson would say if she saw me kissing you on duty?" she asked as she bent to touch his lips with her own.

"I'm sorry. I thought you were still alone——"

The words—the voice more than the words—made Janet swing round towards the door with the thermometer still in her hand and every vestige of colour driven from her face as she met Martin Everett's amused gaze across the width of the room. Had he seen that swift, shy kiss and interpreted it in his own way?

"Good gracious, no, Everett!" Ellis exclaimed. "Come in! I wanted you to meet Miss Ferrier before, when you were at the hospital that first time, in fact."

Martin Everett came slowly across the space between door and bed, seeming taller and even more dominating in the close confines of the small bedroom than he had done in the narrow corrider outside.

"Miss Ferrier and I have already met," he said, without any trace of embarrassment in his cool voice. "We are, in fact, old acquaintances."

An old acquaintance! Yes, Janet thought, that was true, and why should it suddenly sound cold and bitter in her ears? Of course, they were old acquaintances. Even, it might be said that they were old friends.

She was aware that Ellis was looking at her, waiting for her to speak.

"We knew each other in Somerton long ago," she explained.

"Eight years ago, to be precise," Martin Everett added. "We were both very young. Our acquaintance dates back to our schooldays, in fact."

Though you came in to the Minster College and I went to the village school, Janet thought, wondering if that had made all the difference. His father, she remembered, had been considered a very snobbish man.

She found herself looking at Vincent Everett's son as he bent over the bed to speak to her patient and could not imagine that Martin had inherited his father's pride and sense of position. He was more like his mother, with his olive-tinted skin and finely cut features, and there was something of his mother's sensitiveness, too, in his dark eyes as they lifted, occasionally, to watch her across the room.

She plotted her patient's temperature with hands that were not quite steady.

"You needn't go," Ellis said when she moved discreetly towards the door. "Doctor Everett will be in and out to see me most days and at all hours, I expect, till I am on my feet again."

Nevertheless, Janet wanted to go. She felt she could not stay in the room a moment longer than was absolutely necessary to endure the half-mocking gaze of Martin Everett's eyes. She knew now that he had seen her kiss Ellis and it must have appeared surreptitious and clandestine in the circumstances, but over and above all that was the feeling that something had happened to her world in the past half-hour, the quiet, settled world which Ellis Spencer-Wroe had offered her as his future wife. Something had descended on it out of the blue which

58

threatened to tear it asunder with the ruthlessness of all primitive things, and she felt puny and helpless in facing it.

Inadequate. That was the word Ellis had used when he had tried to describe his own feeling of frustration and helplessness a moment or two before, but it was more than that. It was the ineffectual striving to thrust back a tide which swept relentlessly onwards, carrying everything before it.

She walked along the corridor like someone who had gone suddenly blind, hearing the clink of glass and the cheerful clatter of cutlery as the patients' trays were prepared for the ward, and suddenly she wished that she was back on the wards where she might pass Martin Everett day by day without contact, an impersonal unit in the efficient running of the great hospital who might even escape his notice altogether.

"Your tray, Ferrier!" Diana Travers was on duty at the lift. "Mr. Spencer-Wroe's special diet, I suppose?"

Janet lifted the tray without giving the older girl the satisfaction of having goaded her to a swift rejoinder. Diana was harmless enough, in a way, but she had a bitter tongue and a sharp wit that could be hurtful at times.

"Maybe Doctor Everett will be waiting in the corridor to carry it along for you!" Diana suggested as a parting shot.

"Don't take any notice of that half-wit," Olivia Manning counselled as she wheeled her trolley along by Janet's side. "She'd take your job to-morrow if it was going begging. Anybody would!"

Janet supposed that her colleagues envied her the release from the ordinary ward routine, but she would quite gladly have changed places with any of them at that moment. She felt confused and nervous, as if solid ground was slipping away beneath her feet, and there was nothing to account for it. Nothing yet.

Her fingers closed firmly over the tray as she left Olivia at the open doors of the ward and walked on down the corridor to the door at its far end. She was being a fool, a stupid, sentimental fool, to allow the past to take hold of her imagination like this. It's not as if I had a love story behind me, she assured herself. Martin was only a name to me all these years. We were boy and girl together, that was all, and he's had eight years to forget me in. I couldn't have been in love with him—not with so little to go on—his deep-set eyes in his thin, serious

59

face, his voice and the way he carried his head. It had all been nothing more than a trick of memory, a name out of the past persisting to remind me of Somerton.

The door before her opened and Martin Everett stood in the aperture, his tall figure silhouetted sharply against the light, so that he looked suddenly close and demanding and she could not see past him into the room where Ellis lay. In spite of the fact that she was carrying a tray, he drew the door close behind him.

"Well, Janet," he said, "we've both come a long way since Somerton days."

"It's eight years," she mentioned defensively, glad that her face was not now in the full, searching light from the room beyond. "A good many things could have happened in that length of time."

"A good many things have happened to me," he said, making no effort to let her pass. "What about you?"

"As you see, I have become a nurse."

"And I have become a doctor, and in our separate ways we have both returned to Norminster. Or have you always been faithful?"

"I trained here, if that's what you mean," Janet said huskily.

"And you still live at Somerton?"

"No. My family moved to Norminster almost eight years ago."

"Which is near enough, even if it isn't Somerton."

"Did you want to go back to Somerton?" Janet asked.

"I suppose I hoped to go back one day."

He was looking at her keenly, as if he would probe relentlessly beneath the surface of her professional calm.

"What about you?" he asked.

"There's no possibility of my going back."

"Not even by desire?"

"Life isn't governed entirely by desire."

"True," he agreed. "Your family have settled here, then?"

"They live here at the moment. My mother is dead and it is easier for Robin going to school."

"How is he?" he asked with a complete change of voice. "He was the child who was injured the day I first came to the hospital, wasn't he?"

She stared at him incredulously.

"You were here?"

"I helped to get Robin out from under the car, but you didn't seem to recognize me, and I left it for the moment."

Vaguely she recalled the tall man who had stooped to fold the extra blanket over Robin's inert little figure on the stretcher, the half-remembered face that had seemed like a memory out of some distant dream amid all the confusion and anxiety attendant upon the accident, and still vaguely she realized that they had come near to meeting three times during these eventful weeks which had led up to her engagement to Ellis Spencer-Wroe.

A hairsbreadth! A split second in time, a passing mood of destiny! They had met and parted and met again four times in a lifetime, but Fate, with a sharp turn of the wheel, had changed her mind!

"I ought to thank you," she said lamely, "for what you did. I had no idea that you helped."

"There was nothing to do," he said, moving away from the door, "that someone else hadn't done already. Your brother had a narrow escape. If the car had actually fallen on him he would have been badly crushed, perhaps even killed."

And Ellis had saved him! He had taken the risk of being permanently disabled himself in order to shield Robin's frail little body with his own broad shoulders. How much she still owed him! How very much!

Martin glanced back over his shoulder towards the door of her patient's room.

"You appear to be—fond of your work," he said, the slight hesitation before he had found the right word for her enthusiasm holding what seemed to be an intended sting.

She found herself looking into eyes that were deliberately distant and faintly critical, and if she had thought that it could have mattered to him she might even have imagined a certain bitterness in their dark depths. She convinced herself, however, that there could be nothing personal in his regard.

"It's not much use being a nurse if you're not," she said briefly as he opened the door for her.

Her patient's eyes were fixed steadily upon her as she advanced with the tray.

"I had no idea you knew Everett, Jan," he said when she laid her burden down on his bedside table. "But I suppose it might have been expected when you were both natives of Norminster. He doesn't talk much about his earlier days, as a matter of fact. He would appear to be entirely preoccupied with the present and, I dare say, the future. He could have quite a future, Janet. I am beginning to realize that more and more each time we meet. He has a stronger determination to succeed than any man I've ever met, and determination is always half-way to any goal. He might even take my place one of these days."

"That would be impossible!" Fiercely she repudiated the suggestion. "Why should he? Why should anyone wish to usurp your position?"

"Because, my dear," he said, drawing her close, "he has something that I have never had—a ruthlessness, almost, where the future is concerned. He will take what he wants from life and count the cost afterwards, I should say. At least, that is my estimate of the man."

"How can you hope to work with him if you feel that?" Janet asked unsteadily. "You will be showing him all you know."

"I shall be passing on my experience," he corrected her. "But what I have said needn't upset you, Jan. I have half an idea that Martin Everett might end up by being a very good friend. Ruthlessness in a man when he knows when and where to use it and can also curb it on occasion isn't the deadliest of sins, and I am of the opinion that Doctor Everett has learned his lessons in a hard school."

"I don't think you are right there," Janet said, putting the bed-table across his knees. "His father was a very wealthy man and Martin must always have had everything he wanted."

Ellis's brows shot up.

"Yet he has just told me that he wanted to get married as soon as he qualified and couldn't afford to," he observed.

"There must have been some other reason." Janet wondered if he could hear her foolish heart hammering wildly against her ribs as she stooped to set his tray on the table for him. "It couldn't have been lack of money that kept them apart."

She was wondering who it was that Martin had wanted to marry, wondering if it was someone out of Somerton or some stranger whom he had met in London during his student days. She would probably never know. The only definite thing was that he was unmarried now, apparently, and was obviously putting his material success in the future before any second thoughts of love.

While her patient manipulated his fork with his sound left hand she went to stand looking down into the grey quadrangle as if she might find some solution there to her thoughts about Doctor Everett. Almost as if he had appeared in answer to those thoughts, she saw him come out through the swing doors on the east wing and stride across the grass to the row of parked vehicles under the window where she stood.

From that distance she imagined that he was frowning, but she could not be sure until, suddenly, he flung back his dark head and looked straight up at the window, as if he had known she would be standing there.

Their eyes met with the startling effect of shock and he continued to look at her until she turned away.

The whole room seemed tensed and waiting as she stood listening for the starting of a car, and then a door slammed and she heard an engine revving up with a staccato sharpness which suggested an almost vicious stab at the accelerator before the car itself moved off into the stream of traffic at the end of the hospital drive.

She felt shaken and, somehow, taken unawares, and with a swift movement of negation she went round the foot of her patient's bed and sat down on the chair on the far side.

"Ellis," she begged earnestly, "couldn't we drop all this—this secrecy? Couldn't we announce our engagement now and be done with it? I can't see what we gain by continuing to pretend like this."

Her voice was shaking and her hands clung to his one strong one. It seemed imperative, of a sudden, that she should have her way in this, as if she needed some sort of shield or protection to guard her against her own thoughts.

Ellis Spencer-Wroe twisted round in the bed to look at her.

"We're gaining this," he said, holding her trembling fingers in a strong, sure grip. "What do you think Miss Lawson would say if we told her we were going to be married as soon as I am fit again? I'd lose you as my nurse in less than no time! She wouldn't consider it 'the thing' to have an engaged girl nursing her future husband in the sacred precincts of the City General, and you would be back on the wards to-morrow morning!"

His hand moved to her shoulder. "Besides, Jan, there's the little matter of my wretched pride to consider," he added. "I want them to see you getting a whole fiancé, not one that would have to depend on you for most things, my dear!"

There could be no argument against such a decision, and Janet knew it. She bowed before his wish and went on with their secret engagement, although long afterwards she was to be reminded vividly of that desperate little bid for security which Ellis had turned down.

CHAPTER V

WITHIN days of each other Janet's father left for Bristol and Freya went to London. The world seemed full of partings, and soon it would be time for Robin and Mrs. Cass to go, too. She would be alone in Norminster with very few friends to contact outside the hospital and even when Ellis's shoulder came out of plaster there would be very little change. He would need a fairly lengthy period of convalescence before he was really fit, and no doubt he would want to leave the announcement of their engagement until he came back.

She began to wish fervently that she had some confidante with whom to share her secret, some trusted person to whom she could speak openly about Ellis and the future, and quite often she found herself thinking of the sister he had mentioned in distant Taiwan. Doctor Margaret Wroe, she gathered, was a woman of strong character and fixed beliefs and Ellis was even a little in awe of her, it seemed, although their only contact for years had been through the written word. Doctor Margaret had gone out to the island as a missionary eleven years ago and she had not been home since.

"If she came we would have to do something about Minster Close in a very great hurry," he told Janet smilingly when they were discussing Margaret one day. "I suppose I've always given her the impression that I at least have a comfortable home."

Janet felt that she understood Margaret Wroe much better after that, realizing that she was the sort of woman who would have sacrificed her own ambitions to look after her brother if she had thought that he was in need of her care. As it was Ellis had managed to keep her happily in Taiwan all these years by skating over the details of his domestic problems and letting her believe that he was comfortably installed in a suitable home.

"Margaret has always had a keen sense of family obligation," he explained as Janet stood waiting for his washing bowl and towel. "You'd get on well together."

"I wish we could meet," Janet said.

"You will one day. Margaret is sure to come home for our wedding, no matter how quiet we might wish to keep it. I told her, by the way, in my last letter."

"Oh!" Janet said. "I'm glad."

Yet, a moment ago, when he had first mentioned their wedding, she had felt confused and uncertain.

She told herself that she would only be able to express complete confidence in the future when she saw Ellis on his feet again, when there was no longer any fear in her mind about his complete recovery.

In these days he spent a great deal of time with Martin Everett. When Doctor Everett had done his rounds of the wards he invariably sought out his senior in the room at the end of the corridor, bring him news of the cases on which Ellis had been working before the accident and asking his advice on the new ones admitted to the hospital since then.

Janet rarely interrupted these professional conferences, knowing how all-engrossing they were to the two men, and gradually it seemed that Martin was taking up far more of her patient's time than anyone else. They went over symptoms together, checking a diagnosis time and time again in the light of their mutual experience before they would be certain about a case, and more than once, when Martin operated, she felt that Ellis had been there in the theatre with the younger man, in spirit, at least.

She, herself, had ceased to be called into the theatre although she was now a fully-trained nurse, and she was secretly glad of the fact. Martin Everett's presence had an unsteadying effect on her and she felt better when she was able to avoid him.

It was not possible to ignore him all the time, however, and the very nature of their interests and connections with Ellis flung them together almost daily.

Martin was in Ellis's room discussing one of their cases when she came in to say that Robin was leaving the hospital and she would be going home with him for an hour to see him comfortably settled in.

"Have you ordered a taxi?" Ellis asked, always careful for a patient's safety. "He mustn't on any account be allowed to catch a chill at this stage."

66

"Mrs. Cass will have seen to that, I expect," Janet said. "She's very practical."

On this occasion, however, Gladys's practical streak led them into immediate difficulty. She arrived at the hospital on foot, having walked the distance from Lavender Road in the bright October sunshine in order to do some necessary shopping on the way.

"I thought there would be an ambulance or something," she said vaguely when Janet met her on the quadrangle and asked her about the taxi. "I thought you would be seeing to it," she added defensively.

"I mentioned the taxi when you were here on Sunday," Janet reminded her, biting her lip. "But it can't be helped. I can phone for one now. It means, though, that Robin will be kept waiting."

She escorted Mrs. Cass to the visitors' room and went towards the general office to put through the call, but it was several minutes before she received attention.

"What's the matter?" a familiar voice asked at her elbow. "You look worried. Has something gone wrong?"

She turned to find Martin looking down at her, the old mockery entirely missing from his dark eyes.

"I'm trying to phone for a taxi," she explained. "I thought it had been arranged from the other end, but it hasn't. Our housekeeper thought that we could use the ambulance service."

"I think Robin would be happier without the ambulance," Martin said. "Never mind the phone call," he added briskly. "I have to go out and I can quite easily drop you on your doorstep."

Utterly surprised, she did not know what to say, nor could she thank him for a moment. He had come to know Robin on his round of the wards and he was probably making the offer more for her brother's sake than her own.

"It's very kind of you, Doctor Everett," she managed conventionally as they moved towards the foyer, "but why should we take you out of your way?"

He looked down at her with a strange expression in his eyes, half-baffled, half-demanding.

"Shall we say I'm doing it for old time's sake, Janet?" he asked. "It will save a lot of other reckoning."

"It is more than kind of you." The words had sounded stilted and cold, but she hoped that he would understand how grateful she felt. "I'd like Robin to go and say good-bye to – Mr. Spencer-Wroe," she added swiftly. "It won't take him a minute to slip along the corridor and it's just on the visiting hour."

"I'll get the car," he said, not offering to accompany her to Ellis's room.

Robin was so full of excitement about going home, at last, that Janet began to wonder if they would ever get him there safely. He was very thin and he still limped when he walked, but these were details when she considered what might have been.

He was waiting in the ward with Sister Garland, having already said good-bye to the other children, whom he had promised to come and see again.

"I want you to come and say good-bye to Mr. Spencer-Wroe," Janet explained when they were in the corridor leading to Ellis's room. "You could also say 'thank you' in person!"

Robin nodded.

"He pulled me out from under the car, didn't he? I remember that." He was a little white about the mouth as Janet knocked at the door. "I'm sorry he was hurt because of me, Jan."

"He was rather badly hurt, Robbie," Janet said. "That's why I want him to know how grateful we all are."

"I see."

Robin would much rather have gone on down the main staircase to freedom, but he was old enough to recognise his obligations, Janet thought. When she opened the door he went in and thanked Ellis with brief simplicity.

"That's all right, Robin," Ellis said. "Anyone would have done the same thing. All I want you to do now is to look after that leg of yours until it is thoroughly mended. Go slow with the football in the back yard, and no climbing over walls, at least for a bit!" He raised himself slowly on his pillows. "Stand back and let me have a look at you," he commanded. "I always like to see what sort of job I've made."

"It's a perfect job, sir!"

Martin Everett was standing in the doorway looking at

Robin with as much interest as Ellis, and it seemed for a moment as if neither of them remembered Janet's presence in the room. They were craftsmen, keenly critical of the work that had been done, one at the height of his profession but in no way arrogant about his skill, the other on the way up.

"I want you to use your legs as much as possible in the ordinary way, Robin," Ellis advised. "Get out into the fresh air whenever you can. Go for walks in the country if you can manage it, and don't sit about too much."

"We'll see what we can do!"

Martin had clapped a companionable hand on the boy's shoulder and Robin looked up at him with an eager light in his eyes. They had become friends in the ward, Janet supposed, a not unusual procedure between surgeon and child patient, and she found herself wishing a little jealously that Robin could have had the opportunity of offering Ellis some of the youthful hero-worship which he was quite obviously bestowing on the younger man. She was conscious of Ellis watching them keenly, too, as they went out together.

Mrs. Cass was sitting where Janet had left her in the visitors' lounge and when she had been introduced to Martin they all filed out to his car.

Robin rode in the front as a matter of course.

"Hop in!" Martin commanded, helping unobtrusively with the injured leg. "You'll have to direct me, you know. I haven't any idea where you live in Norminster."

"It's called Lavender Road," Robin informed him, "but we're not going to be there much longer." He sounded regretful, yet eager enough for the new adventure. "We're going to live in Bristol!"

Martin turned to Janet in some surprise, but he did not comment on the move as they drove away and Robin began to chatter to him about school and sport.

"I don't know how you'll feel about this, Janet," Gladys Cass said under cover of the animated conversation in the front seat, "but your father and I have decided to get married in Bristol."

It was a shock, but Janet felt that she had almost been prepared for it. Her father's decisions had been so unlike him of late that she was quite sure they were framed by Mrs. Cass in the first place, and it was no use continuing to feel hurt about them. She would apply for leave to attend the wedding in Bristol.

"I don't suppose you will be able to get away from the hospital for the ceremony," Gladys said, "and really there's not much point in it. We'll be getting married at the Registrar's Office, so it won't take more than a few minutes and then we'll just go off somewhere for the day."

"But what about Robin?" Janet objected.

"Oh, we'll get someone to look after him. There's bound to be a neighbour who will oblige."

"I'd rather you didn't," Janet said. "I'd rather have Robin with me."

"But it would mean you coming to Bristol."

"I think that could be managed," Janet said firmly.

"We'll see what your father has to say," Gladys observed almost primly. "He may decide to be married here, after all, and go on to Bristol the following day."

Mrs. Cass remained silent in reflection after that, and Janet found herself staring at Martin Everett's broad back and listening to his deep-toned voice as he explained to Robin how the car worked.

When they reached Lavender Road she turned to thank him, but Mrs. Cass was determined to do the honours in her own way. She had been as greatly impressed by Doctor Everett as Robin was and she invited him into the house for a cup of tea.

Janet's breath caught as she waited for his answer. She would not have dreamed of making the offer, but Gladys was in high spirits these days and had very few inhibitions now that she was reasonably sure of her position as the future Mrs. Ferrier.

"I've got the table all set," she remarked, "and it won't take me a minute to make the tea."

"Please come," Robin added shyly, looking up at Martin as he opened the door of the car.

Martin glanced at Janet.

"Why not?" he said. "I was going to spend the afternoon at Somerton, but that can easily wait for another day."

Robin was overjoyed, and some of his eager happiness must have communicated itself to Janet in the next two hours as

70

she poured out Martin Everett's tea and passed him home-made cakes and thin brown bread and butter spread with honey from her father's bees, because she felt suddenly, inexplicably conscious of an almost overwhelming joy.

"You ought to see our bees," Robin said. "My father keeps them on the moors up above Somerton in the fine weather so that they can work among the flowers, but now that the ling is past he'll be bringing them down again."

"He'll be taking them to Bristol," Gladys pointed out, "if he can find a suitable house."

Again Martin looked in Janet's direction.

"Are you going to Bristol, too?" he asked.

She shook her head.

"My work is here," she said.

"Janet wouldn't dream of leaving the City General to go anywhere else," Gladys said. "Not unless she was leaving to get married, that is."

Janet felt herself flush, but Martin had turned back to her brother.

"We might still have time for a look at the bees, Robin," he suggested. "Tell Janet to arrange about Somerton and I'll come and take you there in the car. It would be killing two birds with one stone, since I want to go there, anyway, on business."

Janet looked up and met his eyes.

"Normanscliff is coming on to the market again," he explained. "The people who bought it from my family eight years ago are going abroad and are anxious to sell."

Would he buy Normanscliff, Janet wondered, and settle down there? Perhaps he was even thinking about getting married, and Normanscliff was an ideal family house.

A swift, heart-catching spasm of nostalgic memory swept through her at the thought and she turned away from the table, saying that she must get back to the hospital.

"Mr. Spencer-Wroe will be wondering what on earth has happened to me," she said.

"I'll drive you back," Martin offered.

"Why should you?" she countered. "It's your afternoon off. There's no reason why you should come back to the hospital because of me."

"No reason whatever," he agreed, "except the fact that I

71

am just as happy at the hospital as anywhere else these days. It will be my home until I have decided about Normanscliff," he added.

They drove back together through the gathering dusk, with the street lights pricking out in a yellow glow above them and some of the happiness they had left behind at Lavender Road still surrounding them.

"I had no idea that you and Robin had become such fast friends," Janet said.

"We have interests in common," Martin laughed, reviewing the events of the afternoon. "It should be quite an experience going to Somerton to see the bees."

"You meant that?" she asked almost awkwardly.

"Why not?" He turned from the wheel for a moment to search her eyes. "Mr. Spencer-Wroe prescribed it as part of Robin's cure."

Ellis's name stood between them for a moment, and then Janet said impulsively:

"Robin will love it, but I hope he won't be too great a responsibility for you."

"Not since I expect you to share it," he told her casually. "Don't you want to visit Somerton again, Janet? Don't you feel that it might be just the right place for a walk in the country, which is what Mr. Spencer-Wroe prescribed?"

"He ordered it for Robin." Janet felt the words choking in her throat as her breath drove out between her parted lips. "I don't think he expected me to be able to go with him."

"I can't see why not. You have days off, haven't you? And, since you are not going to Bristol, it is only natural that you must want to spend as much time as possible with your brother."

"Yes," Janet agreed, feeling suddenly depressed and lonely at the thought of losing Robin's gay young companionship. "It's true enough. Bristol seems a very long way from Norminster when you look at it like that."

"Your father is going to marry Mrs. Cass, I take it?" he queried.

Janet nodded.

"I'm hoping they will change their minds and get married before they leave Norminster so that I can take Robin away somewhere for the day."

72

"Your family matters a lot to you," he said. "Mine did, too."

Janet saw that his mouth was suddenly grim, and it was several seconds before he added:

"There's very little left of it now, I'm afraid."

"I often wondered what happened when you left Somerton," Janet confessed.

"My mother died a year ago." The hardness about his mouth had spread to his eyes now and he kept them fixed firmly on the road ahead. "My great ambition has always been to see her back in Normanscliff, but apparently these things are not left in our hands."

Yet less than an hour ago he had told her that he was about to re-purchase the old family home, but apparently he had nothing further to say on the subject of Normanscliff and they came to the hospital without his offering any added confidence.

The short interlude was over, and although he had suggested that they should spend another day in each other's company, she felt that something might interfere to prevent it.

The remainder of the week passed swiftly enough. The injuries which Ellis had sustained to his legs had healed and he was able to get out of bed for an hour each day, although the plaster jacket which encased the upper half of his spine was still a great handicap to his movements.

By the end of the week, however, he had overruled his colleagues' advice and was appearing in the operating theatre. It was in an entirely advisory capacity, to be sure, but it was forceful and dynamic for all that.

It was quite obvious that his presence was giving Martin new confidence, and indirectly Janet heard rumour of a brilliantly successful operation which it had been thought that only Ellis himself could undertake.

In these days she recognized an unselfishness in Ellis which humbled her, and his dedication to his profession could not have been more pronounced. If Martin was indeed reaping the benefit of his skill and years of experience, Ellis did not grudge it in the slightest, but it also meant that he must have absolute faith in the younger man. Martin Everett had won his laurels as a surgeon before he had come to the City General, but this was specialized work and only Ellis could

73

have taught him its finer points. He could not pass on his actual skill in operating, but he could watch and advise, and he would not have associated himself with such a position if he had not recognized outstanding ability in the other man.

They worked together and lived together, and quite often Janet had to turn Martin out of the room at the end of the corridor when she felt that it was time her patient was allowed to sleep.

"You know what Sir Adrian said when he last saw him," she reminded Martin as they walked along the corridor together on one of these occasions. "They won't really know if Mr. Spencer-Wroe is going to be completely cured until the plaster comes off."

Martin's face darkened.

"Nothing must happen to him," he said beneath his breath. "It would be—too damnable a thing."

Janet watched him walk away, his broad figure in the white surgeon's coat tall and straight as he strode off to his final round of the wards.

Nothing must happen, she repeated in her heart. Nothing that we can possibly prevent.

It was Ellis who finally insisted on the day at Somerton.

"Martin tells me that he has promised to take Robin out for a run to the moors," he mentioned the following morning. "Why don't you go with them, Jan," he added, "and get some fresh air into your lungs? I'm quite sure you are due a day off by now."

The P.N.O. had spoken about her time off the day before, but for a split second Janet knew a strange reluctance to do as she was asked.

"I don't mind not having time off," she told him. "It was a —sort of bargain between Miss Lawson and me when I first came to nurse you."

"All the same," he objected, "I should imagine it is strictly against all the rules."

"I suppose I ought to go," Janet agreed, at which he laughed outright.

"Janet!" he said, "if I didn't know you I would say that you were stuffed with cotton wool and sewn up with the best quality sutures, all duly sterilized and correct in the regulation hospital manner! The City General isn't the only thing in life though I appreciate the fact that you love your work and that it will always be a bond between us. You have your health to consider, though. You've been looking altogether too pale and peaky these past few days, my dear. Go out with Robin and enjoy yourself."

Go to Somerton, he had said in effect. Go back and look into the past. And Janet already knew that she dared not look too deeply.

When Martin came to collect them she had already walked the short distance to Lavender Road, feeling that she did not want to drive there from the hospital with him. Apart from the fact that someone would be sure to see them setting out together, she felt strangely vulnerable in Martin's company now, but after Lavender Road Robin would be there.

Robin hobbled out to the car as soon as Martin drew up at the garden gate and Janet was glad enough to get in behind them and was almost tempted to ask if Mrs. Cass might come too.

Gladys waved them off, and it was only after they were several miles on their way to Somerton that Janet realized that her father's housekeeper had been dressed in her Sunday best.

The fact flickered rawly across her mind for a moment, with its attendant suspicion, and then she forgot all about Mrs. Cass as the car ate up the miles and they turned off the main road and were winding along the twisting by-way to Somerton and Athersage.

"The bees first, I think," Martin decided, putting the car to the hill road that would take them directly on to the moors. "I hope they will all be at home!"

"The queen bee will," Robin hastened to assure him. "She never leaves the hive unless it's time to swarm. It's a young queen that flies away," he added knowledgeably. "An' she takes all the young worker bees with her."

"To form a new home," Martin mused. "Almost life-like in its simplicity, in fact!"

Janet remembered that her father's hives were on the moor not very far from Normanscliff. The moors stretched right up to the houses on the hill, a vast area of rough scrub land golden in the autumn sun, with bracken and heath still glowing on either side of the narrow paths which cut across it and

75

the sky very blue and high above it.

Martin drove the car as far as he could up the uneven road so that Robin would not need to walk too far, and then they set off across the moor in the direction of the miniature valley which cleft it in two and finally ran down to Athersage.

It was a golden day, indeed, and Janet felt the years dropping away from her as they walked on. It seemed that she and Martin were back in the days of their early youth. It almost seemed as if they walked there, hand in hand, with the sun warm on their faces and its brightness in their eyes.

The day had been made for such an expedition, a day snatched from summer, with birds twittering above them and a pair of sulphur butterflies dancing ahead.

Robin hobbled beside them, pointing out the white hives on the hillside to Martin as soon as they came into view, and even while they were some distance away they could hear the heavy droning of the bees carrying across the still air.

The deep, nostalgic sound was only another voice from the past, like the lark singing high above their heads as if it were, indeed, high summer, and the yellow butterflies settling on the path ahead. It was a day carved out of time; an October day holding the sweet, warm breath of June.

Standing beside the hives, they watched the busy progress of the winged inhabitants and were careful not to stand between them and their "front door" because, as Robin explained carefully, they didn't like to be stopped at their work and would probably sting in retaliation.

"Bees have always had a fascination for me," Martin said as they turned back towards the car. "I must keep some when I get back to Normanscliff."

"You could have them on the moor, same as we do," Robin pointed out. "We could have them together. I'm sure our bees wouldn't mind."

"I'm sure it would be all most friendly," Martin agreed. " shall have to come to your father for advice when I do make up my mind."

Mrs. Cass had packed a picnic basket for them and put i in beside Janet in the back seat, and she felt that Martin approved of the idea as he looked up at the sky.

It was certainly the ideal way to have their lunch on such day, and he spread the car rug on the grass for them to sit o and stretched himself out beside Janet as she unpacked.

"We might be a thousand miles away from Norminster," he mused, looking across the valley. "We might be a thousand miles from anywhere!"

"Athersage hasn't changed much," Janet said. "Or Somerton either."

"Places don't change so quickly. It's only people who alter." She did not look around at him.

"Have you found that?" she asked.

"Quite often."

"And it—disappointed you?"

"It surprised me. But perhaps I was looking for perfection."

"Have we any right to expect perfection in others? We're all—vulnerable somewhere."

She looked up at him, at last, and saw that he was smiling, and when Robin came to throw himself down at their side, he said lightly:

"It's too perfect a day to become involved in an argument, Janet. Am I to have some tea?"

"You said that you intended to go to Normanscliff," Janet mentioned when she had poured his tea from the vacuum flask. "Robin and I will wait for you here."

"Why not come with me?" Martin suggested. "There's no reason why you shouldn't. It's only down the lane."

Only down the lane, but somehow Janet felt that it was a world away.

"The present owner won't expect to see a picnic party on her doorstep," she demurred, but he swept her objections aside.

"The present owner is trying to sell the house, and how is she to know that you're not as interested in it as I am? I may be away more than an hour and it can grow bitterly cold up here when the sun begins to go down."

"I'd love to go!" Robin intimated, and so it was settled that they should all go.

Martin drove the car to the end of Horseshoe Lane, parking it on the side of the road where Janet had seen him standing that afternoon when she had first come to Somerton after so many years, and her heart caught at the memory as it might have caught on regret or the bitter realization that she had come upon a precious thing too late.

Normanscliff stood higher than its neighbours, perched on a

natural outcrop of stone which fell steeply to the level of the road, and it was approached by a narrow, zig-zag pathway leading upwards through the density of overgrown rhododendrons and a thick plantation of spruce and pine. The trees left deep shadows on the path and a carpet of soft needles under their feet, and there was no sound as they climbed upwards.

When they were almost at the house a ringdove flew up out of the little wood with a heavy flapping of its grey wings, wheeling above them to find a safer refuge, and somewhere at the back of the house a dog began to bark. Janet wondered if it was the same dog that had barked that afternoon as she had stood down on the main road waiting for the bus, although the sound had seemed to come from farther away.

"Perhaps we should wait for you in the garden," she suggested. "I really don't think we should come in."

Robin had already gravitated towards a shallow lily pond in the sunken garden at the side of the house, and Martin only hesitated for a moment before he said:

"Just as you like. It looks as if these people still keep goldfish in the old pool."

Janet sat on a stone on the rough side of the rock pool and watched the golden fish darting in and out among the broad green lily leaves without really seeing them clearly. She had never been in the Normanscliff gardens before and it did not seem like reality to be sitting there now where Martin had played as a boy.

In many ways it was a boy's paradise, with its closely-growing trees and cave-like outcroppings of stone and the freedom of the moors close to its encircling wall. There was a vast, untidy lawn, ideally suited to a haphazard game of cricket on a summer's day, and an overgrown tennis court which had apparently not been in use since the Everetts had moved away.

Perhaps Martin meant to restore it all one day, and she tried to envisage it when his task would be finished. Somehow, she thought that he would not change so very much. It was a family house, a place where children had always been able to romp freely in the sun, with no danger of spoiling anything or trampling exotic and prized flowers in their haste to retrieve a lost ball or a straying pet. It was the home of her own secret imaginings, a place set apart for laughter and the sound of running feet, and suddenly she was looking at it all through a mist of tears.

"Robin," she said, forcing them back, "are you tired of watching the fish? Do you think we should go back out on to the moor? It's only over the wall."

What wind there was was cold now, coming in over the open stretches of the moor, and some of the gold seemed to have faded from the day. She shivered a little as she drew her coat about her and fastened the belt, and then she opened the door in the lichen-covered wall and led the way out of the garden.

"It's colder here," Robin said, "and not so nice. Why don't we go back, Jan?"

Before she could answer Martin was coming towards them through the doorway.

"I've made up my mind," he said, "to pay them the price they want for the house."

There was frank elation in his eyes as he looked about him, and Janet felt that he must have planned this long ago but that it had only become possible now.

"Mrs. Coupland has asked us to stay to tea," Martin said. "She thought we might like to look over the garden while she got it ready."

Robin wanted Martin to go and look at the fish.

"I've never seen such big ones!" he cried excitedly as he limped back along the path to the pool. "Some of them are nearly orange, and others are quite pale."

"I'm hoping that they might be the descendants of my original pair," Martin laughed. "One of them used to eat bread out of our hands in the old days. My sister trained him to do it and he would swim up and look for her whenever she called."

Robin regarded him doubtfully.

"They all darted away when I tried to catch them," he said.

"Perhaps there's a special word!" Martin suggested. "Or maybe we will have to tempt them with a piece of cake!"

They stood by the pool watching the little golden fish, and the garden seemed peaceful and still and waiting. Janet wondered what Martin was thinking, coming back to Normanscliff after so long a time away. He might even be wishing that he had come back alone so that he might plan his future in the garden of his youth.

Presently they turned and walked through a dense fernery

where the sound of falling water took Robin on ahead of them to a white cascade frothing over a wide ledge of rock. The water went down under the trees in a dark green tunnel, dropping several feet from the level of the house to form the brown stream which Janet remembered went under the road at the far end of Horseshoe Lane. Long ago, as a schoolgirl, she had sat and swung her legs over the parapet of the hump-backed bridge which spanned it, and her heart seemed to turn over at the memory.

To-day had been so full of memories.

Robin's voice came up to them, high-pitched and full of a boy's eager delight.

"There's another pool down here and this one is full of tiddlers! Come down, Jan, and see!"

He was just beneath them, but he was hidden, out of sight, and she hurried towards him over the mossy stones. In the half-light of the tree-shaded gorge, with her eyes still misted by the emotions of a moment or two before, her feet were uncertain and before she realized what had happened she felt herself falling. She had slipped and twisted her foot on a stone, but Martin was close by her side. She felt his arms about her, catching her up and holding her close, and his breath was suddenly warm on her cheek, like the breath of the wind when they had first gone up on to the moor.

For a moment neither of them spoke, and they stood in a silence far more revealing than words. Then, almost violently, he released her, steadying her on her feet again before he led the way down to where Robin was waiting.

Janet could not follow him immediately. She stood where he had left her, white and shaken, feeling the wild beating of her own heart and remembering the throbbing intensity of it as she had stood within the circle of Martin Everett's arms. For one brief, ecstatic moment she had forgotten everything and the whole world had seemed to stand still. Time and even memory had slipped away and there had been only herself and Martin in all the world.

"Jan! aren't you coming?" Robin called for a second time. "There's hundreds and hundreds of fish down here!"

She went without answering, because she knew that she could not trust herself to speak.

Martin was standing beside the pool, looking as young and

carefree as Robin as he bent over the brown water to scoop a handful of tiddlers on to a flat stone at her brother's feet.

"We used to take them up to the house in jars," he said.

Janet made a small, inarticulate sound above them and he stood up to look at her. There was remembrance and laughter and demand in his eyes, but she could not meet them. She turned hastily away, saying in a voice that sounded as unsteady as she felt:

"Surely Mrs. Coupland will be waiting for us by now?"

Martin carried Robin pick-a-back up to the house.

"My mother used to ring a bell when we were wanted at meal-times," he said. "I wonder if it's still there, hanging in the hall. It's the only way to call children when they're scattered about a big garden like this."

There was an old ship's bell hanging in the porch when they reached it, and Janet could remember the clear sound of it echoing down the lane. As children they would know that it was five o'clock, or twelve, or time for bed, when they heard it, and hurry back towards the village. The Normanscliff bell had been a local affair, but it had not rung for them to-day.

Mrs. Coupland was an elderly woman who suffered a great deal from arthritis, and she walked towards them across the tiled hall with the aid of a stick.

"I'm glad you were able to stay for a cup of tea," she told Janet, leading the way into the long drawing-room whose deep bay windows commanded a wide view across the valley to the distant hills beyond.

It was a window which had captured Janet's fancy even from the outside, because she had known that all of Somerton and Athersage would lie down there when you looked over the tops of the Normanscliff pines to the winding road below.

"Doctor Everett told me about your brother's accident and I thought he would benefit by the rest," Mrs. Coupland said, wheeling the tea trolley towards the fire. "I see, though, that he walks better than I do!"

She smiled down at Robin from her considerable height, and Janet thought that she must have been a very handsome woman in her youth. The contours of beauty were still clear in the rounded face, although suffering had etched lines there, too.

"I'm sorry about having to leave here," she said as she poured their tea and offered Robin a glass of lemonade. "I've loved Normanscliff, but now that my family is grown up and scattered and I'm quite alone, it's far too big for me. It's really a family house," she added, giving Janet a swift, confiding smile.

"Mrs. Coupland is going out to South Africa to live with a married daughter," Martin explained.

"Normanscliff isn't difficult to run for someone young," Laura Coupland said. "It stands high and we are very free from dust up here. With a daily help you could run it perfectly."

She laughed, and Janet felt herself go suddenly taut. It was obvious that their hostess thought she was engaged to Martin or at least that they must be contemplating such a happy event.

A bleak spasm of dismay ran through her at the thought. She was engaged. Yes, of course, but not to Martin!

She could feel Martin's eyes upon her from the far side of the hearth and she felt that they must hold the old gleam of mockery, but when she forced herself to meet them it was difficult to say what sort of emotion lay in their dark depths. He was balancing his tea-cup expertly, stirring his tea reflectively, and when he rose to put the cup down he gave her what could only be described as a challenging grin.

It was half-past four when they returned to Norminster and she was due on duty at the hospital at six. There was just time to deliver Robin at Lavender Road and walk back across the park to the Home to change into her uniform and pick up any letters that might have come for her by the afternoon post. She was expecting one from Freya, who had written twice from London during the past three weeks.

"I'll wait," Martin said when he had drawn the car up at the garden gate. "I'm going back to the hospital."

"I—think I would rather walk," she said unsteadily. "I—feel as if I need the exercise."

"After all our efforts on the moors?" he queried. "Don't be silly, Janet! If you're nervous about Matron's eagle eye, I'll let you down at the foot of the drive!"

She could not raise further protest after that, and Robin was already offering his shy but very genuine thanks for the afternoon.

"Next time you must bring your fishing-rod," Martin said,

"and we'll catch some fish!"

He sat back and took out a cigarette, obviously prepared to wait for her in the car, and Janet followed her brother up the path to the house.

A radiant Mrs. Cass opened the front door to them.

"I wondered how long you would be!" she beamed. "We've got a very big surprise for you—your father and I!" She took Robin's flushed little face between her hands and kissed him, and Janet saw the gleam of new gold on the third finger of her left hand. "Aren't you going to come in?"

Janet hung back, letting Robin go ahead. She felt sick with disappointment, not because she grudged her father his new-found happiness but because it had been done in such a secretive way.

"We were married this morning," Gladys informed her. "I hope you're not going to be awkward about it," she added. "You can surely come in and wish us luck."

"Of course."

For a moment Janet had forgotten about Martin sitting outside in the car. All she could make out was her father's tall figure dominating the small sitting-room where her new step-mother had laid out a table with iced fruit cake and wine. He had on a new suit and he smiled tentatively as she went towards him, and then suddenly she was in his arms, clinging to him and telling him that she hoped he would be happy, while he held her more tightly to him than she could ever remember him doing in the past.

"I've asked your friend to come in for a glass of wine," Gladys announced from the doorway, and then Martin was in the room and they were drinking the newly-weds' health and Robin was sitting rather quietly by Janet's side trying not to cry. After all, he was ten years old and boys of ten didn't cry over something they didn't understand which hurt deep down.

When Martin had taken Janet out to the car and had driven the full length of Lavender Road he put his hand unexpectedly over hers.

"Cheer up, Jan!" he said. "It was tough on you that way, but I take it you knew it was coming?"

"Yes." She felt choked and desperately tired, and his unexpected kindness had unnerved her more than she could possibly have imagined. "It wasn't that. It was unexpected, of course, but it hurt Robin——"

"He's young," he said, not indifferently. "He will get over it soon. It's you who have been hurt most."

They did not speak again till he drew the car up just short of the hospital gates.

"I've left it to Robin to thank you for our lovely day," she said, feeling that any further emotion would only break down the hastily-erected defences she had built. "But it's all been wonderful——"

She ran from him with that, across the park and up to the sanctuary of her own room, where she leaned back against the stout door in a confession of weakness which she would not have shown to anyone. The hard panelling pressed against her back as slow, difficult tears welled scaldingly in her eyes and coursed swiftly down her cheeks.

I love him, she thought. I love Martin Everett. It wasn't just a name out of the past, after all. It was all my love and all my life's happiness gathered up into one anguished hope that we would meet again, and now we have met – like this!

CHAPTER VI

THE days which followed were a numbing agony of uncertainty for Janet while she stood aside and watched Ellis Spencer-Wroe binding Martin to him with bonds as unseverable as her own.

With the confining plaster still depriving him of the use of one side of his body, Ellis began to tour the wards again, but it was in his consulting-room and in the operating theatre that the two men really worked as one.

Martin would never have progressed so swiftly if the older man had merely been demonstrating his methods to a highly intelligent pupil, but as things were they worked as a unit. One pair of hands were backed by a sharp, incisive intellect and the experience of years, and the waiting list which had lengthened dramatically while Ellis had been in bed was now being reduced with the utmost speed and vigour.

Janet found herself back on the wards, back on men's surgical, where all the beds were full and Sister Oliphant sat in her little cubby hole of an office just outside the swing doors and made tea at all hours of the night and day.

The ordered routine of ward work was a relief to Janet in some ways. There was so much to do that she often slept from sheer exhaustion at night when otherwise she might have lain awake in the darkness trying to find a solution to what she suspected was an insoluble problem.

She loved Martin, but how could she tell Ellis that when she owed him so much? How could she tell him in face of the secret she shared with Matron and Sir Adrian Pepper?

It seemed as if Ellis might wear the plaster for the rest of his life, although her experience told her that these things were never removed in a hurry. Bones were given time to strengthen and torn sinews were left to knit together, but she knew that the consulting specialist's real fear was the spine. If it had sustained serious injury, then it was already a miracle that Ellis could even walk, and the upper part of his body had yet to be tested.

The days had turned bleak and cold, with an orange ball of

a sun appearing occasionally in a slate-blue sky and hoar frost all along the hedges. The hospital was filling up with seasonal cases of pneumonia and asthma and the sudden icy conditions of the roads brought in its own quota to Casualty.

A good many of these cases found their way eventually to the surgical wards, and work and routine dominated the nurses' lives in consequence. It could not, however, dominate the romantic conception of Christmas as a time for marriages. Two fully trained nurses left within a week of each other, one of them the theatre sister whom Janet had relieved on several occasions during the past year.

News of a wedding was an event and the two brides-to-be were besieged each time they returned from a shopping expedition to the town, but Janet knew how worried the P.N.O. would be over their replacement.

It was more than a surprise to her, however, to be called to the P.N.O.'s office one dull afternoon and offered promotion.

"You may feel that you haven't had a great deal of experience of operative work," Miss Lawson said, watching her closely, "but that will come in time. You are the type for the job. I think I might say I have always found you cool and practical, Nurse, and I do not think that you will fail me or the hospital. You won't be left alone at first. Sister Chard will be there and she will help you all she can."

"Sister Chard?"

Janet had repeated the name without quite knowing why, and then she realized that Marian Chard was senior theatre sister in the west wing and worked mostly with Ellis Spencer-Wroe.

Which meant that she worked, too, with Martin!

"Yes. The main theatre in the west wing, Nurse. You've been down there before and you know your way about." Miss Lawson got up and held out her hand. "Congratulations, Sister," she said with a small, encouraging smile. "I hope you will be very happy in your new work."

She found herself outside in the corridor walking away from the P.N.O.'s office.

It would be expected that she would take up her duties immediately and she knew that she ought to report to Sister Chard at once, but the desire for escape was too strong, even for her sense of duty. She had not seen Ellis to speak to for days, and Martin had seemed too busy to eat in the residents' dining-room, which she passed frequently on her way to the wards, but she knew that neither of them would fill her immediate need.

She thought of Freya, wishing that her friend was back in Norminster, until, as if to convince her of the selfishness of such a desire, Ben Scarriff came smartly along the corridor in his white coat and gave her a fleeting nod as he passed. Then, on second thoughts apparently, he turned.

"Ever hear from Freya Allanson these days?" he asked.

"I have a regular weekly letter," Janet told him frigidly. "Why?"

"Oh—nothing, really. I wondered how she was getting on."

Was that all? Janet waited, but after a moment's hesitation he walked on and she was left looking after him with no doubt in her mind. He was conceited and not at all talented, and detestably sure of himself, but for six months of a golden spring and summer Freya had been deliriously in love with him. It was all over now, but she knew that the memory of that summer would linger, for Freya, at least.

Walking across the grey stones of the quadrangle, she tried to focus her thoughts on her own future, but she could not see any way of making it easier. To work with Martin and Ellis as a unit in the ordinary way would have been the height of any nurse's ambition, but when her heart was torn asunder by love for one and duty to the other how could she hope to give what they both needed? A good theatre sister practically lived inside the mind of the operating surgeon. She had to be practical and cool when they worked together, there whenever he needed her without her mind being dulled by the torture of love and her hands unsteady because of his nearness.

"Hullo, there!" a voice said behind her. "I haven't seen you for days, and Nurse Bennet has taken to giving me sleeping pills in consequence!"

"Ellis!" She wheeled round, feeling that he must surely be able to read her thoughts in her startled eyes. "I had no idea you were allowed out."

"I thought I would take the law into my own hands and come and look for you." He sniffed the fresh air appreciatively. "I saw you escaping as I turned the end of the corridor!"

Escaping! He had used the very word that had been in her own mind since she had come away from the interview in Miss Lawson's office.

"Perhaps I *was* trying to get away," she confessed, biting her strong white teeth on the edge of her lower lip. "I don't know whether you've heard or not, but the P.N.O. has appointed me to your main theatre in the west wing."

"I thought she might do that," he acknowledged with a quiet smile. "You're quite ready for it, Jan. You can do the job."

"I can't! I oughtn't to take it. I'm not really ready!" Her voice was trembling now with her evident distress and she longed to bury her face in her hands because she was not telling him all the truth. "I've not had enough experience, Ellis. I've passed in surgical nursing, but operating technique is quite a different matter. A competent theatre sister does everything but the actual operating."

"And she also has to learn." The blue eyes were looking at her fixedly, willing her to accept his assurance about the future. "This is the sort of thing that invariably happens, Jan. It has happened before and it will happen so long as there are good, conscientious nurses—and doctors, too, by the way— who want to give only their best to their job. Everybody is prone to get the jitters when they find themselves confronted with this sort of responsibility for the first time, and sometimes it even happens to us old stagers! Martin had them less than a month ago, but he got over them—just as you will. Don't worry too much about coming into the theatre. You won't be alone, and nothing is ever the ordeal we first imagine it to be. Don't forget that I shall be standing by."

As he always would, right through life, Janet thought with a catch in her throat. Dear, kind, considerate Ellis, to whom she already owed so much!

They walked back towards the hospital together, and it was as if some sort of pact had been made between them. Janet still continued to feel nervous about her first appearance in the operating theatre, but she did not view it now with the same feeling of dread.

The moment came sooner than she expected, too. She had reported to Sister Chard and found the older woman as kind and willing to be helpful as Miss Lawson had promised she would be, but she also looked harassed.

"It does seem a shame to pitchfork you into the work right away," she apologized with a swift look round her disordered domain, "but Doctor Everett has just operated and we have another emergency coming up in half an hour. Nurse Westlake has reported sick, too." She rubbed her hand across her forehead in a slightly weary gesture which made Janet wonder what time she had come on duty that morning. "If you could help to tidy up in here and push some fresh dressings into the sterilizer it would give me time to snatch a cup of tea."

Janet nodded.

"I'll stay," she said. "You go and get your tea."

She was stacking masks into the sterilizer when Martin came in and he did not appear to recognize her for a moment.

"I left a case of instruments here, Nurse," he said. "I shall be needing them again when we get down to this emergency."

Janet moved the case along the bench towards him and at last he was looking at her.

"Janet," he asked, "what are you doing down here?"

"The P.N.O. thinks I might prove equal to theatre work in time."

She had thrust a calm acceptance into her voice to steady it, but it had all but quivered before she had finished speaking.

"Of course you'll be equal to it! You're a born nurse," he said. "It was something of a surprise seeing you down here, all the same. I thought you were still nursing Spencer-Wroe."

"He hasn't a great deal of need for special nursing now," she pointed out. "Though Sir Adrian thinks he should still remain in the hospital."

His dark brows drew together in a swift frown.

"So I believe," he said. "I'm not quite sure what Sir Adrian thinks about his visits to the theatre, by the way."

"He's only working by proxy. You are doing the major part."

"And what experience I'm gaining in the meantime!" The keen light of ambition and its reflected glow of fulfilment broke in his dark eyes for a moment. "I should never have had the chance of operating on half these cases if Ellis Wroe hadn't given me his confidence and trust."

"It is what you wanted?" she found herself asking.

"It's more than I wanted! It has been the chance of a lifetime, but it has also been something more. It's difficult to explain. I've gained so much in these past few weeks, but I know Ellis doesn't grudge that, and he doesn't look at it as something that should make me grateful to him for the remainder of my days. All the same," he added slowly, "I shall be."

"How long will it take—this emergency you're going to do now?" she asked.

"Not much more than half an hour." He glanced at his watch. "I'm entirely on my own this time," he added with a smile. "It has nothing to do with lungs!"

Even without the evidence of the morning's operating list pinned up on the wall, she could see that he had already had a heavy day. The signs of it were in the small lines of fatigue about his mouth and eyes, yet she wondered if he really noticed it. His keenness on the job would surmount exhaustion. It was the natural attribute of the successful surgeon, and with Ellis's help there would be no limit to the heights to which he might climb in the future.

Suddenly she knew a fierce, overmastering exhaltation at the thought, as if her love had given her the right to be proud, but in the next instant it lay dead against her heart.

In spite of what Martin had said about the emergency operation being a one-man job, Ellis put in an appearance in the ante-room a few minutes before they were due to start. He gave Janet a keen look, nodding his encouragement to her as the patient was wheeled in, and then she had forgotten even Martin as she moved to Sister Chard's side.

The operation lasted less than the half-hour Martin had given himself, and Ellis remained an interested spectator all the time. There had been no need for him to offer advice in this case, but his keen interest in everything surgical kept him on the scene until the last suture was securely fastened and Sister Chard drew her habitual and barely audible sigh of relief. She had been doing it for years and even Martin smiled at it now.

Janet stepped promptly to Martin's side, untying his mask and peeling off his rubber gloves for him. The heat from the great lamp under which he had been working had brought little beads of perspiration out on his brow and the fatigue lines about his eyes were more noticeable than ever, but he had the look of a man who had achieved something worth while and could go on to conquer untold worlds.

Her pulses raced at the thought of the bright future lying before him, at his happiness in achievement which would grow with the passing years, and then she turned to see Ellis looking at them from the far side of the room. His gaze was quizzical but kind, and a sudden rush of tears blinded her as she turned away. How easy it could be to forget one's obligations when love stood close at one's elbow!

With the curtailment of the heavy waiting list came their first opportunity to relax.

"It's high time you had some gaiety!" Ellis declared one evening when Janet had gone to visit him. "I'm not much use as an escort, cooped up here every evening after dark by Matron's orders, and, besides, I don't move fast enough in my strait-jacket!"

She tried to smile, because she knew that he didn't want to discuss the prolonged necessity for the plaster casing which still covered the major part of his chest and arm.

"What would you suggest I should do?" she asked. "I can't go to Bristol because they have the painters in and Robin would have to turn out of his bedroom to accommodate me and sleep on the settee, and there's not a lot of fun in doing a show on one's own." She took a quick turn about the room. "I'm beginning to miss Freya even more than I expected," she confessed. "But I've been too busy to realize it till now."

"I should have thought you would be up to the eyebrows in the nurses' dance," he mused.

"I'm not on the committee. Theatre sisters are never eligible because they work such uncertain hours."

"But you mean to go, of course?"

She looked away for a moment.

"I hadn't made up my mind."

He leaned forward to take her hand.

"I'm sorry, Jan!" he said. "I had no right to tie you down to that promise. Not when I wasn't ready to acknowledge it publicly." His blue eyes looked contrite. "Couldn't you go very well without a partner?"

"Of course!" she said, smiling down at him. "It would be quite in order, kind sir, to go alone! Most of the other nurses will be doing it, but there are always plenty of partners to go round."

"I shall have to ask the P.N.O. for a late pass!" he grinned. "I shall want to keep an eye on you!"

The following afternoon Janet heard that Martin was going.

"I've just sold Doctor Everett two tickets for the dance!" Diana Travers announced jubilantly, coming to stand at the door of the sisters' common-room where Janet and Sister Chard were snatching a hurried cup of tea between operations. "He's bringing a partner."

Janet's cup fell back into its saucer with a despondent little crash and she felt as if her heart had stopped. All morning she had been thinking about the dance, wondering if she had been wise to promise Ellis that she would go, although she knew, deep down, that she had set her heart on it. Apart from the fact that the Christmas dance was an affair to which everyone from the P.N.O. to the newest probationer looked forward with mounting enthusiasm, she loved to dance, and the annual event had always been a bright spot in the hospital year. But now Martin was coming and bringing a partner.

Her thoughts flew to Normanscliff and the care with which he had inspected his former home, and she wondered if this was to be her first meeting with his future bride.

She told herself that she had no right to care. She was not free to care. There was Ellis and the promise she had made.

For days before the dance she did her best to avoid Martin, seeing him only when he operated, swathed in the enveloping white gown and mask which left nothing but his eyes visible and those busy, sensitive hands.

He did not mention the dance. It seemed that it had completely escaped his memory, but Ellis was not so tardy.

On the morning of the twenty-third, as she was pressing the soft folds of her long white evening dress, a young probationer brought a florist's box to the door of the ironing-room.

"For you, Sister," she said, lingering expectantly in the hope that Janet would open it right away, but Janet's fingers were too unsteady for a moment even to untie the silver ribbon bow.

She carried the box to her room, holding the white dress high above her head on its hanger because it was full and sweeping, and when she reached her bed she sat down abruptly on the faded coverlet, staring at the box for several minutes before she opened it.

Inside, on a bed of pale green fern, lay three white gardenias, and the card which accompanied them said, simply: "From Ellis, with love."

She sat gazing at the white flowers for many minutes before she put them carefully back in the box. Her lips were trembling and there was an ache in her heart that held both pity and regret. Ellis always did the right thing. He was so generous and kind, and she had so little to offer him in return.

The remainder of the day passed swiftly. There was only one operation on the list, but it turned out to be a lengthy one, and from two o'clock until four she watched Martin at work, with Ellis sitting quietly in the chair behind the anaesthetist, looking on.

Once or twice, when their eyes met over the concealing masks, Ellis smiled at her, but Martin rarely looked up from his work, except to throw out a brief request for a swab or an instrument as he needed them.

Watching Sister Chard closely, Janet had become more confident, and most of the instruments were now familiar to her. She remembered how afraid and nervous she had been that first day, realizing that her uncertainty had been because she was about to work with Martin. She had been sensitive of his censure, but now she believed that he trusted her to do her part as confidently as Ellis had done right from the beginning.

It was well after five o'clock before the theatre was tidied and left in darkness, and Marian Chard closed the door with her usual sigh of relief.

"I'm always glad when I can do that at the end of another day," she said. "I tell myself that three, or four, or five lives have been prolonged and that I've had some part in it, and that way I get a lot of satisfaction out of my job. It makes you feel that you can go off and live your own life for a few hours with some sort of justification."

Janet had never stopped to wonder before what sort of private life Sister Chard enjoyed. She seemed to be eternally in the theatre or cleaning up, or getting ready for the next day.

"How long have you been doing theatre work?" Janet asked.

"For twenty years." Marian Chard did not look her fifty-odd years with her fresh colouring and jet-black hair. "And for nearly twenty years before that I moved up and down the country, learning my job. Those were the days when a nurse really worked," she added. "Hours were regulated by the hospital's need and you were at the matron's mercy, more or less. The pay wasn't what it should have been, either, but strangely enough nobody grumbled very much. We knew what it was going to be like before we went in for it, I suppose. It was in our blood, I think. Nurses are born and not made. Which you may have heard before."

Janet liked Marian Chard and her reminiscences were always interesting.

"You'll be coming to the dance tonight?" she asked.

"Wouldn't miss it for the world!" Sister Chard said. "I'm not much more than a spectator these days, but there was a time when I could dance most of the young residents off their feet!"

Janet began to dress at eight o'clock. There had been sounds of activity and excitement in the Home since tea-time, and nurses kept running along the upstairs corridors, borrowing this and that. Anne Norman put her head round Janet's door.

"Jan," she asked, her head a mass of giant rollers, "you don't happen to have a stiffened half slip do you? I ironed my dress and hung it up in the bathroom and that idiot, Travers, went in and had a steaming hot bath without having the sense to move it outside! It's gone as limp as an old rag."

Janet turned to the bed.

"I can lend you mine and wear an ordinary one," she offered.

Anne moved into the room.

"Hullo!" she said, "who's been sending you flowers?"

Janet felt her face flame scarlet.

"Don't tell me!" Anne said, laughing. "I bet it was Mr. Spencer-Wroe!"

Anne took her slip and rushed away, and Janet was left to wonder how long her secret would remain her own. There was not very much that happened in or around the hospital that was not fully discussed in the nurses' common-rooms, and although Anne was not really a gossip, it might be too much for her to keep to herself on this occasion.

Slowly she pinned Ellis's flowers into the low neckline of

her dress, feeling them cool and wax-like against her skin. She knew that they would not last the evening out, but she wore them now like an amulet.

The dance was held in the long recreation hall on the ground floor of the Home which had been specially decorated for the occasion. The rather bare lighting pendants had been disguised in long paper lanterns and garlands of evergreens festooned the walls, hiding the dark patches where the damp had come in. There was a reasonably good floor, and a local group supplied the music.

At nine o'clock, when the festivities were due to begin, the P.N.O. came in with a small procession of consultants and their wives, who would dance a few dances and then retire discreetly to the supper-room, and so to bed.

Ellis sat next to Miss Lawson, with Sister Chard on his other side, and nurses and students and residents filled the chairs along the other three walls.

Janet felt a tightness at her throat as the music started. Martin had not put in an appearance and suddenly she wished that she had not come.

"Quite a crowd!" Diana Travers remarked in passing. "All we need to complete it is dear Doctor Everett!"

Janet was looking towards the door, where a tall, dark-haired girl in a striking green dress was standing, and there seemed to be something about her smile and the turn of her head that was strangely familiar.

"I haven't seen him yet," she told Diana. "If he is bringing a partner he has probably gone to collect her."

"It looks as if she's here!" Diana observed with a thin smile as Martin appeared behind the girl in green and led her on to the floor.

They were a perfect match. It almost looked as if they had never danced with anyone else, Janet thought. Height for height, the two dark heads rose above the crowd already on the floor, commanding attention as they moved rhythmically among the other dancers before coming to a halt before the little group at the platform end.

Martin introduced his partner to the P.N.O. and Ellis and then to his other colleagues and their wives, and the girl in green seemed vivaciously at ease in their company. Janet tried not to keep looking in their direction, tried not to acknowledge

95

the ache and emptiness in her heart as she got up to dance with someone else.

Charles Landor was the hospital registrar. Known familiarly as the Merry Widower, he was generally the life and soul of any party, but tonight Janet supposed that she was out of tune, because she had to make an effort to respond to Charles's many quips. He was not a good dancer because he talked too much, and as he swung her round the room in a mad jog she found herself wishing that their dance would come to a speedy end.

There was an encore, however, and away they went again, bumping into other couples right and left and being forced to apologize on every side.

Inevitably, they came upon Martin and his graceful partner, but Martin was able to avoid them with a dexterous movement just in time to prevent a collision. To her horror, Janet caught sight of Martin's partner frowning at them with cold dislike, and although they turned away almost immediately she could not forget the look in the other girl's eyes.

Charles Landor put her down in a chair beside the door and asked her if she would like an ice. His partners generally needed some sort of refreshment when he was finished with them, and he was a liberal man.

"Not just quite yet, thank you," Janet said, regaining her breath. "It's very early."

Yet she was already wishing that the dance was over.

The music started again and Martin came down the room towards them.

"Would you like to dance, Janet?" he asked, and Charles Landor grinned and handed her over with an elaborate bow.

"I didn't see you when I came in," Martin said after a short silence. "I thought perhaps you hadn't come, after all."

She had told him the day before that she had bought a ticket, but that was all. He hadn't even asked if she was coming with a partner, but now he would know that she was here alone.

Well, what did it matter? What did it matter if her heart was beating so swiftly now that he must almost be able to hear it, and every nerve in her body was vibrant to his touch? It was only a form of self-torture to remember how closely it had held her that day at Normanscliff above Robin's clear, brown pool.

"Are you enjoying this?" he asked.

"The dance? Yes—oh, yes!"

"For a moment I thought you looked tired. You had a busy afternoon in the theatre."

She had thought that he had not noticed her, that she was only another cog in the wheel of his success.

"That shouldn't make any difference at my age," she said. "Sister Chard worked twice as hard. So did you."

"When I'm working I'm impervious to fatigue, but then I don't come dancing very often!"

"I thought you danced very well just now."

Why had she to make it so obvious that she had noticed the perfection of his partnership with the girl in green?

"With Vaughan? But that's natural, isn't it? She taught me all I know."

"Vaughan?" Janet repeated. "Then—she's your sister?"

A ridiculous flood of relief was pouring into her heart and her lips parted in a smile.

"Hadn't you recognized her?" Martin asked. "I thought we were so alike that nobody could possibly mistake the relationship!"

"I ought to have remembered," Janet said, trying to keep the relief out of her voice. "Though she was never very much in Somerton."

"She went away to school, and she's older than you are. There are ten years between us," he explained. "Vaughan was an only child for so long that I almost believe she resented my advent at first, but lately she has become quite attached."

It was difficult for Janet to remember Vaughan Everett in any detail. She had always disdained the village children when she had returned to Somerton in the school holidays, and Janet's clearest impression was that of a tall, angular girl on horseback riding out along the ridge of the moors, generally alone. Once again, she mused, it was a name that had lived in her memory.

Vaughan Everett. A strange, remote-sounding name to give a girl, she thought, and one that might easily have coloured her personality from her earliest days.

Half-way through the evening Martin introduced his sister,

and it was then that Janet saw more clearly how alike they were, in outward appearance, at least.

"You lived at Somerton, didn't you?" Vaughan asked distantly. "I suppose you've heard that Martin wants to go back?"

"I knew that he had bought your old home."

Vaughan looked at her in surprise.

"Did you?" she queried. "I rather thought Martin was keeping it quiet until he was ready to move in." Suddenly, her eyes narrowed and she looked at Janet more intently. "I suspect a woman in the background," she said, "but Martin never would play guessing games!"

She waited, but Janet did not speak.

"You did say you lived at Somerton, didn't you?" Vaughan asked almost sharply.

"I lived there all my life till I took up nursing," Janet said.

Charles Landor came to ask Vaughan to dance.

Vaughan won't like Charles, Janet thought. She's not the type to like being pushed around.

Martin swung Janet on to the dance floor.

"It's getting confoundedly hot in here," he objected. "No wonder the P.N.O. and her party have beaten a dignified retreat!"

Janet had not seen the platform party go, but Ellis's chair was empty and she supposed that he must have escorted Miss Lawson to the supper-room. Coffee, sandwiches and cakes were served from ten o'clock onwards, and the buffet supper had always been the most popular form of refreshment with the dancers.

"Do you want to eat?" Martin asked.

"I'm not very hungry."

"I thought all nurses ate whenever they got the chance—by sheer instinct!"

"You don't know us very well, it seems!"

"Perhaps you are right." He guided her among the dancing couples towards the door. "All the same, I think we should eat!"

The supper-room was crowded, however. Couples balancing plates of sandwiches at precarious angles were strewn everywhere, and only after Martin had investigated the possibilities of the disused conservatory were they able to sit down.

"Are you happy here at the City General?" he asked.

Trying to keep herself immune to his nearness, Janet answered quietly, "I love my work."

He put down his cup and crossed to the door, staring out into the night. There was something tense and rigid about his broad shoulders.

"We've all got to be reasonably happy in our work or it would be useless to go on," he said, still with his back towards her. And then, abruptly, "But life isn't all work. There are other things. Other important things."

She felt the tension grow, hard and taut, like a steel rope stretching between them, and then, without warning, he had wheeled round to look at her. There was a naked flame in his eyes as he pulled her almost roughly towards him.

"Janet!" he said. "Janet!"

His arms held her, drawing her close, and then he bent his dark head and crushed his lips down full on her mouth.

For a moment Janet could not move, and then, desperately, she was pushing him from her, and the light behind her and the stars out in the frosty night sky seemed to go out together.

"Janet," she heard Martin say hoarsely. "Janet, what is it?"

"I'm going to marry Ellis Spencer-Wroe."

The deep, pulsating silence which followed her breathless confession lengthened until it seemed to stretch to the ends of the world, and it seemed that Martin would never speak. Her own thoughts stood suspended in a bleak torture of despair as she gazed back at him, and then, suddenly, he laughed.

It was the cruellest thing he could have done, the most insulting thing, and she knew that he wanted to hurt her. He reached out and his hands closed over her arms again, but this time they were like a vice and his eyes were darkly satanic as they searched her face.

"How long have you known this?" he demanded with little mercy. "How long have you been sure of your conquest?"

She recoiled, stricken, before the ungenerous suggestion, but he would not free her. He remained looking straight into her tortured face, his own set and dark, with the mouth drawn into a harsh, relentless line.

"You don't understand." Words would only come with difficulty, haltingly and half afraid because she was fighting back an almost irresistible desire to put her head down on his

99

shoulder and sob out the truth. "Ellis has done so much for me——"

"And this is how you repay him?" He let her go, almost with violence. "How very nice and honourable of you!"

His tone scorned her and her eyes fell before the burning light in his.

"Whatever you think," she whispered, "can't make a great deal of difference."

He laughed for the second time, a harsh, grating sound like splintering glass that cut across her mind with the force of a blow.

"I should be flattering myself unduly if I thought for one moment that it would," he said, feeling in his pocket for his cigarettes and she watched him cup the strong flame of his lighter between his hands and saw it light up an answering flame in his eyes. "It appears that you have your own code of honour in such matters. A woman's code."

"At least it's what I feel to be right," she answered thickly. "I had to tell you this, Martin. You should see that I had to!"

He took a brief turn across the hard floor of the conservatory and then came back to her.

"My conclusions are not so easily arrived at as yours," he said with a lightness which appeared to dismiss them. "They may have been come upon by a more tortuous way," he added coldly, "but that is entirely beside the point. What does matter seems to be the fact that I am usurping someone else's prerogative. Do you wish me to take you back to Ellis, or are you both being discreet till the P.N.O. is informed?"

He might have been the merest stranger discussing her affairs, Janet thought with a sob in her throat.

"I want you to leave me," she said, so near to breaking-point that she felt she could not bear to look at him for one moment longer. "I want you to go now and let me find my own way back to the hall."

"I think," he said with the utmost calm, "that would be most foolish. After all, we came out here together and it would would only cause—speculation—if we returned separately. Even Mr. Spencer-Wroe might wonder and be perturbed by the fact."

"Ellis knows that he can trust me!" There was a shaken sort of dignity in Janet's voice and she was able to hold her head up, at last. "Very well, why shouldn't we go back together, Martin?" she demanded. "My—fiancé is aware that we are old acquaintances."

Dark anger swept in an answering flood across his brow, and then, with what seemed an almost cynical disregard for all that had just passed between them, he took her arm.

Blindly she pulled away from him, afraid her trembling would betray her. Already he considered her shallow and vain and avid for conquest. Her heart twisted painfully at the thought, realizing how singular her love had been down through the years.

She tried to laugh, but it only sounded pitiful and sad, like something breaking into tiny fragments in her heart.

"I don't think I want to dance just yet," she said as he attempted to lead her on to the floor. "I feel—rather tired."

"As you wish." He found her a seat in a corner. "Don't tell me, Janet, that I have upset you? I have misjudged you if I have."

She felt that she could not bear his derision.

"Why should you upset me?" she asked in a cold, flat tone. "You only really came into my life a short time ago."

"Which cuts out the past?" he suggested.

"Completely."

He appeared to consider the point while she wished, beyond anything else, that he would leave her.

"There's something to be said about being entirely ruthless, I suppose," he mused, "but you didn't strike me as being the ruthless sort. However, I am always prepared to believe that I might be wrong, and I freely confess that I know little or nothing of your charming sex. They have always seemed obscure and complex to me, with one exception."

She did not want to know who that exception was. All she wanted was to get away from the gay lights and the music and the rising sound of carefree laughter that seemed to mock the slow tears dropping in her heart. Ellis had gone. She had seen him hesitate in the doorway for a moment as Martin had attempted to lead her on to the dance floor, and then he had turned to follow Miss Lawson down the corridor to the main door.

There was no need for her to stay any longer. It was eleven o'clock and she could make the excuse that she had an early start in the morning.

"I think I would like to go to bed," she said, but long after Martin had left her at the foot of the stairs she stood in the cold of the deserted upstairs corridor listening to the music drifting up to her as if she would never hear music again.

When she turned at last and made her way to her own room her eyes were deeply shadowed and her whole body felt curiously numbed and lifeless, yet she undressed mechanically and got into bed, switching off her light to lie for a long time in the darkness after the other members of the nursing staff had made their noisy way along the corridor outside.

Gradually the sounds of revelry died away. The last car was started up on the drive beneath her window, and the last good-nights were said. The Home subsided into its habitual quiet, but still she did not sleep.

Somewhere in the distance a clock struck two, and the slow, measured beat of the notes seemed to drive her decision into her mind.

"Whatever happens to my heart," she whispered into the unresponsive night, "I can at least make Ellis happy."

CHAPTER VII

CHRISTMAS came, with all its attendant excitement in the wards and its moments of pathos. With the operating lists reduced to the bare threads of necessity, Janet and Marian Chard were in constant demand to help with the decorations and the distribution of flowers and fruit. They kept arriving in constant streams at the main door and Eileen Lawson acknowledged them graciously, but it was left to the nurses to carry them up to the respective wards until every bedside locker and all the central tables were stacked with gifts.

Martin continued to do his conscientious daily round of women's surgical, and because she was responsible for the post-operative care of his patients Janet walked by his side.

The subtle difference in his manner since the nurses' dance kept her silent and uncomfortable in his presence even when they had negotiated the full length of a ward and stood outside the ward sister's door for a final summing-up, and for the first time it seemed that he was adopting the role of the remote consultant. He seemed to be immersed in his work to the exclusion of everything else.

On Christmas Day the resident doctors who were on duty had their lunch together in their own common-room, with the P.N.O. and her senior assistant as guests of honour, and Ellis and Martin were invited to join them.

Knowing that Martin could have taken the day off if he had wished to do so, Janet wondered why he had chosen to spend it in the hospital. His sister was probably still in Norminster, so that there was a suggestion of other company for him outside, but Ellis, himself, did not seem to think it at all strange.

"Martin is making the hospital his whole life," he said when Janet stopped to look in at his bedroom door for a few minutes on Christmas morning. "He appears to have wrapped himself up in his work, but I think he ought to have some sort of relaxation occasionally. Did he enjoy the dance the other evening?"

Janet despised herself for not being able to meet the direct blue gaze fastened on her from the bed.

"It's—difficult to know what Doctor Everett is thinking," she evaded. "If he enjoyed himself, he didn't say so."

"I thought he might have done. He danced with you a great deal."

"I left early." She came towards the bed. "Not long after you went away with Miss Lawson and the official party, in fact."

He moved restlessly, obviously irked by Miss Lawson's edict that he should remain in bed during the morning if he was to be allowed to attend both the luncheon party and the ward concert which was to be the highlight of the evening's entertainment.

"I wish we could be together more, Jan," he said. "The dance the other night made it only too obvious what an unsatisfactory sort of thing a secret engagement really is, but I can't see any other way for it at present. Miss Lawson would expect you to resign if she knew we were to be married, and I don't suppose you want to do that till we've definitely fixed the day?"

"No," Janet agreed breathlessly. "I—don't know what I should do if I hadn't my work."

It was quite true. The work she had always loved was helping her over this moment of heartache and she knew that without it she would have been lost. If it also involved her in closer contact with Martin that she felt able to bear with fortitude, she must find an answer to that, too, in time, but for the present there was Ellis and his obvious need of her.

"I've bought you something," he said, fumbling with his left hand in his locker drawer. "It isn't the sort of thing I'd like to give you, Jan, but it might do till I can get about more freely on my own."

He produced a small, square package wrapped in white paper which he watched her open with a lively interest.

Janet's fingers were not quite steady as she unfolded the wrapper to reveal a white box with the name of a local jeweller embossed in gold on its lid.

"Ellis," she protested shyly, "I'm sure this is much too fine——"

"How do you know when you haven't opened it yet?" he demanded.

"I—it looks expensive."

"You know you should never judge by the wrappings!" He

leaned over on his left elbow. "Open it and see what you think of it. If you don't like it I can easily have it changed."

She raised the lid and stood gazing down at his love gift for a full second without being able to speak.

"Oh!" she breathed at last, "it's beautiful!"

The bracelet lay in a glittering circle, a delicate filigree hoop embossed with tiny diamonds and seed pearls, the like of which she had never seen before, far less owned, and she drew back in confusion, speechless before this first expression of his affection and generosity.

"It's too much, Ellis," she managed at last. "I couldn't really accept it."

"My dear, what nonsense!" he chided gently. "Of course you can accept it! I ought to have been buying you a much more expensive ring, but I think you understand about that. It's you who have been generous, giving in to the whim of a man's pride."

He bent over and took the bracelet out of the box, opening the clasp before he held it out to her.

"It's half by proxy, so I hope it fits," he said. "I had to ask Martin to choose it for me."

Martin! Janet recoiled as if she had been stung, but the man on the bed did not seem to notice. She wondered if he could feel her trembling as he fastened his gift on her arm, but the thought of Martin choosing the bracelet with that new cold detachment of his drove all the colour out of her cheeks and all the sense of responsibility out of her heart. The diamonds seemed to wink back at her mockingly, and suddenly she remembered that pearls were supposed to mean tears.

What had Martin thought as he had gone on his unusual errand? She would never know, but she seemed to see him, suddenly, with his dark head bent over the jeweller's counter and his thin dark face serious in contemplation of the array of jewels before him. Was this, then, what he would have chosen if it had been a personal gift?

Fighting to keep back tears, she touched the bracelet with trembling fingers, and in that instant Martin came to the door. She heard his familiar step in the corridor and saw Ellis look up and past her to where his visitor stood.

"Come in, Martin," he invited. "I've told Janet that we are sharing our secret with you."

Janet's fingers closed hard over the bracelet, almost as if she would protect it from his scornful eyes.

"I've already offered Ellis my congratulations," he said in a voice steely with reserve, "but perhaps I should extend them now." He looked down at the wrapping lying strewn on the bed. "I'm not quite sure about being an envoy in this matter, but I've promised to get it changed if it's not what you want."

His grey eyes were flint-like in the early morning light, seeming to penetrate right beneath the surface of her pretence, and she said stiffly:

"It was good of you to do Ellis's shopping for him. The choice was—all that I could have wished it to be."

He came across the room to stand beside the bed, taking her wrist in his long, lean fingers with a casual movement such as he might have extended to the least interesting of his patients, and when he looked down at the bracelet there was a brief smile on his lips.

"So long as you feel satisfied," he said, releasing her abruptly.

In the ensuing silence Ellis began to gather up the wrapping paper, but Janet could only continue to stare at Martin's unresponsive back as he stood looking out of the window.

"With my love gift on your arm . . ."

The words of the almost forgotten poem rose in her heart and died again. It would never be Martin's love gift, never, so long as she lived. Everything she had to give belonged to the man lying on the bed between them, but even if it had not been so, Martin was not in any way in love with her. He considered her grasping and eager to seize her chance in life with a brilliant man who could provide her with the sort of gift he had been forced to choose for her by a strange irony of fate, and he despised her accordingly. But why couldn't he stop for a minute to think that it might not be true? Why couldn't he see what she owed to Ellis, for all he had done for Robin, the deep and lasting debt of gratitude which had made it impossible for her to refuse his love when he had offered it?

She took off the bracelet and put it back in its box, standing beside the bed without knowing just how to thank Ellis for it while Martin remained in the room. There was the question of her own gift, too. She had not known what to buy for Ellis. She had not even known whether an exchange of gifts would be expected of her, but in the end she had decided on a leather writing-case, a thing which she did not think he possessed.

It was lying on the table beside the door where she had put it down when she had first come in, half nervous about presenting it right away, and she saw Martin look at it as he went out. Was he smiling sardonically at their romantic little exchange of gifts, she wondered, and a brief wave of anger went through her at the thought. Had he no tender feelings at all? Was everything just a matter of work and stern reality so far as he was concerned, with an odd kiss thrown in at a dance with someone who had been willing to play? Had he not time for the heart-warming emotions of attachment and love?

She could love Ellis in a different sort of way, she thought; tenderly and sincerely, with none of the tempestuous agony which seared through her at the very thought of Martin. Love could be placid and gentle and kind as well as being demanding and forceful and strong, and who was to say which was the more satisfying of the two?

She crossed to the bed with her gift in her hand.

"I wondered if you would like this?" she said. "It's the only thing I could think of that you didn't seem to have already."

"You think of everything, Jan!" he said, pulling her gently towards him.

His lips seemed vaguely questioning as they sought and held hers, but Janet did not notice. An overwhelming tide of gratitude and emotion swept her into his arms and she laid her cheek for a moment against his.

"I hope I shall never fail you, Ellis," she whispered. "Because I deserve to die if I do!"

He smiled at the childish little speech, but she did not see. She held tightly on to the white box containing his first gift to her, carrying it with her to the common-room when she left him to hide it safely away in the depths of her locker.

To her unbounded delight and secret relief, she was asked to help with the Christmas tree. It was erected annually in the children's ward and it meant that she would be escaping Martin's round of Women's Surgical in the early afternoon before the regulation visiting hour.

Martin, however, was part and parcel of the hospital these days and had evidently made himself responsible for the security of the tree. A corpulent Santa Claus had entered the ward in the merry person of Charles Landor, and for a moment Janet did not notice Martin amid the general excitement.

A small boy on crutches who reminded her, pitifully, of Robin had claimed her attention, and she had promised to escort him to the tree when the time came, but suddenly she saw Martin and her legs felt weak.

He seemed to be everywhere, dominating her day, although he did not make any effort to cross to her side on this occasion. He stood watching, remote and silent, while she helped to shepherd the children into something like an orderly half-circle round the beds of the dozen or so less fortunate little patients who were still lying on their backs or otherwise prevented from enjoying complete freedom of movement on the floor.

When Charles Landor stepped up to the tree to distribute the gifts, Martin went with him to stand in the background cutting down the toys as each child's name was called. His height proved invaluable as the lower branches were gradually cleared and the toys came down from the top. Charles Landor shook hands solemnly with each child in turn.

They were working in a rather awed silence now, the children not quite sure of the jovial little man in the long red coat and white beard, but gradually the more daring among them began to recover from their shyness and ask questions.

"Where did all the toys come from?" "Why aren't there any presents for the nurses?"

Doctor Landor thought it judicious to answer the last question first.

"There *are* presents for the nurses," he informed the ward at large. "When all the toys are off the tree they are going to come up for theirs. Doctor Everett is sorting them out for me now."

Martin was busy at a table behind the scenes where a few odd pieces of inexpensive dress jewellery lay together on a tray. They were the gifts of the hospital committee and were generally chosen by the P.N.O. and presented when the children had their tree.

Janet was last to go up to the platform to receive her gift. She had found herself hanging back deliberately, feeling that the regular nurses on the ward should have first choice and, if the truth were known, hoping that Martin might even have moved away from the tree before her turn came. She was not to be spared, however. He handed over her present to Charles Landor, standing back to watch as the now perspiring Santa reached the conclusion of his duties.

Janet saw Charles fumble with a small round object and then he had dropped it on the floor at her feet.

"Dear me!" he protested with quite un-Claus-like exasperation. "Where the devil might that have gone? I can't see a blessed thing for this beard, you know, and it's so confoundedly hot!"

"They'll be coming along with ice-cream in a minute," Martin consoled as he stooped to retrieve Janet's gift. "Here you are, and no damage done!"

He held out a curiously carved dress ring with an amber-coloured stone as its centrepiece and Janet experienced a chill sense of recoil as she looked at it. Her heart turned over sickly as Doctor Landor suggested in his jocular way:

"You ought to put it on for her, Everett."

Martin slid the ring on to Janet's finger.

"Until Ellis replaces it," he said under his breath and with a mockery in his eyes that cut her to the heart.

He left the ward in Charles Landor's wake and instantly a hubbub of talk and laughter broke out among the children. Tea was served, but they could scarcely tear themselves away from their new playthings to eat, and for the next hour Janet was kept far too busy to think of Martin and the deliberate hurt he had inflicted.

The Christmas tree ring felt heavy on her finger, as if it bore the accumulating weight of her grief, but she had not removed it, and when she went to change out of her uniform before the concert it winked back at her in her bedroom mirror like a baleful yellow eye. Twice she all but gave way to the impulse to tear it from her hand and bury it deep in one of her dressing-table drawers, but she knew that she would only be questioned about it when the other nurses compared their gifts.

The Christmas Day concert was a democratic affair and she was able to sit beside Ellis in the third row back from the improvised stage.

"I wondered if you'd get here in time to claim this seat," he whispered.

He looked strained and tired, Janet thought, as if the burden of the long day was already proving too much for him.

"What have you been doing with yourself all afternoon?" he asked when she had settled herself.

"I've been watching Doctor Landor playing Santa Claus." She looked down at the heavy ring on her finger. "He did it very well. Doctor Everett helped him."

There was a moment's pause before Ellis said in a low, concerned voice:

"Janet, what is there between Martin and you?"

Her heart plunged sickeningly and all the blood in her body seemed to be driven to her head.

"What could there be between us?"

She felt that she was playing for time, warding off the question because she could not be sure what Ellis really meant by it.

"I've put it badly," he apologized. "What I meant was that there seemed to be a suggestion of—watchfulness between you. I wouldn't like to call it distrust."

"Perhaps it is distrust." Her voice sounded strangled even in her own ears. "Doctor Everett has very little use for my sex, I'm afraid. He told me once that there was only one woman he had ever been able to understand."

"He may not have tried very hard with any of the others," Ellis laughed. "I'd like you two to get on well together," he added, "because I have an idea that Martin and I might form some sort of partnership in the near future. He has far more to offer the world than I have, but there is still a lot for him to learn and I believe that I can teach him." He smiled whimsically. "To be more truthful, I've taken a deep and abiding liking to the man that an earthquake could scarcely shake now, and I don't think anyone could convince me that I am mistaken."

"I don't think anyone would want to," Janet said forlornly. "It will be up to Doctor Everett to prove your trust in him justified."

They were joined by Charles Landor and Sister Chard.

"I see you're still wearing Martin's ring !" Doctor Landor said as he sat down in the next seat to Janet. "It's big enough, isn't it? It looks as if it might be a bit of a burden to you!"

Janet covered the ring with her left hand.

"It's only a trinket," she said. "I don't suppose I shall wear it for long."

All through the first half of the concert she wondered where Martin was sitting, and then, in the interval, she saw him at the back of the hall with his sister. Vaughan Everett was dressed in dramatic black, with jade clips in her ears and a heavy jade bracelet on one wrist, and suddenly Janet wondered if she should have worn Ellis's Christmas gift. It had seemed too elaborate, altogether too expensive, for the simple velvet frock she wore, but now she wished that she had put it on, and the weight of the heavy dress ring seemed to increase as she walked down the gangway to get her tea tray.

The senior nurses who were not taking part in the concert had made themselves responsible for the provision of light refreshments in the interval, and for the next quarter of an hour she carried tea and biscuits up and down the aisles and ran back for the odd ice cream in between times.

When the lights dimmed and she went back to her seat, she found Vaughan Everett sitting there next to Ellis, so that she was forced to retire to the back of the hall and take Vaughan's place beside her brother.

Martin sat through the first two numbers in silence and then he said:

"I'd like a word with you some time, Janet. It's about Ellis."

His lips were tightly compressed as he looked down the length of the long ward to where Ellis sat with his sister, and Janet felt her heart contract at the suspicion that something had gone wrong.

"Do you think that he should not have come to-night?" she whispered anxiously.

"I wasn't thinking of his general health," he returned in a voice just distinct enough for her to hear, "but that may be indirectly affected, too. It was about the plaster casing. It's due to come off in a couple of days."

Something in his voice made her turn to look at him.

"And you don't really think that it should?"

"On the contrary, I think that the sooner it's off the better. I don't think it's doing its job."

She stared at him incredulously.

111

"But Sir Adrian——"

"Sir Adrian looked anything but confident on his last visit, and Ellis is still in pain when he sits up. In almost constant pain."

"What is it you are trying to tell me?" she asked in a low, distressed undertone.

"I want you to persuade Ellis to get other advice."

"And if he won't? If I can't persuade him?"

"No one else could do it but you." He swept her objection aside. "He's in love with you," he added almost impatiently.

The old fear for Ellis rose in Janet's heart.

"What do you suspect, Martin?" she whispered.

"Nothing, at the moment. We haven't discussed the accident fully, and I understand that the X-ray plates didn't show anything serious at the time, so that I may quite easily be barking up the wrong tree. My theories may not even hold water when it comes to the point, but I would feel better about the whole business if Ellis would agree to go to Geneva."

"Geneva? But surely there's someone in this country who can help?" Janet objected.

"Not the man I would like him to see." His mouth closed in a thin, determined line. "Will you make the initial effort?"

"Of course." She moistened her lips with the tip of her tongue. "Of course I'll do it if you think it is the only way."

"We will know whether it is necessary or not as soon as the plaster comes off."

That was all he had to say, except at the end when the concert was over and they stood up to file out with the others.

"Ellis may want you to go with him," he suggested, as if it was already a foregone conclusion that his suggestion would be accepted. "That would mean leaving your job here, but I take it that you would be willing to make the sacrifice?"

If there had been mockery in his tone this time she did not hear it.

"I'll do anything," she said. "Anything in my power."

Vaughan Everett and Ellis came up the aisle together and Janet's heart faltered at the grey look on Ellis's face. Even if Martin had not taken the opportunity to point it out to her, she would have recognized how ill he looked, and she could have shaken Vaughan for her stupid attempt at a flirtation.

"Mr. Spencer-Wroe has promised to come to dinner as soon

as he is well enough to leave the hospital, Martin," she informed her brother, "so that means you must hurry and get Normanscliff fit for occupation before the spring! It's been empty for over three weeks now and you haven't even looked round the house to see what needs doing to it. You really ought to take more interest, unless you are waiting for special advice."

Her words dropped into an odd little silence.

"I don't think there will be any need for advice, special or otherwise," Martin said, at last, in a voice edged with a steely quality of an irrevocable decision. "I have closed Normanscliff for the time being, but Ellis will always be welcome wherever I decide to make my home. For the present, it will continue to be in the hospital."

Vaughan looked aghast and completely taken aback by her brother's decision. It was evident that she had seen herself as hostess in her old home, at least until Martin decided to take a wife. She turned to Ellis with a little laugh, but she was looking at Janet.

"One can only imagine that my brother has been crossed in love," she remarked with calculated cruelty. "Less than a month ago his one desire was to open up Normanscliff and live there, but apparently it doesn't take very much to make a man change his mind about the future."

Martin did not trouble to look at her. Instead, he turned to Janet, saying briefly:

"Get Ellis to bed as quickly as you can. I'll come up and take a look at him before I turn in myself."

"I've never known Martin to fuss like this before," Ellis said when they had reached the sanctuary of the upstairs corridor and Nurse Bennet had gone on ahead to pull the curtains over his window. "I may have overdone things a bit these past few days, but I'll be as fit as a fiddle in the morning after I've had a good night's sleep."

When Kathy Bennet had gone out of the room to fill a hot-water bottle he kissed Janet lightly on the cheek.

"Cheer up!" he grinned. "Everything is going to be all right, Jan, and then we can get down to the more important business of making you happy!"

CHAPTER VIII

THE Christmas festivities over, the nurses were allowed as much free time as possible, but Janet felt that she could not leave the hospital even to go to Bristol.

Sir Adrian Pepper would arrive from London some time during the afternoon to remove Ellis's plaster and reconsider his verdict, and she felt that she had to be within call if she should be needed.

Mercifully, the operating theatre was out of use. There were no emergency cases and Martin was able to remain with Ellis for the greater part of the morning. Janet saw him only when he did his mid-morning round of the wards and she thought that he appeared preoccupied and even worried as he walked away with the P.N.O. and the ward sister in attendance.

There was no reason for professional anxiety among the post-operative cases which were her own special duty, so that she knew he must be worrying about Ellis and the result of Sir Adrian's examination.

Her heart contracted at the possibility of failure. It might mean weeks, even months, in another jacket, and she knew that Ellis would not take kindly to the prospect.

When she went off duty at two o'clock she wondered if she would be able to see him, even if it were only for a few minutes, but Martin preceded her along the corridor and turned in at Ellis's door, and she hesitated. She had no official excuse to offer for being in Ellis's room when she was off duty, and suddenly the whole ponderous machinery of hospital discipline pressed down on her like some dead weight, threatening to crush her. There was nothing she could do but wait. There was no part for her to play, no active part, and she realized how often she had seen a patient's near and dear ones turn away almost hopelessly from a bed with just such a thought in their hearts.

It would have been easier if they had been able to do something. It was the waiting that frayed the nerves and reduced their hard-won courage to fear.

Going slowly down the wide staircase, she became aware of voices in the hall beneath her and saw the P.N.O. and Sir Adrian

114

with a short, thick-set man in a dark suit, who was a stranger to her. She supposed that he was another consultant and stood aside at the turn of the stairs to let them pass.

Miss Lawson looked at her and smiled vaguely, and somewhere at the top of the stairs she heard Martin's voice.

She went on down the staircase like someone in a dream, wondering what she should do for the next half-hour or so. The Nurses' Home was too far away to go there to wait and she decided not to change out of her uniform in any case. Somehow, desperately, she wanted to be needed, although Ellis seemed to have passed beyond her power to serve him.

Disconsolately, she wandered across the quadrangle in a thin drizzle of rain, holding her cloak close up under her chin to keep herself warm.

The minutes began to drag, and once or twice she wondered if the clock on the square tower above her head had stopped altogether, but gradually the hands moved, the hour hand imperceptibly, the large one warily, it seemed, dragging itself reluctantly down the white clock face.

A quarter to three! The rain had gone off, but she hardly seemed to notice the sun's reflection in the tiny puddles it had left between the grey paving stones. Suddenly she realized that she was standing beneath Ellis's window, but when she raised her eyes there was nothing up there for her to see. It looked down at her blankly, but she could not move away.

Other windows faced out on to the quadrangle and she knew that she would be seen from them, but she was past caring. Nothing mattered now but the fact that Ellis must get better.

"He may want you to go with him," Martin had said, "and that would mean leaving your job . . ."

Well, she would do that, too, if need be. She would do anything to prove to Ellis how much she cared about his future.

Slowly, she turned away. It was five minutes to three, and she had made her final decision. Whatever happened, whatever the result of this past hour should prove to be, she must keep faithful to the promise she had made.

Sounds of voices and subdued laughter came from the wards as she passed them. The hospital seemed full of warmth and kindliness and belonging, while only she walked alone.

The door of Ellis's room was still closed when she reached

the upstairs corridor, but at any minute now Matron might open it, wondering why she was standing there hours before she was due to come on duty again. Yet it did not seem to matter. There seemed nowhere else that she could wait. The sisters' common-room would be full and her colleagues would wonder why she had not gone out or gone across to the Home. Even kindly Sister Chard, who rarely asked questions, might consider it strange that she should want to forgo her off-duty time when there was nothing happening in the theatre.

She thought of the theatre in an abstract sort of way, of her work there which would throw her more and more into Martin's company if she remained at the hospital, and then she remembered that he had offered her a way out. She could go with Ellis to Geneva.

Slowly, she walked along the corridor to the door of the operating theatre, feeling its coldly sterile atmosphere strike at her through the glass portholes cut in the swinging doors. She might work here for years or only for a few weeks longer, and always there would be Martin coming and going in his white surgeon's coat with the grave expression on his dark face and the look of mockery in his eyes.

The door of the ante-room was ajar and she pushed it open and went in. This, in a way, was her own domain. There would be no one to question her right to be here.

While she waited she began to occupy herself with the routine tasks of checking and replenishing the stores, but she had hardly turned to the glass-shelved cabinet on the far wall before she heard a step in the corridor outside.

Martin! She knew that he was there before she looked round, and she knew that he had come to find her. He came in and closed the door behind him.

"You needn't tell me," she said, looking at his set white face. "Something has gone wrong."

He came and stood beside the cabinet for a moment, looking at the array of bottles and instruments behind the glass.

"It was what I feared," he said in a voice she hardly recognized. "There has been trouble going on beneath the plaster for the past two weeks, the sort of thing that would be least expected."

"Yet you suspected it," she said.

"I can't take any credit for that. I saw it happen less than

116

a year ago, in Switzerland."

"And—the cure?" Her lips felt almost too stiff to move. "You said Ellis should have other advice. Was this other case you have just mentioned your reason for advising it?"

"Partly."

"Then—there is something to be done?"

For a split second he did not answer her and she saw a pulse hammering high in his cheek, as if he were trying to keep some emotion in check by the greatest effort of willpower.

"There must be something to be done," he said, at last. "And quickly."

"You still want him to go abroad?"

"I'm taking a risk on it," he confessed. "The operation has only been done half a dozen times before to my knowledge and—it is not always successful."

"Martin——!" Her voice trembled, but she steadied it with an effort. "We can't let this happen to him! He's got to be cured. We've got to get him the use of his arm back, somehow. It means so much to him. It means – all his life!"

He turned sharply away.

"Do you think I don't know that?" he said harshly.

"What are we to say to him?" she asked after a moment. "How are we to tell him the truth?"

"He'll expect no less from us, but I think he already knows." His mouth was more grim than she had ever seen it. "After all, he is a surgeon and all the signs of failure were there when the plaster came off. We're waiting for the second lot of X-ray plates now, but I doubt if they will tell us much more than we already know."

"What does Sir Adrian think?"

"His reactions are much the same as my own. He is disappointed and without the necessary skill to do much more about it. Paralysis is a strange thing, Janet, and it has many different facets. No one can be sure that he has the key even in the simplest of cases."

"This operation you speak of," she asked with difficulty, "will it mean that he might be worse—more severely paralysed —if it isn't the success you hope for?"

"No." He was quite definite about that. "Ellis will be pretty much as he is now. He will be able to get about, able to move freely, but with no real power in part of his right side."

117

Suddenly, she buried her face in her hands.

"All these weeks," she said in a dry, harsh whisper, "while he's been hoping for a complete cure there's been—this!"

He had crossed to the window and he stood with his back to her when he said:

"I think he knew, all the same. I think he had an idea that things might not work out quite so simply for him. He was severely crushed and there was considerable internal haemorrhage at the beginning, but it is never possible to say what the outcome will be in these cases and Ellis would know that."

Numbly Janet wondered if that had been part of Ellis's reason for wanting to keep their engagement a secret, if he had faced the prospect of being crippled for the remainder of his life and had reserved the right to make a second decision with the least public humiliation to herself.

It seemed to have very little to do with the present, however, and she could only face Martin with another demand on her lips.

"He mustn't know about the other operation only being a fifty-fifty sort of chance," she said. "You can promise me that, Martin."

He turned from the window, looking at her now with a curious expression in his eyes, but he neither made her the promise nor denied it to her.

"How am I going to see him?" she asked when the silence in the room had become almost unbearable.

"I think it's time you went to the P.N.O. and told her the truth," he said unemotionally. "You have every right to see the man you are going to marry."

She let her breath go in a small, scarcely audible sigh.

"Yes, Martin," she said. "That is the only way."

He opened the door for her.

"I'll tell Ellis you are coming," he said.

On the way to the P.N.O.'s office she wondered why Martin had been so kind. Perhaps he felt sorry for her, sorry and trying to help. It was a side of him that she had not suspected and his sudden gentleness hurt even more than the habitual brusqueness.

Miss Lawson was seeing the two consultants off at the door leading to the quadrangle where they had parked their cars, and Janet was forced to linger in the foyer near the front entrance

118

until they had shaken hands and said their final goodbyes. She knew that she should have approached her assistant before seeking this interview, but she felt that time was far too precious for that.

Before Eileen Lawson could close her door behind her she hurried towards it, saying as calmly as she could:

"Will you excuse me, Miss Lawson? There is something I have to say—something urgent. May I speak to you right away on a private matter?"

Miss Lawson glanced up at the array of small electric light bulbs set in the wall above her door and saw that her own colour combination was unlit for the moment.

"I can give you five minutes," she said, "if that will do?"

"Thank you."

You could burn all your boats behind you in five minutes, Janet thought, or change the entire shape of the future.

"Now," Eileen Lawson said, seating herself behind her desk in the chair of authority. "What is it you wish to say to me?"

"It's—just that I should like to see Mr. Spencer-Wroe." Janet was aware of the surprise—almost the shocked surprise —in the P.N.O.'s eyes, but it hardly registered in her tormented mind. "You see," she explained swiftly, "we are engaged to be married."

Eileen Lawson made an abrupt movement, as if she could not quite credit such a fantastic statement, before she said briefly:

"Can you be a little more explicit, please, Sister?"

"We have never announced our engagement," Janet explained. "I—it happened just after my brother's accident when I was nursing Mr. Spencer-Wroe, and he thought it best that we should keep it as—something between ourselves for the time being, because of hospital discipline and because—I think he wanted to be completely well again before we announced it publicly."

For exactly three seconds Eileen Lawson remained silent, weighing up this difficult situation as she watched the girl sitting across the desk from her, and then she began to gather up the reports lying on its polished surface.

"I think the best thing for me to do would be to see that you are put back on the wards, Sister," she said. "In that way it could be arranged for you to relieve Nurse Bennet almost immediately."

"Oh—thank you, Miss Lawson!"

The flood of relief in Janet's heart was overwhelming because she had not known exactly what to expect.

"You understand, of course," the P.N.O. said, "that I am doing this largely because I respect and admire Mr. Spencer-Wroe and feel sure that I can trust your own discretion. I realize that—your fiancé has suffered a very bitter disappointment this afternoon. A smaller plaster casing has had to be put back on to his arm to support it for the time being, and the knitting-together process which we had hoped for has not materialized. It is a very great tragedy for a man of his outstanding ability and I can only hope that you will do your best to make life as easy and pleasant for him as possible under the circumstances. I wish you both luck."

Janet's eyes filled with tears as she walked away. Walled round by the need to enforce discipline among those who served under her, Eileen Lawson could rarely show the generous heart that beat under her formal dress, but once or twice there had been glimpses of it at a time of special need and today had not been the least of these.

The senior ward sister was coming off duty when Janet reached the upstairs corridor.

"You are to relieve Nurse Bennet," she told Janet in a surprised tone. "The P.N.O. has just rung up. I thought you were permanently on Theatre?"

"I was," Janet confessed, inwardly thanking Eileen Lawson for making the way easy for her. "But you're short-staffed, aren't you, and no doubt the P.N.O. thinks I can do a bit of both."

"I never did think that Theatre was a full-time job," the ward sister sniffed as she turned away. "You can report to Sister Oliphant after you've seen your patient."

Janet hesitated at the door of Ellis's room. She could hear voices inside and hoped that it would be Kathy Bennet talking to Ellis, for somehow she could not quite face Martin just now.

Kathy Bennet came to the door in answer to her knock, balancing a tray of dressings in one hand.

"Oh, it's you!" she observed. "Am I really off duty, or is it only another false alarm?"

"The P.N.O.'s orders!" Janet said. "You're free to go."

Kathy gave her a swift, searching look as she passed.

"You all right?" she asked.

"Yes, I'm all right," Janet assured her. "I've not really been doing anything very strenuous all day."

Kathy lowered her voice as she stepped out into the corridor.

"Have you heard?" She indicated the bedroom with a movement of her head. "About the plaster, I mean? An awful shame, I call it. It's had to go on again, and I guess he's had enough, suffering all these weeks and keeping cheerful the way he did."

Janet knew that Ellis would still be "keeping cheerful", at least to all outward appearances, and she had to bite hard on her lower lip to keep it from trembling as she went in to him.

"I wondered when you would come," he said, holding out his left hand in the old gesture of eagerness. "It isn't too good, is it, Jan, being trussed up like this again when we expected our freedom?"

Freedom to announce their engagement, he meant, to take up their life together like any normal couple in love.

"Ellis," she confessed, sitting down on the chair at the head of his bed, so that he might keep her hand clasped in his. "I've had to tell Miss Lawson. I had to tell her to get to see you. It was the only way, and I think she understood."

For the first time in her memory of him she saw his eyes cloud, their vivid blueness overshadowed by doubt and pain.

"I'm beginning to wonder if I have any right to hold you to that promise," he said. "You've heard the verdict, I suppose?"

"Yes," she said, "and it doesn't make a scrap of difference. It wouldn't make any difference to the future so far as I am concerned if this was final. It would only seal it."

He looked away from her steady eyes.

"It's pretty final, Jan," he said. "It's only Martin who seems to have some strange sort of hope left."

"Why should it be strange if it's hope at all?" she cried. "Martin would never have suggested a final opinion if he hadn't some sort of assurance to offer." She slipped on to her knees beside the bed. "Oh, Ellis, give this a trial," she begged. "Let Martin write to this friend of his in Geneva and make an appointment for you. We can't go down without a fight. It

121

means so much, my dear! It means so much to all of us."

He put his hand under her chin, tilting her face up so that he could look deeply into her eyes.

"I believe it does," he said, at last. "All right! Fix things up with Martin and I'll go along."

She got up and stood beside the bed, great waves of relief sweeping through her at the thought of his capitulation.

"You won't regret it," she said. "Martin has such faith in this man. He may even be a worker of miracles!"

Ellis said warily:

"We mustn't hope for too much. Paralysis is a strange thing and there has never been any accounting for its peculiar vagaries, though we have come to know quite a lot about it in these latter days. But for a particularly savage trick of fate my shoulder should have healed by now and I should have back the use of my arm, but these things happen. We know the reason for them, but sometimes not the remedy, and even Martin's miracle man is still very much at the experimental stage."

Janet's heart contracted with sudden fear.

"But surely Martin wouldn't let you take an unnecessary risk," she whispered. "He told me there had been a percentage of cures——"

"Martin doesn't promise anything. He's not the sort of man who would make such an offer without being sure that I understood all the facts. So far, this theory of Professor Hochsolden's is in its trial stage and I may as well act guinea-pig as the next fellow. I know what he is going to attempt and I shall accept it if he fails. Martin has really very little responsibility in the matter, you know. He only made the suggestion. It was up to me to make the decision. You can't very well blame a man for offering you hope."

Janet wondered if Martin would blame himself if Professor Hochsolden failed, but she did not expect to be given any indication of his feelings either way.

When Ellis informed him that he was willing to go to Geneva, he set in motion the machinery for the interview by writing personally to his Swiss colleague of a few years back and making all the necessary arrangements for the journey beforehand so that very little time would be wasted. He seemed quite certain that the Professor would agree to see

Ellis at once, and within a week he had a letter back from Geneva saying that everything could be arranged for the end of the present month.

Ellis took the news quietly.

"It's a long way to go for a disappointment," he observed in a mood of unusual depression. "I wonder if it is really worth it?"

Janet and Martin were both in the room, and Janet left Martin to reply. It seemed that he could handle the situation better than she could, and there was a determination about him that would brook no regret at this stage.

"We've made our decision," he said firmly. "All that remains to be done now is to carry it through."

"I'm reacting badly," Ellis confessed immediately. "I'm sorry! Can you forget that I ever said that?"

Martin put a friendly hand on his uninjured shoulder.

"We'll make it as easy as we can for you," he promised.

"When do I go?" Ellis asked after a pause in which Janet took his temperature and marked it carefully on the chart beside his bed.

"Next Tuesday." Martin sounded implacable now. "There's no use wasting any more time."

"None whatever."

Ellis was looking at Janet, as if he had something of importance to say to her, but he seemed to change his mind as Martin went on:

"I've asked the P.N.O. to see to everything for you—pyjamas and an extra suit and that sort of thing. You will need warm clothing to travel in, but it should be milder down there than it is here. You may have to stay for a week or two if Hochsolden agrees to operate right away."

Once again Ellis glanced in Janet's direction, but again he seemed to be silenced by some inward thought. Martin continued to study him intently and Janet hurried from the room, fearful that she might betray the sudden, terrible sense of foreboding which had clamped down on her spirit in the past half-hour.

When Ellis had gone she would have nothing to do but wait. The days would pass and lengthen into weeks while she remained here, waiting for letters, waiting for a telephone call, waiting for any scrap of news that might tell her which way their future was to go. She might even be dependent upon Martin for that news for a time if Ellis could not write, and he would tell her only what he considered it was good for her to hear.

The ruthlessness in him would be uppermost if he thought for one moment that she would endanger his patient's recovery by any sort of weakness, and he would no doubt hold her responsible for Ellis's state of mind when an exchange of letters was finally possible.

In some ways there was no pity in Martin. In some ways she found him without personal frailty at all.

It was Saturday when he announced that the last details of his plans were completed. Ellis would leave London by air for Geneva.

Suddenly Janet determined to go to London. Why shouldn't she go and see Ellis off? She had several days of her annual leave to take, so why shouldn't she ask for this special favour?

The P.N.O. granted her the interview.

"I was about to send for you, Sister," she commented when Janet reached her office. "Doctor Everett thinks that you should be given leave of absence to go to Switzerland with your fiancé. I must say that it is a flagrant breach of all our rules, but if things go right for Mr. Spencer-Wroe in Geneva, as we all hope they will do, you will no doubt be handing in your resignation when you return."

A small, inarticulate sound escaped Janet as she got to her feet.

"I don't know how I can thank you for letting me go, Miss Lawson," she said after a moment. "I have leave to take. It is part of my annual holiday, so it wouldn't be necessary to apply for special leave of absence if I could take that."

The P.N.O. made a note on the pad in front of her.

"I shall see that it goes through," she said.

Not until she was well away from the hospital did Janet realize that she had hurried out without telling Ellis her wonderful news. But perhaps he already knew. Martin had arranged everything, so carefully and in such minute detail, that there could scarcely be any room for surprise. Suddenly she had felt the need to get away, to be by herself for a while so that she might straighten out her thoughts.

She would have to pack, and send off word to her family in Bristol so that her father would know where she was going. "On a private nursing job." That would be the best way to put it just now, she decided. Ellis had not said anything about making their engagement public and although he might not have expected her to keep the news from her family, she had not yet passed it on to Bristol.

For the moment, however, she felt the need to put distance between herself and the City General, for some strange reason which she could not quite define. Perhaps she was too close to her problems there, but whatever it was it sent her almost breathless in the direction of the city walls and through Clifford's Bar to the north way bus terminus, where buses left for Somerton and Athersage every hour.

She looked at her watch, seeing that it was almost three o'clock, and suddenly she was trembling from head to foot. Why had she decided, out of the blue like this, to go to Somerton?

She did not know. What she did know was that she would not turn back now.

Almost inevitably, she found herself in the bus heading for Somerton.

She did not know why she should have chosen this moment to go back, but the familiar way seemed to ease some of the tension within her.

As they drew near Somerton she purposefully averted her gaze from the houses on the hill in case her eyes should betray her and fill with tears. The conductress had come down the bus and was asking conversationally:

"You for Somerton village? We go right through to Athersage before we turn, you know, but perhaps you're a stranger to these parts?"

"I know Somerton very well," Janet told her automatically.

"I'll put you down at the Green, then." The conductress pressed a bell. "Unless you want to go further on?"

"The Green will do very well."

The bus stopped and Janet got out. It was several minutes before she realized that she was not the only visitor to Somerton that day, and the girl who watched her from the garden of the post-office hesitated for a fraction of a second before she came forward.

"I thought it was you," Vaughan Everett said casually. "I had no idea I would meet anyone I knew, apart from the locals, of course."

"I am a local in a way," Janet said, conscious of the fact that Martin's sister was surveying her most critically. "I had time off from the hospital and there isn't much to do in Norminster in this weather."

Vaughan glanced about her.

"There doesn't appear to be much to do in Somerton, either," she declared. "Strange how one expects so much from the place where one spent one's youth, yet when one does get back it's all rather flat and uninteresting, after all."

"I've always thought Somerton was beautiful, and Athersage is a show place, isn't it ?" Janet said. "The typical Cotswold village."

"I suppose so, if you like that sort of thing." Vaughan took out a packet of cigarettes and offered one to Janet. "No ?" she commented, helping herself. "I thought nurses smoked by instinct ?" She flicked her silver lighter, inhaling deeply before she asked: "How long does the bus take to go to Athersage and turn ?"

"About ten minutes."

Vaughan waved her lighted cigarette vaguely in the direction of the hill.

"I've been up having a look at the old homestead," she observed. "A closed house can look hopelessly derelict, but Martin doesn't appear to be going to do a thing about it. He isn't making the slightest effort to put it straight. I've offered to help, but I just come up against a blank wall of refusal, and all because some girl or other has walked out on him!" She gave a short, unsympathetic laugh. "I didn't think that Martin was the type to let any woman influence his life to that extent. He's always wanted to go back to Normanscliff, and now that he seems to be fairly settled at the City General it would be an ideal country house for him. But perhaps he isn't really settled at the hospital," she added, giving Janet a sidelong look.

"I think he could settle there," Janet said, moistening lips that had gone suddenly dry. "He is needed, and—Mr. Spencer-Wroe has great faith in him."

"All the same," Vaughan said, "I've never known Martin to

126

be quite so restless as he is now. I've even offered to come and keep house for him, but he won't hear of it. Perhaps he suspects that I should get fed up after a bit and want to go back to London."

The bus hurtled back round the corner, coming to a stop before the red painted doorway of the Black Bull on the far side of the road.

"See you some time!" Vaughan announced vaguely as she dashed across the road, and Janet watched the bus drive away, dazed and a little confused by this unexpected encounter.

Who was the girl who had turned Martin down? Was there a reason for it and would they meet again and realize how mistaken they had been to let love go? Nobody who had been loved by Martin could ever really want to give him up!

Turning almost blindly in the direction of the moors, she found herself standing on the spot where they had picnicked that day when they had taken Robin to see the bees. It seemed ages ago, and the beehives had gone and the moor looked cold and deserted where once it had worn a carpet of purest gold. The wind blew chill, too, striking coldly against her cheek with a breath of ice in it which must have found her heart.

Martin and the girl he loved.

She could not get away from the thought. The tall chimneys and grey roof of Normanscliff were just visible above the bare trees and they had a deserted, almost a forlorn look.

She walked towards them along the narrow pathway which finally skirted the high garden wall and went down beside the house itself to the main road where she would be able to rejoin the bus without walking all the way back to Somerton, and suddenly she felt very near to Martin as she stood gazing down at his old home.

What would he do with it, she wondered, now that the woman he loved and had counted on had refused to share it with him?

The uncurtained windows of the upper floor stared back at her like blank eyes without giving her an answer, but suddenly there was a movement ahead of her, a rustle of dead leaves as someone on the far side of the wall struggled with the opening of a door.

She knew a wild desire to run, to put miles between her and that opening door, but within seconds it was flung back and

Martin stood in the aperture, looking out at her.

His face was quite grey in the cold northern light, with a tightness about the mouth which she had seen once or twice before in moments of stress, and there was a bitterness in his eyes which he could not disguise at first. He was so utterly changed from the suavely composed consultant whom she met every day in the hospital that she drew back involuntarily, conscious of looking into the depths of some wild despair which she would never have been permitted to see in the ordinary way.

He held the garden door open for her.

"Better come inside, Janet," he said in a voice she hardly recognized. "It's the quickest way back to the main road."

Her limbs all but refused to obey her, but what reason could she give him for not wanting to enter the garden of his disillusionment? She walked before him down the overgrown path leading to the sunken lily pool where Robin had sat that afternoon watching the goldfish swimming in the sun. It was all so different now. The sun had gone, hidden by a low, dark cloud on the horizon, and the lilies in the pool had withered long ago. Even the flat green leaves floating on the surface were decayed and brown and curled up at the edges, and there were no golden fish visible today.

Martin stood staring down at the pool.

"Well, this is it," he said. "Not a very pretty picture, after all, is it? People are the soul of a garden, I suppose. The people who tend and care for it. Just as a woman is the soul of a house."

He threw his head back, looking towards the uncurtained windows where the dust of weeks had gathered and rain and wind had streaked and marked the glass, like tears dried on an expressionless face, but Janet felt that she could not look.

All that he was suffering, all that must be passing in his mind behind the mask that he now wore upon his face, seemed embodied in the deserted garden where they stood.

Not a flower to be pressed of the foot that falls not;
As the heart of a dead man the seed-plots are dry. . . .

They turned to walk in silence along the deserted path, with the sound of Swinburne's impassioned words beating a merciless tattoo in Janet's brain, chaining her mind to the past.

This was where Martin had planned to bring the girl he loved, the garden where they were to have walked hand in hand down through the years, but something had gone wrong and now it stood empty and forlorn as the house it guarded, where, in the fullness of time, children's voices should have echoed from room to room.

Perhaps it would stand there for ever, a mute and unhappy monument to his loss.

> *Only the sun and the rain come hither*
> *All year long.*

Beneath them the path dropped down to the rock pool where Robin had seen the brown fish darting between the stones, but Martin did not go that way and the bitter pain of remembering pierced Janet's heart like an ice-cold blade. It was down there that he had held her to him for a moment, but it could not have been with love in his heart when all his thoughts were already centred on the future he had planned with someone else.

> *Only the wind here hovers and revels*
> *In a round where life seems barren as death,*
> *Here there was laughing of old, there was weeping,*
> *Haply, of lovers none ever will know . . .*
> *Years ago.*

Martin turned, looking back towards the house, but he did not speak and, somehow, she knew that he had not gone in. The garden had held too poignant a memory for him to go on to the house it sheltered, where memory would await him beyond every door, and so he had turned his back upon it, shutting a dream out of his life with a deliberation which had left him shaken and weakened afterwards.

> *And or ever the garden's last petals were shed,*
> *In the lips that had whispered, the eyes that had lightened,*
> *Love was dead.*

Her steps lagged and the silence between them became intolerable. She felt that she had stumbled upon Martin's innermost soul as it lay bared for a moment for all to see.

"I'm sorry, Martin," she said in a voice harsh with emotion. "I'm so desperately sorry—about this."

He wheeled round, his face ravaged with the extent of his emotions and the bitter hopelessness of his grief.

"Are you?" His eyes sought hers, burning with an impassioned scrutiny which she found it difficult to meet. "Sorry! Isn't that a tame sort of word to offer over something that might have meant so much?"

She recoiled before the look in his eyes, before its ruthless demand which sought to strip her own heart bare, and then his face changed, all the anger and bitterness going out of it as he said:

"Now it is my turn to say I am sorry! I had no right to speak to you like that, Janet, but this thing meant a great deal to me. I was arrogant enough to imagine that I couldn't lose when my own love had gone so deep."

He walked a step or two farther down the path, reaching the great iron gates that gave on to Horseshoe Lane and opening them for her to pass through.

"Don't feel too badly about it, Janet," he said. "You had nothing to do with it."

He was dismissing her kindly, telling her in so many words that she could not even offer him the consolation of understanding, telling her that she had "nothing to do with it".

"Can I give you a lift back to Norminster?" he asked when they reached his car. "I'm going back to the hospital."

She could not refuse to go with him, although she wondered what they would find to say to each other on the journey, but Martin was evidently determined to thrust their visit to Somerton behind them.

"About Tuesday," he said. "I think I have made all the necessary arrangements. There's only the question of your passport—seeing that it is up to date. I think you told me that you went across to Paris for a holiday a year or two ago."

"I went with Freya Allanson," Janet said automatically. Freya and their light-hearted jaunt to Paris seemed far enough away now, in another world. "It was only two years ago, so my passport should be all right."

"Have you flown before?" Martin asked.

"No, but I don't think I'll be a bad traveller. It's Ellis who really matters." She clasped her hands tightly in her lap. "So long as he can weather the journey it doesn't matter about me."

He made no comment on that.

130

"Ellis will go straight to the clinic in Geneva, but he has the name of your hotel and the reservations." He was completely himself again, composed and deliberate in his planning as he steered the car away from Somerton and the past and set their faces towards the future. There was no present, except where it concerned Ellis. "I stayed there when I first went to Switzerland three years ago, so I know you will be comfortable. If not, Professor Hochsolden will look after you. The main thing is to make sure that Ellis gets there without too much strain and fuss. I would have gone with him myself," he added, "but we have two important cases on the lists next week which Ellis doesn't think should be left to hang fire till he gets back."

"You'll operate alone?" she asked.

"Yes," he said without hesitation. "I feel that I can manage on my own now. In these past few weeks Ellis has taught me more than I could have learned elsewhere in as many years."

He was grateful, humbly grateful, as only a man like Martin could be because Ellis had put the final seal on his skill.

CHAPTER IX

MARTIN saw them off at the airport.

The two men shook hands with a firm, sure grip, looking deeply into each other's eyes, and Janet's heart beat fast and hard at the thought of their continuing friendship. Martin would come to Ellis's future home as one of its most honoured guests, and through the years she would have to steel herself to receive him as nothing else. In time, he might even bring his wife to Minster Close and she would receive her, too, as if love for Martin had never touched her life.

The great plane hovered above the airfield for a moment before it set its course southwards across the sprawling chequer-board that was London and flew out towards the Channel.

Ellis sat silently, looking down at the last of the land as the broad band of the sea came up to meet it.

"I'm glad you wanted to come, Jan," he said after a while. "If it does nothing more, it will put Martin's mind at rest. He thought I would be better with someone I knew rather than a stranger."

"Was it—entirely Martin's idea?" Janet asked.

"In one way—yes, though I had toyed with the suggestion myself. I wondered, though, if you would be willing to give up your job for such a—temporary post."

"I had leave to take," she told him. "Part of my summer holiday, as a matter of fact. It made it easier for Matron to let me go, I suppose, but if Martin feels that I should stay longer I'll do that gladly, too."

The air hostess came down the plane with coffee and sandwiches and she held Ellis's cup for him while he drank.

"This should have been a holiday for you in the fullest sense of the word, Jan," he said. "Not a sort of busman's spree, attending to an invalid on your first air trip."

"I'd just as soon be kept busy," she smiled. "It keeps one's mind off being air-sick!"

"After the first half-hour you won't feel it," he assured her, "and in next to no time we'll be there." He looked down from the window to the white clouds rolling beneath them. "Thank goodness I can get about on my own two feet!" he commented. "I should have loathed a stretcher, and ambulances meeting us everywhere. If I close my eyes and concentrate on you I could almost imagine that this was our honeymoon!"

"Ellis," she said, not knowing why she should ask, "were you ever—in love with anyone before?"

He kept his eyes closed for a moment and then he looked at her with a quizzical smile.

"What a question to ask a man of my age! If I told you 'no' you would never believe me!"

"Then you have? Would it be cruel of me to ask what happened?"

"You could never be cruel, Jan," he said, looking down at the clouds again. "Not intentionally cruel, and why shouldn't I be able to tell you what happened? It was so long ago, that sometimes it seems a part of another life when I look back on it. We both had our careers, and Irene's took her one way and mine took me another. She married a missionary and went out to Africa. I haven't heard from her since."

There was nothing in voice or expression to tell her what he thought now, whether the old love still lingered or whether time had mercifully erased its memory. His blue eyes were as serene as they always were; his generous mouth was curved in a smile.

"Have you heard from your sister?" she asked, changing the subject. "You mentioned that you had written to her about—about us."

He shook his head.

"But don't worry about that!" he said. "Margaret might be hundreds of miles from her base. These missionary doctors are all alike. They're so wrapped up in their outpost jobs that letters often accumulate for months before they get down to the task of answering them. Margaret was never a good correspondent at the best of times. She'll write when she has news enough to fill half a book and expect me to do the same by return of post!"

"You're very fond of one another," Janet guessed, smiling at the thought of Margaret.

"It was touch and go whether we went out East together," he admitted. "She did her best to persuade me, but specializing in my own line won in the end." He sat engrossed in his

133

own thoughts for a moment. "As one grows older it's surprising how often one looks back and wonders about the other road, the way we might have chosen when we came to our own particular crossroads in life."

"Regretfully, do you mean?" Janet asked.

"Not particularly. We never really know how the other way would have gone, do we?"

"No, I suppose not."

Janet was trying not to think what would have happened if she had met Martin that day at Somerton when he had stood at the far end of Horseshoe Lane while she had waited for her bus at the other. Would it have made a difference to her promise to Ellis, the promise which bound her so closely now? "We never really know how the other way would have gone . . ."

It was true. She forced the thought of Martin from her mind, looking out through the thick glass to the fleecy pattern of cloud etched sharply against the penetrating blue of the sky and saw, far beneath them, the first powdering of snow on dark earth.

As they approached the first serrated barrier of the Alps they climbed higher and she saw a long, unbroken line of glittering peaks flushed pink in the rays of the westering sun. The white majesty of them took her breath away as she watched the dark shadow of the plane hovering on their flanks and saw a blue lake opening up before them.

"It's wonderful, Ellis!" she breathed, but she still couldn't say that it was like a honeymoon.

Again and again lakes gleamed like tiny mirrors on the snow far beneath them, dwarfed into insignificance by the mountains on every side, and lazy rivers coiled like dark snakes through the deep valleys. Roads branched and spread everywhere like the arteries and veins of the human body, until they came at last to Lac Léman and their destination.

The great lake was like a vast inland sea, lying tranquilly in the last of the January sunshine, its southern shore already deeply shadowed, the lights beginning to prick out along its entire length.

Geneva sprawled beneath them, a fantastic, glittering city steeping her feet in the tideless water. Janet could see great white buildings and wide avenues spread out like a map and her heart began to beat with a sudden mad excitement.

What had this strange white city sleeping beside its blue lake to offer her? What could it promise her for the future? Heartbreak or joy? A measure of happiness leavened by tears?

"We're almost there." Ellis was looking out over her shoulder. "Is it too early to ask what you think of it?"

Trying to stem the tears that misted her eyes, she turned towards him.

"How I wish that we needn't have been seeing it for the first time like this !" she said.

He took her hand and carried it to his lips.

"There will be other times, Jan," he said. "At least, we can hope for that."

The plane circled and lost height and they came in to land on the white tarmac. White was the predominating colour everywhere: white buildings edging the snow-covered airfield; white mountains fringing the sky with white clouds over them, and the long, straight white roads radiating in all directions into the heart of the Alps.

"I wonder if we will be met," Ellis said. "I forgot to ask Martin whether we should expect a car or not."

"Mr. Spencer-Wroe, if you please?"

A smart, uniformed chauffeur was touching his peaked cap and relieving them of their luggage while he explained in perfect English, with just the barest trace of an accent, that Professor Hochsolden deeply regretted not being able to come to the airport in person because he had two emergency operations on his hands. One was a small matter of a penetrated lung, and he knew *Monsieur le Docteur* would understand and excuse him.

Janet almost began to feel at home. This was the work that Ellis knew and he would not feel strange in the atmosphere of the clinic.

He helped her into the car and they drove away down into the wide heart of the town with its many bridges and out along the lake shore where the palatial buildings gradually gave way to lovely, isolated villas dreaming behind their high stone walls.

The chauffeur turned the car in between the gateposts of one of these and ran up a short, gravelled drive from which the snow had disappeared, though it still lay white and glistening

135

on the lawns and gardens on either side.

"We are arrived, monsieur!"

The door immediately in front of them was lit by a lantern encased in wrought iron and the trim figure of a nurse appeared as the car drove up to the foot of the steps. She ran briskly down to greet Ellis in English.

"We are worried because the plane is a little late, Mr. Spencer-Wroe," she said, "and because the Professor is not yet through with his operating, but perhaps you would care to come up to your rooms and be settled in before you meet him?" She turned to Janet with a welcoming smile. "You are the little nurse who has come from England with your patient and whom we have arranged for at Le Manoir? You will be quite comfortable there, I hope. It is not too large an hotel, and many of our profession stay there when they come to Geneva for a conference. I am French," she added as she led the way up a broad, uncarpeted staircase to the floor above, "but I know your country very well. I live in Hampstead with a friend when I go to London."

She ushered them into a sitting-room gay with multi-coloured chintz whose long windows gave on to a balcony overlooking the lake, and beyond an inner door Janet caught a glimpse of a more austere bedroom, clinically white from floor to ceiling, its bare pine boards devoid of any covering.

Ellis looked round his sitting-room and smiled.

"They mean to keep me here," he said.

The Professor came in almost on their heels. He was a small, bespectacled man in an old-fashioned morning coat and striped trousers, with a scrubbed look about his rotund face which appeared to make him shine. He shook Ellis warmly by the hand and turned to acknowledge Janet with an encouraging nod of his grey head.

"Doctor Everett has told me about you," he said. "Soon we will see what can be done, but first it is necessary that you should rest to recover from your journey. It is not so cold in Geneva as it is in London and you will find many places of interest when you drive round our so lovely Lac Léman. I have put my automobile at your disposal," he added. "André will drive you wherever you wish to go."

Janet moved towards the door.

"Perhaps I should find my hotel," she suggested.

"Ah, yes! Doctor Everett was very concerned that you should be made comfortable," the Professor assured her. "He said: 'It is necessary to make Miss Ferrier feel at home in Geneva in case she must stay there for some time.' But nobody wants to go away from our lovely city once they have come, and you will not prove the exception!" He looked towards the nurse still hovering in the doorway. "Marie will take you to Le Manoir to Madame Belfrage."

Janet was relieved to discover that her hotel was not too far away from the clinic, and she followed Marie back down the stairs and out by a side door to a narrow road leading back from the lake.

"We all remember Doctor Everett," Marie said conversationally. "A very handsome man and a very clever doctor, but oh, so English!"

And so frigid, Janet supposed, the thought of Martin rushing in upon her as if he had been walking behind them.

That evening, as they sat quietly in Ellis's sitting-room overlooking the starlit lake, she thought of Martin many times. His name seemed to have dominated the conversation ever since they had arrived in Geneva, and there was a suggestion of loss as the Professor spoke of him which she fancied even Ellis noticed.

"You who have yet much to teach him will understand what I mean," he said, and Ellis nodded.

Presently Ellis rose to his feet and stood beside the window looking out over the velvet-dark water.

"Debts are curious things," he mused. "They sometimes work in reverse."

In the next two days they drove as far as they could into the mountains, coming back by the lakeside in the evening when the lights were strung out along the shore like fallen stars and the glittering constellation that was the city itself lay reflected in the water at its head. And each evening, when Ellis retired early at the Professor's expressed wish, Janet bade him good-night and walked slowly back to her lonely room in the nearby hotel.

It seemed ages since they had left Norminster, and the following morning, when Ellis remained behind the closed door of his bedroom with the Professor, she tried to write home. She filled three pages with descriptions of the places she had visited, enclosing some coloured post-cards for Robin, but she found that she could not tell them much about her job.

There was so little to tell up to now.

Nervously she waited for the Professor's verdict, wondering if he would convey it to Ellis direct, but when she went back to the clinic after posting her letter the Professor himself was waiting for her on the doorstep.

"Please to step in here for a few minutes," he requested, opening the door of a small office on the ground floor. "I have something that must be said before you go upstairs to your fiancé."

Ellis—or Martin!—must have told him the truth about their relationship, Janet thought. She wondered which, but it did not really matter now. It made her position easier and the Professor seemed relieved that his patient had someone closely connected to him near at hand.

"I have made my examination," he said, "and also my decision."

The last remnants of colour receded from Janet's cheeks as she waited for him to continue, and her heart seemed to be hammering loudly in the stillness.

"I shall operate at once."

"Then—you think there is a chance?" Unbounded relief and thankfulness flooded across her face, filling her eyes with tears. "It must come right, Professor Hochsolden! It must, for Ellis's sake!"

"And for you, also, *ma petite*!" He put his hand under her chin, tilting it to look into her eyes. "You are very fond of him, although there is much difference in your ages?"

"That doesn't matter," Janet assured him quickly. "I owe him so much, Professor." It was strange how truthful you had to be with people like Professor Hochsolden when they looked at you in this particular way.

"So!" the Professor said, passing a thin hand over his grey hair. "It is a matter of great debt and a little affection?"

"No! Oh, no, not really!" she cried. "Ellis is the sort of person you couldn't help being in love with. He is so kind, and generous to a fault."

"So!" said the Professor again, but that was all.

Janet found Ellis reading quietly in his room. Now that the final decision was made he looked happier and he greeted her

138

with his old, fond smile.

"They've decided to carve me up," he said.

"I wish Martin could be here!"

The desire had been a passionate heart-cry uttered almost before she knew it, the conviction that nothing could go wrong if Martin's strong hand was on the helm.

"Would it help?" Ellis asked.

"It would help you."

"He has a great deal to do at Norminster. The list I left with him might well have daunted someone with twice his experience, but Martin has never been afraid of hard work. In fact, these past weeks I have been forced to the conclusion that he is putting work before everything else in life." Ellis had spoken with his eyes on the grey rectangle of the window where the light outside filtered through an atmosphere heavy with the promise of more snow. "It's the sort of thing a man invariably does when other ways of life have failed him."

The words were almost a question, but Janet did not think that she had any right to divulge Martin's secret. Her one hope was that Martin would not plunge into an orgy of overwork to kill the pain of loss, but she thought that Ellis would watch out for that, too.

"When will Professor Hochsolden operate?" she asked anxiously.

"About the beginning of next week, he thinks." Ellis looked at her speculatively. "Which gives us three whole days to see some more of the countryside," he suggested. "Would you like to go to Chamonix and see the Mer de Glace and drive round the lake to Montreux, to the Château de Chillon? They're all story-book stuff, Jan. Things you ought to see. I only wish I could take you to the very top of a mountain, but I think the Professor would put his foot down about that! We could go so far up, though!"

They drove round the lake again, past Nyon and Rolle and Morges to Lausanne, where they had lunch in a deep-roofed chalet on the edge of the town and lost themselves afterwards in its maze of interlacing streets. There was so much to see that Janet almost forgot that Ellis was an invalid, but she had promised the Professor that he would be back in the clinic before dusk and they left the romantic Château de Chillon to be visited another day.

In some ways it was almost impossible to believe that less than a week ago she had been busily engaged on the wards at the City General, and if it had not been for the recurring thought and anxiety of Ellis's forthcoming operation she might have felt as if she were indeed enjoying a holiday.

The crystalline Alpine air had whipped new colour into her cheeks, and the breathtaking beauty of the snow-bound countryside through which they passed could not fail to find response in her eager heart. The seeking, wondering spirit which reacted so spontaneously to all she saw was her greatest charm for the man who sat quietly by her side, watching the changing expressions fleeting across her face and the wonder deepening in her eyes.

It was at such moments that Ellis Spencer-Wroe wondered if he had any right to claim her youth, but always Janet would convince him that she was happy with a word or an impulsive gesture which was entirely her own.

The following day was Saturday and they took the opposite way round the lake to Chillon, crossing the frontier and driving leisurely along a road which the mountains almost crowded into the sea.

It was a clear day, with keen frost in the air, and the lake was very blue. From St. Gingolph they looked across the eastern end of it to the fabulous castle on its green island with its turrets stained with the golden fire of sunlight, and Janet thought how often she had wondered what it would be like to look across at Chillon without ever dreaming that she would one day go there.

"How lovely it is!" she said, standing beside Ellis in the sunshine. "Like something out of a romantic fairy-tale!"

"It has a chequered history," Ellis said, drawing deeply on the cigarette she had lit for him. "It isn't all a story of love and romance, I'm afraid. People were imprisoned there to rot away their lives in hopeless agony in the bad old days, but it must have been built originally with the conception of beauty."

In these few minutes the castle's turbulent history had become far more real to Janet. Lovers had been imprisoned there, men and women who had never known the fulfilment of their love, and suddenly she turned away, feeling that she could no longer bear to look on its isolated, moss-grown towers.

140

Ellis followed her in silence and they got back into the car and drove across the Rhône, a rushing giant of a river, white-cascaded with ice-water from the mountain fastness from which it had sprung.

At Villeneuve they stopped for tea.

"I'm playing truant to-day," Ellis declared, "because I'm quite certain Professor Hochsolden is going to order a complete day's rest for me to-morrow!"

Neither of them had spoken much about the operation after Ellis had told her that it had been fixed for nine o'clock on the Monday morning, but it could not be entirely forgotten, although they each did their best to push it into the background for the other's sake.

"I don't think he will mind," Janet smiled, "if we're a minute or two late. He's the most understanding person I know, Ellis! And he loves this beautiful lake of his so much that he wants to share every corner of it with us!"

"I'd like to make the round trip and go back by Chamonix," Ellis suggested, "but André thinks the roads might be difficult after dark. There has been quite a lot of snow in the mountains, so I suppose we had better keep to the lake shore."

André, however, suggested a short detour through Aigle and Monthey, which would take them close to the Dent du Midi and some of the lesser giants which had bounded their horizon all day long, and Ellis nodded and told him to go ahead with an eagerness which successfully disguised the fact that he had seen it all many times before.

"Happy?" he asked as they began to climb and the cold increased. "Have you enjoyed your day?"

"Need you ask if I have enjoyed it?" Janet's eyes were shining with gratitude as they looked into his. "I could never have dreamed anything could be so wonderful, Ellis. Nothing—no photograph, not even the cinema—can show these mountains as they really are. You have to see it all, the living colour, and the height and majesty, and the clear distances, to realize what it is really like."

He took her hand in his, clasping it gently.

"This need only be the beginning," he said.

Janet could not answer him. Ellis was looking forward to their future life together, seeing it as something he had longed for, perhaps seeing it, even, as perfection, and how could she

141

do other than try to make it so for him?

The car began to slow down and after a minute or two Ellis released her and bent forward to the glass partition to speak to André.

"What is the matter, André?"

"I do not know, m'sieur." The chauffeur drew up at the side of the road. "There appears to be some trouble in the carburettor, but it may be slight. A matter of minutes, m'sieur. Please do not get out of the car in order to assist me."

The minutes passed, however, and presently there was an exasperated sound from under the bonnet.

"Parbleu!" said André expressively.

Ellis got out and they spoke swiftly in French for several minutes before he came back to Janet.

"It's rather a nuisance," he said. "The petrol pump has ceased to function and it looks as if André will have to return to the nearest town or go on to Vouvry to have it repaired."

Janet's thoughts flew to the Professor waiting at the clinic for their return.

"How long will he take?" she asked. "Professor Hochsolden will begin to wonder what has become of us if we don't put in an appearance before it gets dark."

"We'll get back all right," Ellis said. "I don't think anyone will start to worry till after ten. They'll probably think that we have decided to have a last meal together on the way home."

André came to the door, touching his cap.

"It is a long way for you to walk, André," Ellis said.

"N'importe!" André assured him with his ready smile. "It is all downhill and if I am lucky I shall get a lift back. I am sorry to cause you this inconvenience at so late an hour, but it is something that has not happen to me before."

He walked disconsolately off along the road and Janet and Ellis settled down in the car to wait.

"There's no use worrying," Ellis said. "It's not as if we're on an isolated mountain road where we might be marooned for hours."

It was the best part of two hours, however, before André staggered back towards them through the snow.

The blizzard had come upon them swiftly and unexpectedly half an hour after he had left, sweeping down out of the pass behind them, cruelly persistent and piling the snow up against the car in a white shroud so that they could not see out through the windscreen at all.

"Malheur ne vient jamais seul!" André declared, blowing on his hands as he took off his gloves. "One trouble is never enough. It was not necessary to look into the pass to see this coming. I should have felt it in the air and stayed on the lake road, as you suggested!"

"It's no use worrying," Ellis assured him. "Have you got the pump welded, that's the main thing? The blizzard will only hold us up a little on the way back."

While they fixed the pump Janet got out and began to walk backwards and forwards along the short strip of road to keep warm. The snow was falling thickly now and the wind whipped it against her, but it was almost colder in the car. She wondered how long it would take them to get back to Geneva, but would not ask in case they would think that she was over-anxious.

"You're frozen stiff!" Ellis said, coming back from the bonnet to find her. "André has almost got it fixed now, so it shouldn't be too long before we can push off again."

"He has taken it all very badly!" Janet smiled. "Like a sort of personal disgrace. I'm quite sure he prides himself on the perfect running of the Professor's car."

"Accidents can happen, but so long as we're not stranded in some inaccessible spot for the night, why worry?" Ellis returned. "All that's happened is that you've got bitterly cold, so we may as well be hanged for a sheep as a lamb and have dinner on the way back."

Dinner would be over at the clinic by the time they got back, Janet realized, but she still felt uneasy about the journey ahead of them.

They stopped at Evian, and André indicated a comfortable hotel where they would be well served. The wind had dropped now and the snow was falling in big, soft flakes that settled thickly on the windscreen, but it was not nearly so cold. When they had finished their meal Janet felt a good deal happier about the situation, although she could not quite dispel her former restlessness.

They raced along the lakeside road with the lights of Geneva glittering ahead of them like brilliant stars on a black backdrop and the white-mantled peaks of Mont Salève rising ghost-like beyond, and to Janet it seemed, suddenly, as if she was coming home. There was a warmth, a passionate nearness in the night which she had not noticed before, and when they turned in at the clinic gates it seemed to be intensified.

The sound of the returning car brought Marie running to the door in her white wrapper and floating head-square and in the light of the lantern above her head her face was very pale.

"They've been worried," Ellis said. "We should have phoned from Evian."

Janet could not answer, for suddenly, beyond Marie, a tall, broad-shouldered figure had come into view.

"By all that's wonderful!" Ellis said. "It's Martin!"

Martin's eyes seemed to hold Janet's, even from that distance, with a look in them which she could not fathom. At first she took it for anger, but gradually she realized that it held more than that. Concern for Ellis? The surgeon's swift reaction where any suggestion of strain for his patient might be concerned?

He came straight down the steps towards the car.

"Are you all right?" he asked harshly. "We imagined a score of possible accidents."

"I'm sorry, Martin!" Ellis apologized, and for the first time Martin turned fully towards him. "I should have phoned when the car broke down, but we thought we would make it. We went farther than we planned, as a matter of fact. Right round one side of the lake as far as Villeneuve. It was a glorious run and I thought Janet should see some of the Swiss countryside while she was here."

"Of course," Martin said stiffly, and it was then that Janet imagined his anger to be directed chiefly against herself.

As far as Martin was concerned she had come to Geneva as Ellis's nurse, someone who would see that he obeyed orders and took the necessary rest before his operation, and it would not seem at all important to him that she should be shown the local beauty spots while she remained there. He would indeed think it extremely foolish of Ellis to have taken the risk of driving so far, but hers would be the real responsibility.

He preceded them into the clinic, walking towards the stairs, and Janet hesitated in the hallway.

"I won't come up," she said to Ellis. "Martin thinks that I have kept you out of bed too late as it is."

Ellis laughed, pulling her with him towards the stairs.

"Never mind Martin!" he said. "Just come and tell him how pleased we are to see him and everything will be all right! He's a stickler for obedience where his orders are concerned, of course, but I shall promise him to rest all day to-morrow!"

"He has come to see you," Janet protested. "And it's almost ten o'clock."

He put a firm hand under her elbow.

"Come up and share the bed-time cocoa!" he insisted. "I refuse to be browbeaten, even by Martin, and so should you!"

Janet tried to smile, but she was far too concerned over Martin's anger to be able to treat the situation as lightly as Ellis was apparently doing. It was possible that Martin considered that she had betrayed a trust, and the thought hurt.

He stood with his back to the stove in Ellis's sitting-room while she went to help Marie with the supper tray.

"I have never seen Doctor Everett more worried than he was this evening," Marie said. "When you did not return before dinner he said that we must wait—half an hour, one hour! When you did not come he began to pace up and down in the Professor's room. 'Something has become of them!' he said, when still you did not arrive, and he would have gone out himself to search only the Professor persuaded him that an accident would soon be reported if one had, indeed, taken place. *Enfin,* Doctor Everett, he eat a little *diner* and go back to his pacing. Back and forward, back and forward he go across the Professor's carpet, like the lion before the bars of his cage who long to strike out with his great paw but cannot do so because he is confined. Then, when he hear the car arriving, he bound down the stairs, two at a time, in case you have come to harm!"

"He would be worrying about Mr. Spencer-Wroe," Janet said. "We should never have stayed away so long, but—but we had no idea that Doctor Everett would come."

"The Professor was not surprised to see him," Marie informed her. "For Doctor Everett Mr. Spencer-Wroe is a very special case."

"Yes," Janet agreed, "that is true. He would want to be here in person because he persuaded Mr. Spencer-Wroe to come. It means so much to them both," she added in a whisper.

"And also to you, *n'est-ce pas?*" Marie gave her a little,

145

sidelong glance. "Which one are you going to marry, Miss Ferrier?"

A vivid flush which she could in no way control stained Janet's cheeks.

"There's never been any suggestion that I might marry Doctor Everett," she said unsteadily. "We are old acquaintances, but—nothing more."

Marie put the steaming jug of cocoa on the tray and arranged some wheaten biscuits in a meticulous design on a plate before she spoke.

"In France we say it is a dangerous thing for a man and woman to admit to an old acquaintance!" she smiled. "But perhaps love is not so easily recognized in your country when it is so well disguised!"

"In France you are far too romantic!" Janet managed to say with a lightness which she was far from feeling. "And at the moment we are all going to be much more prosaic and drink cocoa together!"

"Ugh!" Marie commented, but whether the sentiment expressed her dislike of their nightcap or her complete contempt for the English way of falling in love, Janet was never to find out.

"Here comes the Professor's panacea for every ill!" Ellis greeted the arrival of the tray. "He must have consumed gallons of cocoa in his time."

Martin took the tray from Janet without looking at her, and he left it to Ellis to continue the conversation as they settled round the stove to drink the warm beverage and dispel the chill of their late drive.

"I've been telling Martin that this ought to have been our honeymoon trip, Jan," Ellis said when he had drained his beaker to the dregs. "No girl ought to find herself in such wonderful surroundings without a romantic reason attached, or so I imagine." He turned to the silent man on the far side of the stove. "What do you say, Martin?"

"I think it's time you went to bed!" Martin got abruptly to his feet. "You do understand about this rest business, don't you?" he added, whipping the conversation away from the romantic beauty of their surroundings to the real reason why they had come to Geneva. "You must have prescribed it before an operation yourself dozens of times."

"Ah, but being the patient makes all the difference!" Ellis declared. "All right, Martin," he added more seriously, "it looks as if you and the Professor win! I stay in bed all day to-morrow and give you a chance to do your best for me on Monday morning."

"That's what we want," Martin said, putting a friendly hand on his shoulder.

"That needn't apply to Janet, though," Ellis suggested. "Staying put here, I mean. She ought to get out and make the most of her sight-seeing while she can. She ought to have the experience of climbing a mountain, right to the top, if possible!"

Janet felt as if her heart had turned over. Ellis was going to suggest that Martin should take her to the mountain-top and he did not want to go!

"We'll see what can be done about it," he said briefly, "but for the present you must get some sleep. I shall send Marie up to you and be back again myself within half an hour to make quite certain that you have obeyed orders this time."

Janet walked ahead of him along the corridor and down the wide marble staircase, her hands trembling on the tray. She had taken off her coat in the hall when they had come in and it lay on a chair near the door. Martin lifted it and held it out.

"Never mind about the tray," he commanded. "Marie will collect it when she comes past. I am going to take you back to your hotel."

"No, Martin, there's no need!" she cried. "I can walk back," she added almost desperately when he did not speak. "I've been walking back from the clinic alone every evening since we came."

"But not at this late hour." He seemed to be well acquainted with her movements since she had arrived in Geneva and probably he had asked the Professor about her efficiency. "It shouldn't take more than five minutes each way."

A task to be completed as swiftly as possible, Janet thought. Something expected of him, in fact. The kind of small courtesy which Ellis himself would have offered!

Tears stung her eyes as they went out into the night, tears of mortification and disappointment that were as foolish as the joy that had flooded into her heart at the first sight of him. They walked close together, with the falling snow drifting lightly against them and the sounds of the great city behind them. The wind had gone and the lake lay very still, circled by the snow-clad giants above it so that the falling snow was like a gossamer curtain veiling a scene of fantastic loveliness. It was a night of enchantment, but there was no joy in it for Janet now. Martin had come to Geneva only to see Ellis, and he had come to find her wanting.

"Ellis must have been relieved when he saw you just now," she said to break the heavy silence between them. "No matter how much faith he had in your Professor, the known face is always a help at a time like this."

"He had you," Martin reminded her almost stiffly.

"It isn't quite the same."

"Isn't it? I thought the presence of the beloved liquidated every form of loneliness."

"It should do," she said in a shaken undertone. "When it is the right sort of love."

"Isn't yours the right sort? Yours for Ellis?"

She drew back as if he had struck her.

"I've tried to make it that sort of love," she cried. "If I haven't succeeded it is because Ellis deserves nothing but the very best." Her voice all but faltered. "I haven't had a great deal of time to show him how grateful I am for all he has done for me, but that will come."

He swung round to face her in the arched gateway of Le Manoir.

"Gratitude!" His voice was chill and scathing, his eyes like steel as they looked down into hers. "My heaven, Jan! what sort of answer is that when a man has given you his life? Ellis won't want your gratitude if that is all you have to offer him."

"I can offer him love and affection, the sort of love you probably don't know anything about." She wanted to hurt him now, but her voice was still not quite steady. "Ellis has never had a home—not a real home in the true sense of the word—and I can give him that. I can give him loyalty and trust and the service of my life, and I have a feeling that he will be content."

"Content!" He threw the word back at her. "What sort of weak-kneed half-measure do you think that is? Do you imagine that any full-blooded man would be satisfied with such an offer? Do you think Ellis would, if he knew?" He

148

caught her by the wrist, holding her when she would have attempted to run from him towards the house. "Are you incapable of love, Janet? The sort of love that might be strong and passionate and demanding? Have you ever known that sort of love?"

She strove to free herself, great sobs breaking from her throat, but he held her for a fraction of a second longer, looking down at her with absolute demand in his eyes before he let her go.

"You've no right to say these things!" she sobbed. "You've no right to ask them."

Suddenly he laughed, and it was not a pleasant sound.

"No," he agreed, "I have no right. I have no right whatever, Janet, even though I know the answer to them as clearly as if it had been put into words for you to hear! Go on loving Ellis, Janet, in the only way you can," he added savagely. "Perhaps, after all, it is the way he wants."

What had he said? What did he mean? Her mind could not grapple with the mood of the past few minutes, but suddenly she felt as if the world had gone black all round her and there were no stars left. She felt Martin near her, but he was saying lightly, almost provocatively:

"Ellis is a spinner of dreams. He wants you to feel that this might have been a honeymoon trip. To-morrow I am to take you sight-seeing while he obeys orders and rests. To-morrow we will climb our mountain, Janet, but I don't know what sort of view I'm to promise you from the summit!"

He was gone before she could answer him, disappearing into the shadows cast by the tall oleanders overhanging the garden wall.

CHAPTER X

JANET went to see Ellis early the following morning. She had not slept well and had walked down to the lake shore before making her way to the clinic, drawing in deep breaths of the keen, fresh air as if to fortify herself for the need of the hours ahead.

She found Ellis already up and dressed. He was having breakfast at his sitting-room window and Martin was with him, drinking a companionable cup of coffee as they discussed events at Norminster since Ellis had left the hospital.

Janet hesitated in the doorway, not quite prepared for Martin so early in the morning.

"Come in, Jan!" Ellis called immediately. "We've been waiting for you. I've told Martin that he must take you up to Chamonix. It's just the day for a climb, though I think you should stop before you actually come to the top. The view from Le Brévent is one of the finest bits of mountain scenery in the world and easily my favourite. Martin knows where I mean. He has been there many a time."

Without looking in Martin's direction Janet said:

"I'd rather not go. I'd much rather stay here with you, if you don't mind."

"But that's ridiculous!" Ellis objected, although he seemed pleased that she should have thought of it. "I've got to rest, the Professor says, and visitors are barred. You would only have to sit and worry about to-morrow all by yourself." He lowered his voice a little as Martin moved towards the breakfast trolley to pour another cup of coffee. "Martin understands how I feel. I want to stop you worrying."

When he came across the room with her coffee, Martin seemed to have accepted just that view of the situation.

"The gods appear to have favoured us," he observed with a glint of mockery in his dark grey eyes. "It is a day in a thousand, with clear skies and a rising temperature. By midday it will be positively warm on Le Brévent and we should be able to see the whole of the Mont Blanc range from the Aiguille de la Tour right down to Notre Dame de la Gorge. I can assure you that Ellis will rest far more contentedly if he feels that you have something interesting to do."

"There must be heaps to do in Geneva," she suggested feebly, but Martin pointed out reasonably enough:

"The routine of the clinic would only be upset if we hung about. I think we might be permitted to have dinner here in the evening, though."

Perhaps he had already seen to that. Things seemed to be running pretty much as Martin desired, even in this distant hospital in a new country, but he could not force her to go with him against her will.

Against her will? Something deep down in her laughed mirthlessly at the irony of the suggestion. It might be against her better judgment that she would go with him to Chamonix, but the will of her heart would have taken her into Martin's arms to remain there for ever.

Her hands were trembling as she turned to Ellis to say good-bye.

"I hope they will let me see you when I come back," she said.

"Martin will arrange that," he assured her confidently. "Even the Professor gives way before his blandishments!"

Martin held the door open for her and she had no choice but to pass out before him and walk along the corridor and down the wide white staircase by his side.

"I can't come with you," she said when they reached the hall. "I can't come to Chamonix," she added almost desperately.

"No?" He turned towards her musingly. "Why not, Janet? Are you suddenly afraid of the mountain-tops?"

The colour ebbed from her cheeks, and then, suddenly, she lifted her head proudly and was looking straight into his mocking eyes.

"Why should I be afraid?" she asked defensively. "I've never climbed to such heights before, but I don't think I need fear their effect. Ellis has said that he will feel happier if I go, so why should I decide against it?"

"Why indeed?" He took down his thick coat from the circular stand behind the front door. "Are you sure you will be warm enough on the first part of the journey? I have told you that everything will favour us when we reach the heights."

"If we're going to climb," Janet decided, "I ought to have

another pair of shoes. I bought some yesterday in Geneva because Ellis said I would need them for longer walks. They're ankle boots, really, and are quite tough."

Ellis, she remembered, had wanted to make her a present of the lamb-lined, goatskin bootees they had seen in a shop in one of the main thoroughfares of the town before they had set out for Chillon, but she had been firm about buying them for herself. They were to be her one extravagance in a city whose shops were among the most glittering and spectacular in the world, but she had not thought to wear them for the first time climbing to a mountain-top with Martin Everett.

While she changed, Martin went to see about the car which the Professor had offered to lend them for the day, and he was waiting for her at the gate of Le Manoir when she came out.

To her surprise she found him sitting in front behind the steering-wheel.

"André has the day off," he explained. "It is most convenient all round."

How implicitly the Professor trusted him, she thought as they threaded their way into the foothills, and then she relaxed and gave herself up to the breathtaking beauty of the way ahead.

Following the dark channel which the swift-flowing Arve had cut deep in the snow-bound countryside, they took the road to 'Annemasse and Cluses, with the mountains coming closer with each mile they covered and finally crowding in upon them by the time they had reached Sallanches.

Everywhere Janet looked the Alpine giants lifted their snow-clad shoulders against the sky, sometimes even shutting out the sun as the road wound close beneath them, and Martin named peak after peak for her—the Roc d'Enfer and Haute Pointe and grey old Tête Pelouse brooding in the west—but the unfamiliar names faded swiftly before the accumulated grandeur of the whole and she felt too enthralled even to breathe.

Once or twice Martin looked down at her and laughed, but there seemed to be a grim sort of quality about his mirth and when he suggested that they should eat an early lunch at St. Gervais-les-Bains, which was off the main road, she was only too willing to agree. The keen mountain air had whipped up her appetite, but there was also the unsettling fact of Martin's nearness in the enclosed space of the car which made it essential that she should have a respite.

At St. Gervais they had climbed into a white fastness girt about by glittering snow, and for a long time she sat silently looking out of the hotel window at the scene before her, as if she would imprison its crystalline beauty in her heart for ever. The whole world seemed new and still and white, and Martin and she the only people in it.

He ordered their meal with a confidence she had come to expect in him, and they sat out in the sun on the wooden verandah to drink their coffee.

"I wish Ellis had been able to come," Janet said impulsively. "I wish he had been able to see all this just once— before his operation."

"You forget that he has seen it all before," he said. "It would not be new to him, except for the fact that he would be seeing it for the first time with you, of course."

"Ellis and I can come again." Her voice faltered over the words. "Though perhaps he may want to choose somewhere else. Geneva may hold too many memories of his illness for him to revisit it often in the future."

Martin rose abruptly, striding to the verandah rail where he stood for a moment without speaking.

"You'll marry him, of course, either way?" he asked, at last.

"You mean, whether the operation is successful or not?" Her voice was quite steady now, as her eyes would have been if he had turned to look at her. "Need you ask, Martin?"

It was a full minute before he answered.

"No," he said. "I suppose not."

Beyond him she could see the towering peaks, the wild rampart of pinnacles and granite buttresses which thrust up against the blue sky with black rock splinters tearing jagged rents in its mantle of snow, and suddenly Martin seemed a part of it all, remote, inaccessible, cold.

It was minutes before he turned, and then he came towards her with a strange look in his eyes. Something seemed to have been torn away from an inner depth of loneliness which he had not yet been able to cover up with a veneer of cynicism or pride, and for a split second he looked vulnerable.

"There's just one more question," he said. "Did you know in the beginning that Ellis might not get well, Janet? Did you

153

know that first day at Somerton?"

She felt the blood pulsing in her veins and a dreadful numbness in her limbs, but there could only be one possible answer to the question he had asked.

"Yes," she whispered, "I knew."

He turned abruptly, standing aside so that she might walk ahead of him down the verandah steps to the sunlit street below, but it seemed to Janet that the sun had already gone from her magic world. In one blinding moment of revelation she had looked into a man's eyes and known the truth.

Martin loved her. He had always loved her, but he would never tell her so. They were bound by the same bond, and she must never let him know that he had betrayed his benefactor's trust in a moment that had been too strong and too poignant for both of them.

After that it didn't seem to matter whether they reached the mountain-top or not. They knew the way they had to go, and no view from the heights could ever alter it.

"We'll push on to Chamonix," Martin said. "Ellis thought you should see the view from there. Chamonix is the conventional way up. There's a mountain railway almost to the top."

The conventional way! Yet, when they had first set out from Geneva, Martin had thought of taking her up by another way!

The view might still be the same. She must ask him about the view, she thought desperately. They must speak about anything now rather than about their two selves, thrusting convention between them because of the promise she had made and her sense of obligation, which was as great as his.

"Ellis said that we should be able to see the Mer de Glace from above Chamonix," she said, wondering at the calmness of her own voice. "He seemed to think it is something I should not miss."

He glanced swiftly up at the sky.

"I think there might just be time," he said. "Though we will have to be quick."

There did not appear to be anything amiss to Janet. The sky was still blue and innocent-looking above the highest peaks and Mont Blanc still reared his hoary old head in the golden glow of the sun. Only in the east was there a faint dimness, a grey cast over the sky with the blue still showing through, like a diaphanous scarf drawn across the horizon which might be only the effect of distance.

They left the car at the station where they boarded the funicular, and presently they were gaining height, pulling steadily up and out of the town towards the edge of the tree-line and up over it to the white snowfields beyond.

It was an entirely new experience for Janet, but her heart felt like lead and Martin's very nearness made her quiveringly afraid. If she betrayed her own love she would precipitate them all into a dark abyss from which there might be no escaping, but every minute she spent alone with him was a trap for her will.

It was late to travel to the top of their mountain and they were practically alone on the upward journey. The ski parties had all travelled earlier in the morning and would be well on their way down to the valley by this time, and only a few sightseers like themselves would remain at the top, making the most of the sunshine while it lasted.

They walked along a narrow path banked high and white on either side with a hard snow rampart, and then Martin drew her forward to a narrow log platform to look down on the distant valley at their feet and out across it to the mountains on the other side.

She looked and saw a glittering river of ice, the great mass of the Mer de Glace cleaving its slow and tortuous way down the deeply scarred side of the mountain, its fissures gleaming like sapphire, its polished crest shining in the sun.

"It's like a shield," Martin said, but Janet thought that it was like a sword.

She saw it one minute and the next it had gone. Before she could look again the scarf of mist that had hung in the sky on their upward journey had come down over the peaks, obscuring their view and shutting off the sun.

Involuntarily she shivered. There was nothing to be seen now but the greyness of obscurity, like a grey mist of pain drawn between her and Martin's promised vision from the heights.

"Cold?" he asked when the sun went in altogether. "I'm sorry it has turned out like this, but it's often the way. We can't always have everything to order."

Like views from a mountain, and love, and faith, and honesty!

155

He took off his scarf, wrapping it about her throat in spite of her protest, and his kindness was like a knife thrust deep in her heart.

"Shall we go back?" His face was inscrutable. "Ellis will expect us to keep our promise."

The mist had penetrated to the valley when they reached Chamonix.

"It's all so different," Janet said. "So cold and—lost-looking."

They motored rapidly towards Geneva, but the first lights were strung out along the lakeside before they reached it. The stillness of the snows was everywhere, their coldness penetrating deep into Janet's heart.

Ellis was waiting for them when they reached the clinic.

"I'm on a special menu," he announced, "but you needn't be. How did you get on?"

"A mist came down," Janet explained, not quite able to meet his eyes with the smile expected from her. "It hid most of the view, but we saw the Mer de Glace for a few minutes. It was like a sword in the sun."

She hadn't meant to say that, but it had slipped out. It had been the sharpest impression of her day.

"Janet was disappointed," Martin said lightly. "But I have told her that she can always go again."

It wouldn't be the same, Janet thought. There would always be the memory of to-day.

She stood by the window, unwinding Martin's scarf from about her throat, running the soft wool through her fingers with an unconsciously caressing movement before she parted with it, and when she turned back into the room she found Ellis watching her. He had been resting all day, but suddenly he looked tired and a little despondent, and she went to him immediately, putting her hand in his in a small gesture of confidence and affection as Martin crossed to the door.

"I'll leave you two together," he said. "You must have quite a lot to say to one another."

Ellis watched him go out.

"Martin's a strange sort of person in some ways," he mused. "He's sensitive, really, though he would never want anyone to guess it. He doesn't want to think he's butting in on a love scene!"

Janet wondered how dead a human heart could feel while it had to go on beating, while everything had to appear the same as usual when it was all so desperately changed. She wondered, too, if she had been wrong about Martin, if the very force of her loving had tricked her into imagining that he loved her in return.

When their dinner was brought in and the two covers set out on the small table near the stove it was evident that Martin had decided to take his alone or with the Professor rather than make a third during their last evening together before the operation. She supposed that Ellis was aware of the thoughtful gesture and was suitably grateful.

At ten o'clock, however, Martin came back, saying authoritatively:

"Time's up, I'm afraid. The Professor wants you to be asleep before eleven."

"And has supplied the necessary sleeping draught!" Ellis grinned across at the bottle he had set down beside the glass on the table near the window. "All right, Martin, I'm not going to be awkward. I've given the same sort of order dozens of times myself and I know it has to be obeyed!"

Janet put her hand in his for a second time.

"We'll soon be going back to Norminster," she said steadily, "and this time I shall expect you to be taking care of me!"

He put his lips to her hand in an odd little un-English gesture of farewell.

"That will be up to Martin and the Professor," he said.

Martin followed Janet to the door.

"You needn't come down with me," she assured him swiftly. "I can manage quite well on my own."

"Nevertheless," he said, "I intend to come."

"Yes," Ellis agreed, "see her back to the hotel, Martin." He smiled across the width of the room into Janet's distressed eyes. "Chin up, Jan!" he grinned. "We'll know the worst by this time to-morrow!"

"Is that true?" Janet asked Martin in a low, constrained whisper as they left the room.

"More or less." His mouth was grim, the line of his jaw inflexible as he gazed purposefully ahead. "There should be almost immediate response if the pressure is lifted. Otherwise we will know that we have failed."

157

"It can't happen," she protested passionately. "It mustn't happen to Ellis! He lives for his work, and half measures would never do for him. It's been all right for him to pass on the result of his experience to you in the past few weeks, to operate by proxy, but he could not go on doing that. He would need to be sure of a full-time job, the utmost need for his specialized skill, and without the power of his hands, how can he?"

They had reached the hall and he followed her out into the night before he spoke.

"We've got to face this," he said. "I've never pretended that it was more than a fifty-fifty chance, and quite candidly I'm not thinking beyond to-morrow morning at nine o'clock."

Janet felt that he was advising her not to think far beyond that fateful hour either. Uncertainty and fear of the result would not gain them anything. The Professor had asked Martin to help him with his task and she knew that he would need all his confidence for the job.

"I envy you," she said, "being with him. If only I could be there too!"

"It isn't possible." He turned to her in the uncertain light of the cold, starless night. "You will have your part to play when mine and the Professor's is finished."

"Yes," she whispered, "I know. Ellis is looking forward to our marriage."

The sudden wind that had sprung up and was whipping over the lake seemed to be blowing chill against her heart, as chill as the icy breath of doom, and her one instinct was to run from Martin and find lonely sanctuary in the house whose white bulk gleamed among the laurels just ahead of them.

"I'll come for you when it's all over," he promised, halting at the arched entrance to the garden. "Get out, Janet, if you can. Get out into the sunshine. The time will pass more quickly that way."

Janet did not think that the time would ever pass, but she could not tell him so. Her utter loneliness of spirit was her own to bear and it would stretch far beyond the events of to-morrow, in which he had his part to play.

"Take care of him, Martin!" she begged huskily as she fled from him into the darkened garden.

CHAPTER XI

A FROND of palm leaves loomed starkly against a grey back-cloth of sky when Janet opened her eyes next morning to the limited view from her pillows, and she supposed that it must be just after dawn. There was a heavy stillness outside which suggested that more snow had fallen in the night, but presently the sounds of activity in the narrow street on the far side of the garden wall told her that the rest of the world was astir. She had apparently slept longer than she had expected to, possibly because a kindly *concierge* had sent her up a hot drink "with something in it to take the chill out of her bones".

If only it could have taken the chill from her heart!

She got up and began to dress, feverishly at first and then with the dispirited accuracy of someone who knows that there is all the world of time between them and the major issue of the day. There were hours to spare, hours yet before she would know the result of the operation. Waiting hours and hoping hours; hours of praying that a miracle might happen.

It would be impossible for her to see Ellis, or Martin either, before nine o'clock, which was the time set for the operation, and as the minutes ticked away she began to envy Marie, who would be taking an active part in it all.

Even now Marie would be busy preparing the theatre, starting the sterilizer, laying out the necessary gowns and masks and the trays of instruments which the Professor would use. There would be an air of quiet purpose about all Marie did and a sense of challenge in the white tiled room which awaited their patient when all the preparations were complete.

How often she had felt that challenge back in Norminster when she had stood in the theatre at the City General with her own mask adjusted, waiting for the surgeons to complete their task of scrubbing up! The rows of carefully chalked rubber gloves would be lying in readiness, the subsidiary lights would be on and the silent group round the operating table would be waiting for the patient to be wheeled in.

She wondered if Martin would give the anæsthetic or if he

would be taking a more active, surgical part with the Professor. They had worked together in the past. They were aware of each other's methods, and Martin had all the steady confidence of youth.

At eight o'clock she went slowly downstairs, drinking the cup of coffee that was brought to her but leaving the basket of crisp French rolls untouched. To eat would have choked her, or so she felt, and presently she was out in the bleak January wind, muffled in a thick coat but still feeling cold and lonely and depressed.

Travelling in the stream of city-bound pedestrians, she found herself on the fringe of Geneva's busy main streets, crossing the bridges over the turbulent Rhône and walking aimlessly through its tree-lined squares. Traffic missed her by inches on more than one occasion and the hurrying citizens of Geneva threw alarmed glances in her direction as she made the pavement just in time to avoid an accident.

Nothing registered with her for the moment, not even the fact that she had walked so far until she found herself at the station and saw that it was twenty minutes past nine.

It would be ten o'clock before she got back. An hour after the operation had begun. Would there be news for her then? Would she know what Martin and the Professor had achieved?

She dared not take a tram in case she went in the wrong direction, and she had come out without enough money to hire a taxi, so there was nothing for it but to walk.

Her sense of direction was helped by the gleam of distant water every now and then as she hurried in the direction from which she had come, and a clock somewhere struck the hour as she reached the lakeside promenade. The slow, heavy strokes seemed to be pounding out in her brain, ten deliberate hammer blows directed at her by malignant time. Only one hour. Would she have further hours to wait?

Suddenly she made her decision. She had waited long enough. Her place now was by the side of the man she had promised to marry, and even Martin could not decree otherwise. She had taken his advice up to a point.

The usual sounds of activity met her ears as she pushed open the clinic door and passed into the sterile whiteness of its tiled hall, but as she paused in indecision for a moment she seemed to detect an undercurrent peculiar in its usual smooth-running

160

efficiency. A nurse hurried past her, giving her little more than a cursory glance as she stood there, and someone wheeled an empty stretcher towards the lift.

Her heart stiffened, as if a cold hand had been laid over it, and little beads of perspiration broke along the line of her upper lip.

Not that! she prayed. Not failure in the utmost, final sense!

Her limbs felt cramped and refused to obey her and there was a rushing, roaring sound in her ears, like some relentless tide rushing up over dry sand.

Not Ellis! a voice within her cried. Not Ellis! It would be too cruel to let him die. Too cruel after all that has happened!

She did not know how long she had stood there staring after the hurrying nurse. It could have been seconds; it might have been hours before she realized that she was no longer alone. Someone was speaking to her in a quiet, encouraging voice, as if she had been a child.

"It's all right," Martin said. "It's all over now and there's nothing to fear."

She stared at him, not really hearing what he had said. He was still in his shirtsleeves with only his operating gown missing, and she knew that he must have come straight from the theatre to find her. He had known that she would be there, and he had kept his promise and come to tell her his news right away.

"The stretcher?" she said indistinctly. "I saw it being taken up in the lift. I thought—there must be some sort of emergency. . . ."

Her words trailed off into silence and she saw that he had averted his eyes from her questioning look, but he guided her towards the stairs, saying firmly enough:

"There's nothing wrong. The operation is over and Ellis has been taken back to his room."

"And the stretcher ——?"

"Had nothing to do with him."

She smiled nervously, perilously near to tears in the first flood of relieved tension.

"I've been imagining all sort of things! What a fool one can be when one's on the receiving end of all this!"

He went on up the wide staircase without replying, leading the way to a door immediately ahead of them when they reached the top. It was not Ellis's room.

161

"I can't promise to let you see Ellis right away," he explained. "He hasn't come out of the anæsthetic yet, so there wouldn't really be much point in it, anyway. We can have no idea, of course, about results until the Professor has examined him when full consciousness has returned."

There was a curious reserve in him which might have suggested checkmate in a lesser personality, and sudden fear beat hard and fast against Janet's throat.

"Something has happened," she whispered. "There's something wrong, Martin!"

He thrust her into the room and closed the door. It was the sitting-room of a private suite much the same as that which Ellis had occupied for the past six days and she supposed it must be his own.

Without answering her almost frenzied appeal, he strode to a wall cabinet and mixed something in a medicine glass which he held out to her as he came back across the room.

"Drink this," he commanded, "and try to pull yourself together, Janet." His voice was curiously gentle and kind, more like the Professor's than Martin's. "There was an accident in the theatre not long after the operation began," he added swiftly. "The Professor collapsed. He went out like a light, and there was nothing to do but get him sent downstairs as quickly as possible."

"But Ellis ——? You said just now that the operation had begun!"

"Yes," he admitted. "It was up to me to finish the job."

"Martin ——!"

He smiled without a great deal of mirth.

"I'm sorry, Janet," he said. "There was no other way for it."

Dumbly she stood before him, not able to speak, hardly able to think in that first moment of overpowering shock. It was something so unexpected, so far removed from the bounds of possibility that it seemed as if her tired brain would not register the facts at first, but even in that moment she knew that there was no actual fear in her. Martin had seen the Professor operate before. He knew the older man's technique, and his own hand would be firm and sure. He had probably discussed the operation step by step with the Professor before they ever entered the theatre, and Martin would have been conversant with every intricate detail of the older man's plan.

"What an ungrateful little beast you must think me," she whispered at last. "You stepped in when things might have gone wrong—seriously wrong, and I haven't even tried to thank you. You probably saved Ellis's life."

"There would have been someone else there to do it if I had not been on the spot," he said briefly. "No surgeon ever works alone. You know that, Janet."

"But this was a special operation, needing specialized skill!" She would not let him detract from what he had done. "Oh, Martin!" she cried, "I'm not doubting you — I never could do that! — but if anything had happened to him —"

He turned abruptly to the window when she could not finish her sentence.

"Nothing sensational has happened," he repeated. "It only remains to be seen whether I have operated successfully or not."

"Ellis will be for ever in your debt!"

He swung round to face her.

"These things have no connection with debt or repayment or anything else," he declared almost angrily. "They are beyond gratitude, if you like, but they are also a surgeon's job. His everyday job. He doesn't think in terms of owing, and Ellis least of all. A doctor's life's work is a matter of service, and how he performs that service is largely a thing for his own conscience to decide. He has something to give, and if suffering humanity benefits from it here or in Timbuctoo, he has discharged his obligations and justified his living."

"I suppose that is the way Ellis thinks, too," Janet agreed, "but—ordinary people still feel indebted, Martin. When a surgeon's skill and tenacity has given them back a life they almost despaired of or made their own life possible again, they would never be able to overlook it or take it all for granted."

For a moment he stood looking down at her in the harsh northern light that came in across the snow-bound mountains, and then he said abruptly:

"I suppose that's just one of the things that we doctors must learn to accept."

He stood over her while she drank the contents of the glass, his dark brows drawn together, the line of his jaw set and hard, and it seemed that he had come to some unalterable conclusion in these few minutes while he waited for the stimulant to have its effect.

163

It steadied Janet's nerves, but it could not banish the anxiety she felt.

"When shall I be able to see Ellis?" she asked.

Martin glanced at his watch.

"In about an hour, perhaps. Have you had any breakfast?" he asked perfunctorily, dismissing the subject of his patient because there was no more he could tell her about Ellis for the present. "You've probably made do with a cup of coffee," he added, "and that's getting us nowhere. Marie is bringing me up a tray and I shall tell her to put something on it for you." He moved towards the door, rolling down his sleeves. "Excuse me a moment, Janet, while I go and find a coat. I came straight from the theatre to look for you."

He must have told Marie about the extra breakfast when he went along the corridor because, ten minutes later, she appeared in the doorway with a laden tray which Janet helped her to set out on the table near the stove. Marie was a tireless worker and never seemed to mind what kind of task she tackled. It was all done with a will and a smiling disregard of lengthy hours, and she seemed completely immune to fatigue.

"Doctor Everett!" she exclaimed as soon as she saw Janet. "But he was wonderful! Wonderful! Never before have I seen such presence of mind in the operating room! He just took over where the Professor left off as if nothing had happened, as if it was all a part of the plan arranged before they come to operate at all! He was magnificent, but also it could be seen that he was working under a great mental strain. It was of great importance, this operation, both to his patient and to himself."

"Yes," Janet said, "I know. If anything had gone wrong Doctor Everett would never have forgiven himself. But the Professor? What happened to him, Marie? I should have asked Doctor Everett, but I was—too upset at the time."

Marie shook her head.

"It is impossible to say," she declared. "He had what you call a complete black-out, and that is something terrible for a surgeon. It is a warning that he must go slow, that he must not continue to burn the candle at both ends. For months he has been overworking because there is so much to do here in the clinic, and never has he taken a holiday in the past three years. Always it is the progress of his work here in Geneva that is in the forefront of his mind, but now Doctor Everett will order him to go away, to rest for a little while so that he will come back 'a new man', as he says!"

"I'm so sorry," Janet said. "Somehow one takes it for granted that a surgeon can go on performing miracles indefinitely with no ill effects on his own nervous system. We expect too much, I suppose, unthinkingly."

"That is true," Marie agreed, laying Martin's table napkin carefully in place and standing back to see that all was in order on the table. "But everything will be all right now if the Professor takes notice of this warning he has received and rests a little."

Martin came in, watching as Marie served up a steaming hot egg dish from under the silver covers. Janet poured two cups of coffee, but she still felt unable to eat. Martin, however, was calmly insistent.

"We have an unexpected patient on our hands," he pointed out. "You may be able to make yourself useful helping with Ellis to relieve Marie and the night staff. We can't afford to have you cracking up on us, too."

"I don't think I shall be a nuisance to you, Martin," she told him with quiet dignity. "I don't crack easily, but to-day has been a strain—for all of us," she added. "Marie has just told me about the magnificent way you stood up to things in the operating theatre."

He smiled deprecatingly.

"Marie tends to exaggerate," he said. "You must not take all she says too literally, my dear Janet. She is one of those distressing people who make idols of their doctors and suffer endless disillusionment when they discover the feet of clay."

"Now you are just being cynical to cover up your embarrassment!" she told him. How close she seemed to have come to Martin in these past few minutes! How well she seemed to know him. "Marie is only telling the truth. You met the situation as she expected you would, but she doesn't see any need to keep quiet about it."

"Marie thinks I am made of steel or carved from granite, perhaps, like her guardian mountain over there." He nodded towards the snow-capped summit of Mont Blanc just visible above the low-trailing wisps of mist which encircled the lesser peaks at its base. "And there really wouldn't be any point in disillusioning her in this case."

"Must you always wear a mask?" she asked involuntarily. "Must you always appear to be—far more invulnerable than you really are?"

He looked up, surprised at the intensity of the question, his eyes holding hers for a moment with a strange expression in them.

"A mask is necessary occasionally, Janet," he said slowly. "Otherwise we would run the risk of finding ourselves without protection of any kind."

As they finished their breakfast he went over the details of the operation with her, thrusting the professional angle of their relationship between them deliberately, it seemed, and when he looked at his watch again he told her that he thought she might see Ellis whenever she was ready.

"There's a mirror in the bedroom and a bathroom beyond that," he said as he went towards the outer door. "You may want to freshen up first."

She knew that he was offering her a moment to compose herself before he took her to Ellis, and when his footsteps had died away along the corridor she went towards the inner room and through it to the black and green-tiled bathroom beyond.

Ice-cold water straight from the mountains gushed from the tap she turned on and she plunged her face into it, thankful for its cool touch on her flushed cheeks and the astringent quality of it on her brow. If it would help to clear away some of the haze of pain and indecision in her mind she would be thankful, but when she had patted her face dry on one of Martin's towels she wondered if anything could ever do that for her.

Going slowly through to the bedroom, she found herself standing before his dressing-chest looking down at an array of brushes and the odd possessions which a man of Martin's type invariably possesses. There was the old and well-worn tobacco pouch, the silver lighter, the favourite pipe, and beside them the current issue of *The Lancet*, which he had probably read on the plane coming over. His shaving gear was there in a zippered leather case which he had forgotten to close, and yesterday's handkerchiefs in an untidy, crushed pile beside the mirror, but it was the final, unexpected possession that caught and held her eye.

166

Behind the shaving case was a leather folder holding two photographs, one a portrait and the other a group. The portrait she recognized instantly as one of his mother taken several years ago, and she gazed at it for a moment, realizing once more how very much alike they looked. There was the same fearless, wide-set eyes, the same high, intelligent-looking forehead and a similarity about the whole facial structure which must surely have been reflected in their individual character to some extent, at least. Dorothy Everett had been greatly respected and universally liked in Somerton both for her kindliness and impartiality of judgment, and she had been known to possess a rare courage which could face up to self-criticism and even to defeat. She had carried out her many commitments unfalteringly and with a quiet dignity, and that, Janet knew, would be the way with her son.

When she turned to the second photograph a small gasp of amazement escaped her. She had thought to find a boys' school or college group, but instead she was looking down at a badly taken snapshot already fading at the corners with age. It was something she had quite forgotten, a group posed at the net after a game of tennis on the public courts at Athersage, and Martin and she were standing together in the centre.

She continued to stare at it, shaken and unnerved, with all her new-found resolution reduced to nothingness and the ache of longing uppermost in her heart again. Why had Martin kept it? This was so long ago, and reason should tell her that he did not care, but here seemed to be the negation of all her doubts, the proof that what she had seen in his eyes for one brief moment on a mountain-top had existed for a long time for both of them.

Blindly she turned away, the tears she must not shed obscuring her vision as she hurried back to the sitting-room to stand rigid before the window looking out on a drift of falling snow till Martin came to her.

"Ten minutes, Janet," he said. "It's all we can spare you at present."

"I won't disturb him."

Ellis was lying propped up with pillows in the high clinic bed, still a little dazed from the effects of the anæsthetic but able to smile in his own inimitable way as she went in.

"Everything is O.K., Jan!" he told her. "You mustn't worry.

Martin has his fingers very firmly on my pulse!"

Janet heard Martin walk away along the corridor and her lips quivered uncontrollably for a moment as she bent to kiss his patient.

"Of course, Ellis," she said. "You came through wonderfully."

He roused himself to consider her more closely.

"You have been worrying!" he said.

"Everyone worries just a little, especially over an operation of this magnitude," she answered. "We are certainly all glad that it is over."

"I haven't seen the Professor," he mused. "Where is he, Jan?"

"He's—resting." It was obvious that Martin did not want him to know about Professor Hochsolden's collapse just yet. "He's been working very hard these past few months. Overworking, Martin says."

"Martin pulls everyone up for the very thing he is most apt to do himself!" Ellis smiled. "He proposes to go back to England with the first available plane after he has made quite sure about me in case Norminster and the City General have blown up in his absence!"

A cold stab of loneliness went through Janet at the news, but she told herself that she should have expected this of Martin.

"He can't leave the hospital without two of its consultants indefinitely," she said, and was surprised to see a vaguely regretful look come into Ellis's eyes.

"I'm not so sure about Martin staying on at the City General," he said. "He has some idea that he wants to come back here, to leave the General and Norminster to take care of themselves."

"No!" Janet protested as his eyes closed. "No, he mustn't!"

"When Martin once gets an idea into his head," Ellis said without opening his eyes again, "he will carry it out if he believes he must, however wrong it might be. He might even think that it is his duty, you know," he added.

Janet waited till she was quite sure that he was deeply asleep, and then she went out into the corridor, moving like someone in a dream towards the head of the stairs. Was all that Ellis had just said true? Was Martin really planning to leave Norminster and return to Geneva? And if so, why?

It would be throwing away so much that he had set his heart on, all that part of his career which had already shown so much promise of brilliance under Ellis's guidance. He might make a name for himself here in Switzerland, too, but somehow it would not be quite the same. It would not be in connection with the work that was nearest his heart.

What had changed him? What had made him alter his mind since he had come to Geneva? He had spoken about the future with confidence so often, and here he was ready to throw it all up for some idea of necessity or pride, or whatever it was.

At the foot of the stairs she met Marie.

"Will you give me something to do, Marie?" she asked. "I can't go on wandering aimlessly about like this when everyone else is busy."

Marie promised that she would speak to Matron and no doubt Janet would be permitted to help with Mr. Spencer-Wroe.

Janet wondered if Martin would agree to that and found herself waiting impatiently for his decision. He seemed to be the arbiter of all their destinies now and the stern adjudicator of his own.

She was allowed to help with Ellis the following day, and was almost relieved that the Professor, and not Martin, was standing by her patient's bed when she went into his room.

"We have been a little remiss in our duties!" the Professor confessed, his dark eyes twinkling as she came forward. "I have been asking Mr. Spencer-Wroe what he thinks of a surgeon who—how is it you say?—'falls down' on his job!"

The joviality of the remark covered a deep concern for his failure as the short, thick fingers remained fastened on the other man's pulse.

"I have only just heard the truth of the whole affair," Ellis told Janet, "and Martin appears to be avoiding me in consequence. He does not wish to be thanked, apparently."

"You must recognize your debt to him in some other way," the Professor suggested. "I could not have completed the job more skilfully if I had been permitted to finish it myself. These things are inevitably in the hands of *le bon Dieu*. So small a thing it was that made nothing of my plans!"

Ellis remained thoughtfully silent till the Professor had left the room, and even then he did not bring Martin's name into the conversation again until Janet appeared in the doorway round about midday with the English mail.

"Martin arranged for our letters to be redirected to us," she explained as she sorted them through. "I expect they are mostly for him."

"Martin thinks of everything," he mused. "And quite often not of himself."

"There's one letter for you," Janet said, "and a periodical. They have both been sent on from Minster Close."

She handed over his mail and he laid aside the periodical to scrutinize the letter. Janet had noticed that it bore a foreign stamp.

"It's from Taiwan," he said. "Margaret has taken time to write at last!"

Ellis was turning over the flimsy sheets of his letter with the eagerness of a boy, but suddenly he laid it down and looked at her across the bright blue counterpane.

"She's coming home!" he said. "This has been on its way for some time and she's probably half-way to England by now."

There was no doubt about his delight at the prospect of this meeting after all those years of parting, and Janet tried to visualize their reunion.

"Tell me what Margaret is like," she demanded a little nervously. "Does she say anything about our engagement?"

"I haven't come to that part yet. Margaret's letters are like a serial. You're given an instalment every day and then the whole thing is posted off in volume form when she realizes that it is taking on alarming proportions and you might not have time to read it all!"

Janet laughed.

"She sounds delightful. Is she like you to look at, Ellis?"

"Good heavens, no! Can you imagine any woman looking like me?" he grinned. "She's slim and *petite*. At least, she was when I last saw her and I don't think she has changed so very much in the interval. She still describes herself as pint-sized when she thinks about it!"

"Yet she's doing a giant-sized job," Janet mused.

"She's wrapped up in her work," he agreed, "but I think she always meant to come home one day, if only to check up

170

on my domestic arrangements!" He lay back among his pillows, smiling ruefully. "It's going to be something of a showdown when she arrives, isn't it?"

Janet looked perplexed at the question and he added swiftly:

"About Minster Close, I mean. She's going to take a poor view of the way I've been living there, and, come to think of it, there's not much to offer her in the way of home comforts, either. She'll refuse to go to an hotel, though."

"I don't think she should have to," Janet said. "After all, she is coming home for the first time in years and she deserves somewhere comfortable and pleasant to stay."

"Which isn't Minster Close." He heaved a long-drawn sigh. "Jan, I've been hopelessly lacking in foresight for a great many years. I've let my job fill my life and bound my horizon to the exclusion of a great many things that are equally worth while, but maybe I can do something about it before it is too late. We could," he suggested, "tackle Minster Close first and foremost!"

Janet's heart gave a sudden, apprehensive leap, as if something which had been standing in the shadows at the back of her mind for a long time had suddenly come forward to claim her attention.

"What would you like me to do?" she asked, knowing even before he spoke that he was going to ask her to make a home for him at Minster Close before his sister got there.

"I thought you might be able to do something about the flat," he admitted. "You know what chaos it's in. The sitting room is an absolute barracks and my bedroom is little better. There's a spare room, too, with nothing in it but a lot of junk—dismantled microscopes and all sorts of things that have outlived their usefulness. The average man can't bear to throw things away, you know, even though he's pretty well aware that he'll never find a use for them this side of the grave!"

"I'll see what I can do," Janet promised. "How much time do you think we have?"

It seemed that time itself was slipping away from her, that she was being precipitated to some strange, swift destiny which she could not avoid and must accept without protest.

"I'm not quite sure about that point," Ellis said, trying to make out the date stamp on his sister's letter. "She won't be flying home, that's a certainty, but this may have been posted when she reached the boat. She would have to come via Hong Kong and Singapore, I suppose, so that gives us a week or two yet."

"You'll be home before then," Janet assured him. "You might even be able to do some of the planning yourself."

"I'm not going to count on that, though," Ellis said firmly. "I'm going to send you home in advance, Jan, and let you make a start. If you go on ahead of me there can be absolutely no fear of Margaret landing at Minster Close unwelcomed. I should never forgive myself if that happened. Not after all those years!"

It was impossible to refuse him because it meant so much to him.

"When do you want me to travel?" she asked as Martin came into the room.

"Almost immediately." Ellis looked up at the younger man, debating something in his mind before he continued: "Martin is going back tomorrow. You can go with him, and he might even be persuaded to help with Minster Close."

Janet recoiled at the suggestion, but she could not make any outward protest. She would go with Martin because Ellis wished it and he would agree to put his services at her disposal for the same reason, but how could she bear to see him, day after day, in Norminster while she awaited Ellis's return? How could she bear to go with him to Minster Close, to what was to be her first real home, with the thought of lonely, isolated Normanscliff for ever in her mind?

CHAPTER XII

JANET and Martin flew out the following day. Ellis's arm was still in its plaster casing, but he had been able to move his shoulder quite freely since the operation and the Professor had advised him to stay on in Geneva until the appropriate massage could be started and the cure completed.

"Professor Hochsolden seems convinced of an absolute cure," Janet said as they circled the white airfield buildings and turned northwards. "I know we shouldn't look back, but when I think of all that it might have meant I feel that it has been almost a miracle, Martin."

"Yes," he said, "it's what we prayed for, isn't it? Everything ought to take its normal course now, and you should be married within the year."

The words stabbed at her hurtfully.

"All these preparations for Margaret Wroe's arrival are a two-fold affair, I gather," Martin went on relentlessly. "You and Ellis intend to set up house at Minster Close, I suppose?"

"Ellis hasn't been definite about it," she answered unsteadily.

"But it will be your home," he persisted. "At least till you find somewhere more suitable."

"Yes," she admitted in a choked whisper.

He did not refer to Minster Close again till they had stepped off the plane.

"If you will let me know what you want me to do," he suggested, "I'll help where I can. Does it mean that you won't be coming back to the hospital?"

Did he wish that? Was he telling her indirectly but as plainly as he could in the circumstances that he would prefer her not to be at the City General in future?

"I shall have to work my month's notice whatever I decide to do," she said, feeling her spirits sinking at the thought. "This has been annual leave, you know."

"I had forgotten that." He helped her into a waiting taxi. "When are you due back?"

"On Monday. It gives me three days to see what can be

done about Minster Close."

"Will you stay there in the meantime?"

"I hadn't thought of that. I—just expected to go back to the Nurses' Home."

He glanced down at his watch.

"That gives you till eleven o'clock this evening, then," he said lightly. "It means that we have time for a meal in London before we catch our train."

She felt that he was being merely polite and could not bear the thought.

"I'd rather go back, Martin," she said, "if you wouldn't mind."

"It's for you to say," he assured her briefly.

They travelled to Norminster by the five-fifteen train, arriving there shortly before eight o'clock. The train had stopped at most of the smaller stations on the way and Janet had found it the most trying part of their long journey home. It seemed to represent the slowing-up of the brisk pace at which they had lived during these past few days in Geneva, underlining the fact that all things returned to normal, in time.

"There may be a letter at Minster Close from Ellis's sister," she said when they turned out of the brightly-lit booking-hall to look for a taxi. "He has asked me to open it if there is one, so perhaps I should go there first."

"I think you can safely leave well alone till to-morrow, Janet," he told her firmly. "You could do very little about it to-night, even if there was a letter, and you look all in. I'm going to take you to Coulson's for a hot meal and then you're going straight to the hostel to sleep."

She could not argue with him. His sudden kindly protectiveness was almost more than she could bear, and more than once during the meal, tears threatened to make a swimming mockery of her smile.

If Martin saw them he made no comment, but as soon as the waiter had brought his bill he paid it and drove her to the Nurses' Home.

"I'll phone you in the morning," he said, "at Minster Close."

Utter exhaustion made Janet sleep that night and she realized when she woke next morning that she had not slept

174

really well for over a week. There had been all the anxiety about Ellis and the worry of his operation, but that was in the past now, with so many other things.

She forced herself not to think of Martin as she made her way to Minster Close, and the news she received there was certainly startling enough to make her forget him for a moment.

"There's one of them cablegrams arrived for Mr. Spencer-Wroe," the caretaker's wife advised her as soon as she appeared at the head of the stairs. "It came yesterday and I didn't rightly know what to do with it. I wasn't sure if you could redirect them like you do with a letter."

"It's all right, Mrs. Carling," Janet assured her as she tore the flap of the envelope. "I'll see to it right away. You couldn't really have done better."

She took out the message and unfolded it, seeing that it had been handed in at Colombo two days ago,

> Flying home from here with a friend [she read]. Will phone from London.

It was signed "Margaret", and there was no doubt that Ellis's sister was all but on the doorstep.

Janet's heart began to pound with great, sledge-hammer blows. What am I to do? And how can I possibly cope? Should Ellis be told, or should I go ahead with his plans for the flat and hope for the best?

The momentary panic subsided as soon as she thought of Martin, however. She would leave it to him to decide what should be done about telling Ellis. There would be no way of bringing him back to England immediately and Martin would wish to safeguard his patient before he considered anyone else.

The telephone bell rang and she went to answer it.

"Martin here," the voice said from the other end. "Is everything in order, Janet?"

"Nothing is," she confessed, though she did not feel quite so flustered now. "It looks as if Margaret Wroe might be in London before the week-end."

He caught the urgency in her voice immediately.

"Stay where you are," he commanded. "I'll be with you in under ten minutes."

Janet decided to leave everything till Martin got there, but she could occupy the time making him some coffee.

Mrs. Carling obliged with a tin which she declared she had only opened the day before and Janet found cups and saucers and a percolator in Ellis's study. She discovered that he possessed most of the essentials but none of the luxuries of living and he had amassed all of them in one room, together with his books, presumably to save himself the inconvenience of moving farther afield when he found it necessary to eat at home. It was one of the principal reasons for the study's air of confusion and she felt that there was material enough here to furnish two rooms.

Ellis's bedroom she decided to leave as it was for the time being.

There was a strong aroma of coffee in the air by the time Martin arrived, and all the windows in the flat had been flung open.

"What is it?" he asked lightly as Mrs. Carling ushered him in. "A chest clinic?"

"Did you know about this?" Janet asked when Mrs. Carling had disappeared.

"I knew that Ellis lived rough, but I've never seen the full evidence till now. It won't do, Janet. You have a right to a home."

"So has Ellis. He never had one, and I suppose this was the next best thing."

Martin bent to switch off the percolator, standing with his back to her while she set out the cups.

"When you have changed all that he will notice the difference," he said.

"It will have to be changed quickly, Martin." There was an echo of desperation in Janet's voice which had nothing to do with Margaret Wroe's homecoming. "His sister has cabled from Colombo, where she has been staying with friends, and she is flying on the last lap home. It means that she may be here this coming week-end, and, at any rate, it looks as if she will be home before Ellis."

He whistled softly.

"Ellis has given you a free hand, I gather?"

"I am to spend what I like. His credit is good in most of the

176

local stores." She looked about her uneasily. "There seems so much to do."

He put down his half-finished coffee.

"You'll do it, Janet," he said almost stiffly. "You're made that way."

"I suppose the bedroom will come first—Margaret's bedroom, I mean," she said with a deep flush. "I feel almost as if I know her already," she hurried on. "The room will have to be cleaned out, of course, and there ought to be curtains at the windows and new bedspreads."

"Don't forget that your Doctor Margaret has come straight from missionary work in the field!" he reminded her dryly.

"I am remembering that," Janet said. "It's the reason for the softly feminine touch. I want her to feel that she has really come home."

He turned towards the door.

"Phone me when you want the furniture moved," he said laconically. "I can't promise to help with the pretty curtains, but I promised Ellis to take care of the heavy jobs."

Janet worked all that day. Mrs. Carling came in to scrub the spare room floor and ended by distempering the walls in a pale shade of apple green which was cool-looking and a perfect foil for Janet's mauve-patterned chintz.

In a whirl of mingled apprehension and excitement she visited the local shops, hurrying back to Minster Close when her arms were too full of parcels to carry more. She might only have another day, but already Margaret's room was ready for the divan bed and crinoline-skirted dressing-table which she had bought at Greal's in the High Street, and if she worked harder than ever in the morning the living-room would be ready for its new furniture by the time Greal's van arrived round about midday.

She thought that she could safely leave the kitchenette and bathroom to Margaret's sense of proportion. Ellis could not be expected to take an interest in the state of kitchen paintwork and electric gadgets, and these things could be installed gradually.

Martin, however, appeared to have different ideas. He arrived shortly after two o'clock complete with an ancient surgery coat and operating cap in which he declared he was about to tackle the bathroom walls.

"Baths are an essential to people who have been forced to live without them half their lives," he said. "I phoned half a dozen painters and decorators, but nobody would take the job on at such short notice." He struggled into the white coat. "Pass me the scalpel, Nurse!"

Janet gulped and obeyed. Here was a side to Martin she had never seen before, one that she might never have guessed at in a thousand years, and the bitter-sweet poignancy of working with him in such a way brought a constriction into her throat which kept her silent.

While she snipped and sewed at curtains he put a first coat of flat on the bathroom walls, covering himself in apricot paint in consequence, but the very fact that he had done it badly endeared him to her all the more.

"You may be a good surgeon," she said, trying to fight back the hopeless longing in her heart with humour and friendly banter, "but they would never enrol you as a master painter on the strength of that end wall!"

She followed him into the living-room, where he had gone to take off his coat.

"Will you let me make you some tea?" she asked.

"No, thank you." His refusal had sounded almost brusque, although he had tempered it with a brief smile. "I'll push off now. You won't want me till the morning."

The furniture had arrived and the men had carried it into the appropriate rooms. Janet stood looking about her with an odd feeling of anti-climax, the dreadful, empty feeling of having fallen from the heights. For half a day, for an infinitesimal spell in a lifetime, she and Martin had worked on a home together, but it was not their home. It was hers. Her home with Ellis.

She saw Martin to the door and he said good-night rather abruptly and went swiftly down the outside stairs.

The next day Margaret Wroe telephoned from London.

"I've just arrived," she said when Janet had explained her own presence in the flat. "I'm so terribly sorry about Ellis—and worried. Ought I to put up in London if he's not in Norminster?"

"Please don't," Janet begged. "He wants you to come straight here. He wants you to come home."

That seemed to settle it. Margaret said she could be in

178

Norminster by six o'clock that evening.

Janet phoned Martin, catching him just before he left the hospital.

"One of us will have to meet her at the station," he suggested. "Do you want me to go, Janet?"

"Perhaps that would be best," Janet agreed. "I'd like to have a meal ready when she gets here."

He rang off, and Janet went through to the kitchen, thinking that Martin had accepted most of Ellis's responsibilities these days. She peeled potatoes and opened a tin of peas and the jar of jellied chicken she had bought for just such an emergency, trying not to think that it was as if Martin was bringing a first guest into his own home.

Clamping her teeth firmly on her lower lip, she decided on chilled tomato juice before the chicken and a savoury afterwards. It was a safe sort of meal to offer two people whose tastes she did not really know.

Shortly before six she made her way to the bathroom to wash and tidy her hair, but the smell of new paint and the sight of the end wall where Martin had applied the apricot colouring far too thickly caught her off her guard and she found herself standing in the middle of the floor with her hands tightly clenched while dry, shattering sobs shook her from head to foot.

"Martin! Oh, Martin!" a thin, weak voice in her cried. "If it could only have been you!"

The bell rang as she put a final layer of powder under her eyes. She had not heard the car, but Martin might have left it out beyond the cobbled yard where there were better facilities for parking than in the square itself.

Drawing in a deep breath, she opened the door to Ellis's sister.

"Janet, my dear!" Margaret Wroe said, taking both Janet's hands in hers, "how glad I am to see you! Ellis wrote me all about you, but I was determined not to believe one half of it till we met!"

She was slim and *petite* as Ellis had said, but no verbal description could have done justice to Margaret Wroe's eyes. They were, without doubt, her most arresting feature and they sparkled in her piquant little face like sapphires. They were a deeper blue than her brother's and Janet had the suddenly

179

disconcerting impression that they missed very little that went on in their owner's immediate vicinity.

"You'll stay and have a meal with us, Martin?" she invited. "Ellis would expect it."

She wondered why she had found it necessary to add that bit about Ellis when Martin had obviously been prepared to stay.

"This is all a tremendous surprise," Margaret said when Janet had shown her to her room. "I always understood that Ellis kept a typically bachelor establishment, and I know what that can mean! Odd meals cooked over a gas-ring and books and instruments everywhere. I expected to find cultures growing in the bathroom and a skull on the kitchen bench!"

"I thought it would be nicer if you didn't find it that way," Janet smiled. There was no point in pretending with Margaret Wroe. She would have guessed the truth anyway. "Ellis was going to re-furnish the flat, in any case."

"Of course! It was going to be your home."

Margaret turned to look at her brother's fiancée in the full light of the wall sconces on either side of her dressing-table, and Janet felt reserve in her for the first time. The candid scrutiny was critical, and somewhere behind the deep blue eyes lay a suggestion of regret. It would seem that Margaret was struggling to like her, but it was a tussle with a personal bias which she had held for years.

"You're much younger than Ellis," she said, "but I suppose that doesn't count at all if you're in love!"

"I've hardly noticed it," Janet returned truthfully. "Ellis is such a helpful person when it comes to surmounting obstacles."

Margaret looked at her rather sharply through the mirror, but she did not say anything as she took off her hat and coat.

"The bathroom is through here," Janet said, leading the way. "Martin has just painted it, so I haven't been able to hang up the towels."

"Martin?" Margaret queried. "Oh, of course—Doctor Everett! I should have understood. Ellis wrote about him, too. It was very kind of him to come to meet my train."

"Ellis and he are colleagues."

"So I gathered." Margaret paused with a towel in her hands. "He told me coming from the station that he owed a great deal to my brother," she added.

"Ellis has taught Martin practically everything there is to know in their particular sphere," Janet said, unaware that her voice had betrayed her admiration for both men to the woman who stood listening.

"And Martin will carry on for Ellis while he is away and perhaps afterwards, while he completes his convalescence?"

"I'm not quite sure." Janet found sudden difficulty in meeting the searching blue eyes. "I don't know whether Martin will stay in Norminster or not."

Martin was pouring drinks when she reached the living-room.

"Well?" He looked up as she came in.

"You mean, what do I think of her?" Janet asked. "She seems a wonderful sort of person."

"But shrewd, for all that," he remarked dryly. "Those eyes have become accustomed to weighing people up in the shortest possible space of time. It's part of a missionary doctor's stock in trade, I should say. Otherwise, they would be hopelessly exploited."

"All the same, you like her?" Janet suggested.

He looked down at her with a crooked smile.

"How did you guess?"

"You went out of your way to be nice."

"And when I don't do that?" he queried.

"You can be hurtful or—indifferent."

He held out her glass.

"You know a great deal about me, Janet," he said, "but not all."

"Would that be a disadvantage, Doctor Everett?"

They turned to find Margaret standing in the doorway. She was smiling, but as she came forward to accept her drink from Martin her blue eyes were watchful.

"It might be in certain circumstances," Martin agreed, "although Janet is never likely to encounter them."

"Which means that they occur mostly when you are alone?"

"Mostly."

Margaret sipped her drink, considering him in the frank way she had.

"Tell me about Ellis," she suggested. "He wrote to me about
181

his accident, but why had he to go to Switzerland for this operation?"

"I advised him to see a colleague of mine there," Martin explained. "Paralysis had set in after the shoulder had been set and put into plaster and Professor Hochsolden was the one answer to the problem."

"I'm afraid I haven't kept up with my surgery," Margaret said as they moved towards the dining-alcove.

"Your brother weathered the operation all right," Martin told her, "but it was too soon after it to bring him back with us. He must have extensive massage to his shoulder and arm, but that can be arranged over here. He won't want to stay in Geneva a moment longer than he can help now that you have arrived."

Margaret glanced at Janet, who was carrying in the chicken and vegetables.

"Can I help?" she asked. "Or is everything so beautifully arranged that I would only be hindering?"

"It's all here on the tray," Janet smiled. "Go on talking shop with Martin!"

For the moment, however, Margaret had no more to say to Martin on the subject of her brother.

"I came over to London with a friend," she mentioned. "We met unexpectedly in Colombo and she persuaded me to fly back on the second lap of my journey. She had been staying in Ceylon with her brother, who is manager of a plantation out there. I have promised to meet Irene again in London, so I expect I shall be going up there again quite soon."

Irene! The name struck a deeply resounding chord in Janet's memory, and suddenly she seemed to be sitting by Ellis's side with the muted roar of a plane's engines in her ears and thick clouds spreading under them as they flew high above the English coast.

It was so long ago, Jan, that sometimes it seems a part of another life.... She could hear Ellis's voice as if he had spoken now in the lamp-lit room behind her. *We both had our careers, and Irene's took her one way and mine took me another. She married a missionary and went out to Africa. I haven't heard from her since.*

Could this be Ellis's first love, returned to England for the first time in years? Janet felt her throat go dry as she served

182

the meal, and even when Martin had carried the coffee tray across to the fire and set it down on Ellis's book table, Irene's name seemed to echo through the room as if it had been the most important thing in their conversation.

Martin stood drinking his coffee with an arm along the high, carved mantelpiece which was a feature of the lovely oak-panelled room.

"I have a round of the wards to do at eight," he excused himself a few minutes later. "Two post-operative cases from yesterday and two that should be going out tomorrow." He turned to Janet. "By the way, the P.N.O. expects you to work that month's notice," he said. "There's no way of talking her out of it. Rules, apparently, are rules."

"I'd rather go back," Janet assured him swiftly. "I think Miss Lawson knows that. I spoke to her yesterday on the phone."

She wondered if she should go with Martin to the door or if that was Margaret's prerogative now that she was duly installed in her brother's flat.

"I'll see you to the door," Margaret said, as if she had already made up her mind.

"I hope you will come again," she told Martin as they shook hands. "Even before we get Ellis back. I expect Janet to visit me often."

"It's kind of you," Martin acknowledged, but he did not make her any promise.

When Margaret came back Janet was clearing the table.

"Leave it for a minute," she said, "and come and have another cup of coffee, Janet. It's still quite hot. When have you got to be back at the hospital?"

"We're allowed out till eleven, unless we have a late pass for something special." Janet settled herself on one of the low chairs which Greal's men had delivered that morning, wondering what her companion would say if she knew what a scuttle there had been to make the flat comfortable before she arrived. "I won't be going on duty till tomorrow afternoon."

Margaret lit a cigarette, studying its gleaming scarlet tip when she had drawn on it for a second or two in silence.

"Is Martin Everett a native of Norminster?" she asked.

"He's more or less a native. He was brought up at a place called Somerton about eleven miles north of here."

"Did you know him at that time?"

"Yes." In spite of herself, the colour deepened in Janet's cheeks. "You see, I was brought up in Somerton, too."

Margaret seemed to be content with the explanation, for she turned the conversation to nursing and the medical world and very soon it was ten o'clock and Janet said she must go.

"And not a dish washed!" she exclaimed.

"Don't worry about those," Margaret assured her. "I'll paddle around in my dressing-gown and fix them after you've gone. I'll have to find out where everything goes, you know, and just as well now as later."

"You won't feel nervous, staying in the flat alone?" Janet asked. "The caretaker and his wife are just below you."

Margaret laughed.

"I've slept in a mud hut in the middle of a jungle before now," she said. "I won't feel lonely, Jan, but come back and see me as quickly as you can. It's the days with very little to do that will seem strange and long at first, I guess, and we ought to get to know each other for Ellis's sake."

After that Janet spent all her spare time with Margaret.

Back on the wards she was kept busy enough, and she rarely saw Martin except when he walked between the rows of beds with his attendant retinue. He seemed remote then, and beyond her reach, and he made no effort to seek her out.

Margaret went to London and met her friend, Irene Swallow, but she did not bring her to Norminster as Janet had half expected her to do, and at the end of the month Ellis came back.

Martin went to London to meet him at the airport, taking Margaret with him, but Janet was on duty all that day and could not go.

She tried not to look on the fact with relief, tried to convince herself that it was still possible to make something worth while out of her marriage to Ellis, but a gnawing uncertainty at the back of her mind mocked constantly at the suggestion.

If only I knew what to do, she thought. If only . . . !

When she went off duty at six she made her way to Minster Close, some strange instinct which she could not quite define keeping her in uniform. It was as if she wished to underline the fact that she was still part of the hospital, still a member of its working staff and would continue as such for another fort-night. It was almost, she felt, as if she were playing for time, thrusting the day of her acknowledged engagement to Ellis as far into the future as possible.

In moments of self-scorn, she told herself that it was a coward's way out, but the thought of Martin lay against her heart like a dead weight and she could not hope to reason sanely or wisely while it remained there.

When she went in Ellis was sitting in the chair she had occupied that first evening when Margaret Wroe had come home, but he jumped to his feet as soon as he saw her.

"I'm so sorry I couldn't get to the airport to say 'welcome home'!" she told him, holding fast to his outstretched hand.

"You've managed to say it most effectively with Minster Close," he assured her, his eyes sweeping over the improve-ments she had made to what he remembered as a bare and cheerless room. "You and Martin," he added. "You've been quite a team!"

Margaret said: "Yes, haven't they?" and poured Janet a drink, but after that she was almost conspicuously silent.

Janet saw that Ellis's shoulder and arm were both out of plaster now, although he still could not move them as freely as he would have liked. Martin had said that it would take time.

"Professor Hochsolden has forbidden me to operate for at least a year," Ellis remarked when they had gone over the events of the past few days in detail. "It means that Martin will have to take over at the City General."

Janet looked at Martin directly for the first time, but there was nothing to be read from his expression. Would he still leave Norminster? Would he still hold to his decision to go away?

Supposing she went instead? Supposing she persuaded Ellis that they should marry immediately and go off on a lengthy honeymoon, as he had suggested once before?

All her thoughts seemed to stand still there and she could not see the future that lay ahead of them at all.

When the party broke up at ten o'clock she would not let Martin run her back to the Nurses' Home.

"I feel that I want to walk," she said.

"Ellis," Margaret Wroe asked when both Martin and Janet had gone and they were alone in the flat, "how long have you known Janet?"

"Since my accident. Possibly before that. She has been a nurse at the hospital ever since I came to Norminster. Shall we say that I noticed her in a different way after the accident?"

"Why should your accident have made so much difference?"

He paused for a moment, as if this was the first time such a question had ever occurred to him.

"Janet's brother was pinned under a car," he said slowly. "I happened to be the person who pulled the child out."

"And the car collapsed on top of you while you shielded him?"

"Exactly."

"Then it was largely a question of gratitude?"

His sister's blue eyes were very steady as they met his.

"Haven't you felt it, my dear?" she asked. "Didn't it ever occur to you?"

"Yes," he confessed after the briefest of pauses. "Yes, I think I have always known."

Margaret did not ask what he was going to do about it, but the next day, when Janet came to tell Ellis that the P.N.O. had arranged his first appointment with the hospital masseur, Margaret found that she had some urgent shopping to do.

"Go in and chatter to Ellis till I get back," she said. "I won't be long."

"Janet," Ellis said in the first pause in their conversation, "do you feel that we might be making a mistake?"

She looked up at him, not quite grasping what he meant.

"About us," he said. "About our immediate marriage."

Something leapt to life in her that was hope and unutterable relief rolled into one, and then she crushed it as she said:

"I have given you my promise."

"But not your heart? Forgive me, Jan," he added swiftly as she drew back, "but it's the only way. We've got to talk this over."

"It won't do any good," she said. "We've—everything is settled."

He got up and crossed to the fire, stirring the reluctant coals into a blaze.

"Supposing," he said, "the reason for all this has outlived its usefulness?" He had spoken in a quiet, measured tone which held both kindness and understanding. "I think the time has come, Jan, to set you free from that promise of yours. You see," he added with a half-smile, "the reason for it no longer exists."

She met his eyes with sudden tears in her own.

"That isn't true," she said. "I could make you happy, Ellis."

"And I you?"

"Yes," she cried passionately. "Yes, you could make me happy. You have always been so kind—so dear!"

"Kindness isn't the same, Jan." He drew a thin hand over his hair where the first threads of grey were beginning to show. She saw that it was his injured right hand, and it shook a little as he repeated: "No, Jan, it isn't the same. For both of us it would have been only half measure—second best, if you like. I think I've known that you've been in love with Martin right from the beginning."

A sense of shock kept her speechless for a moment, and then she said almost desperately:

"Did you know that Irene Swallow was in London?"

"Yes. I must go and find her out. Margaret tells me that she has been widowed for several years." He came over to stand beside her. "Don't vex yourself about this, Jan," he said kindly. "It has worked out this way and we have got to accept it. If we had both been in love, passionately and completely in love with one another, nothing would have stood between us, not even the difference in our respective ages, but as it is I have no right to take your youth, my dear, even when it was offered in pity and gratitude."

She stood beside him, feeling that her heart must break, feeling empty and forlorn because his friendship had meant so much to her, and yet he had said the things which she had known in her heart to be true all along. Without love—love on both sides—marriage was a mockery.

"There never was a ring," she said unsteadily. "I have nothing to give you back, Ellis."

"I think you have." He put his arm lightly about her shoulders. "I want you to make me another promise."

She looked up at him, hardly knowing what to expect.

"I want you to go to Martin and tell him that he must stay

here," he said. "Tell him that you love him."

The colour fled out of her cheeks and her eyes were full of tears as she shook her head.

"How could I? How could I tell him that when I don't know what he thinks?"

"Don't you?" he asked, tilting up her chin to look into her eyes.

The sound of a key in the lock of the outside door saved her an answer and Margaret's voice sounded from the hall-way.

"I've brought you a visitor, Ellis," she said, coming into the room and glancing searchingly from one of them to the other before she added: "Irene came down from London by the afternoon train."

"Irene!"

If Janet had needed any further justification for the break-ing of her engagement that one word would have given it. Years of longing and suppressed love, and hours of fruitless yearning were all there, and Ellis seemed to have forgotten everything else as he stood in the past, seeing Irene Swallow as she was then, a lively, independent fellow-student with all the future before her and a shining ideal clasped in both her eager hands. If the years of hard work and frustrations had aged her he did not notice it. Time had slipped away as if it had never been and they were back in their youth again. Janet thought that she could safely leave them there.

"I've got to go," she whispered to Margaret who had gone out to the hall to hang up her coat. "I have to be back on the ward at six."

Margaret went with her to the door.

"Janet," she said, "is it all right? You weren't in love with Ellis, were you?"

"No." Janet's voice was not quite steady. "Though we would never have had the courage to tell each other that we had made a mistake if it had not been for you!"

"I've made my own mistakes in my time," Margaret admitted. "It's strange that it nearly always takes the onlooker to see most of the game. I knew you were in love with Martin Everett almost from the first moment I saw you together, and then I began to wonder about Ellis, remembering how he had felt about Irene when they were both young. It didn't seem to me as if Ellis had changed much, and Irene was free to marry again. Besides, you were so inevitably Martin's that it didn't seem fair."

"To Ellis?"

"To all of you. Irene will take Ellis back to Africa with her for a time and he'll be able to work there with her. He won't feel out of it in the same way as he would if he remained here and wasn't able to operate. And that should leave you quite free to marry Martin!" she added with finality.

How easy Margaret thought it was, Janet reflected as she made her way across Minster Square, realizing that it was still early and that she couldn't face the general confusion of the nurses' common-room. Her own thoughts were in too great an upheaval to listen to the idle chatter that generally went on there during the tea break, but there did not seem to be anywhere else to go.

It had started to rain, a thin, mist-like rain that fell across the surrounding shrubs like a veil as she turned in at the hospital gates.

She heard a car turn off the main road behind her, but she did not move aside immediately. She stood there caught in its headlights until it drew up and she heard Martin's voice.

"For heaven's sake, Janet, what are you doing standing there in the middle of the drive? Are you trying to commit suicide?"

She smiled at him in a vague sort of way.

"I was going on duty," she said. "I have to report at six."

He glanced down at the clock on his dashboard.

"Get in," he commanded, opening the car door on her side. "Get in out of the rain."

He would drive her up to the hospital, she thought, but instead he turned the car in the limited space of the drive and went back out through the gates again, nosing his way through the tea-time traffic till they reached Clifford's Bar and came on to the broader and more deserted north way out of the town.

"Now," he demanded, "can you tell me what has gone wrong?"

"There's nothing—nothing to tell."

"I'm afraid I can't quite believe that." He pulled the car up at the side of the road where there was a broad grass verge suitable for parking. "Not after I found you standing in the

189

middle of the hospital drive as if the end of the world had come."

She felt stifled, with tears choking against her throat, but if he saw her distress he was ruthless about that, too.

"Where had you been?"

"To Minster Close."

"To see Ellis?"

"Yes."

There was a brief silence.

"Janet," he asked at last, "are you still engaged to marry Ellis?"

"No."

"Was that all settled this afternoon?"

She nodded miserably.

"And you care? You really are in love with him?"

In the tense, waiting silence which followed his question it seemed to Janet as if her heartbeats must be heard, beating out her denial.

"It needs an answer, Jan," he said.

"I've—never been in love with Ellis," she whispered. "Not in the way you mean."

"Then you know the way I mean?" His voice was suddenly vibrant, yet he still appeared to be keeping his emotions in check. "What is going to happen?"

"I think Ellis will eventually marry—someone else."

"This friend Margaret has been meeting? This—old acquaintance?"

She thought that he had used the last word deliberately, but she could not reason about Martin now.

"Yes," she admitted. "It seems that they were in love long ago, in their student days."

"As you loved me?" His voice had softened, although the ring of determination still remained as he turned her round to face him in the limited space of the front seat. "Answer me, Janet," he commanded. "I've waited almost as long as Ellis for this, you know!"

Words choked in her throat, words that she longed to utter, and finally her hands went up to grasp the strong hands that held her.

"Martin!" she whispered. "Martin! Surely you've always known?"

190

For answer he swept her into his arms, kissing her fiercely and possessively full on the lips.

"Have I?" he said. "Have I? I don't know, Janet. A man is never sure of this sort of thing. I've always loved you. I've always wanted you. Nothing could be surer than that, but I thought that I had come back too late. You see, there were —debts to clear up for me, too." He held her close, speaking above her head. "My father died an undischarged bankrupt while I was in my last year in hospital, and it was as much as my mother could do to see me through to my degree. She had to sell Normanscliff to do that, and I vowed that I would pay every penny back. I'd almost done that, Janet, when I came back to Norminster, and then I set out to find you. My mother had died, but I still wanted to buy our old home back, even though I wouldn't be able to see her living there again, as I had planned." His words dropped into a long silence in which she knew he was thinking about his mother and all he had wanted to do for her by way of compensation. "By a stroke of amazing good fortune," he went on, "the house came on to the market last September and I meant to have it to offer you. I wanted it to be my home again, but it meant nothing to me unless you were going to be there, too. I wanted you there in my mother's place."

"If only I had known," Janet whispered. "But how could I? You came back after I had promised to marry Ellis."

"The one man to whom I owed so much!" His arms tightened possessively about her. "That first day at Normanscliff when I held you like this beside the waterfall. Do you remember it, Janet? I think I knew then that it couldn't end any other way than this, but afterwards it seemed that you thought otherwise, and how could I step in and take what you considered belonged to someone else?"

"Someone we both respected and admired so much," Janet said.

"I think Ellis knew," he said. "I think he suspected all along, and I had to fight the temptation to put my cards on the table on more than one occasion. The trouble was that we both owed him too much to want to see him hurt in any way, but what we should have realized was that we would have been doing him a graver injury by our silence."

"I couldn't have told him, Martin!" Janet said, feeling it

strange, even now, that she should be here in his arms, at last.

"Neither could I," he said. "I suppose we're just not made that way, but, thank God, it's come right in the end!"

He held her for a moment longer in silence and then he bent forward and switched on the dashboard light.

"Jan," he said, "it's not quite five o'clock. We've got time to go out to Somerton and back before you go on duty. We've got time to go to Normanscliff."

He drove swiftly through the rain, and it was still raining when he pushed open the garden gate of his old home and they walked up the steep pathway through the trees.

"I've always wanted to hear you say you loved me—here at Normanscliff," Martin said as he drew her tenderly into his arms.